Praise for Deadly Rescue

Deadly Rescue is a story c   it. A fascinating look at lesser k.   ᴐ my enjoyment of this stellar series. I eagerly await its next installment. *Cozy Up With Kathy*

I especially loved the authentic atmosphere of **Deadly Rescue**. Everything throughout the story felt true to the period, from dialogue to thoughts to the setting. *Terry Ambrose – Mysteries with Character*

Deadly Rescue's entangled, gripping mystery will keep you so entertained that you won't want to put the book down. *Christy's Cozy Corners*

I have to say that I really look forward to each new addition to this fun historical cozy mystery series! Parker has a true skill when it comes to researching the past in order to get the setting just right while also keeping your attention with a wide range of characters, a mystery to keep you guessing, and enough surprises to really have you turning the page all the way until the very end. *Books A Plenty Book Reviews*

Also from Kate Parker

The Deadly Series
Deadly Scandal
Deadly Wedding
Deadly Fashion
Deadly Deception
Deadly Travel
Deadly Darkness
Deadly Cypher
Deadly Broadcast
Deadly Rescue
Deadly Manor

The Victorian Bookshop Mysteries
The Vanishing Thief
The Counterfeit Lady
The Royal Assassin
The Conspiring Woman
The Detecting Duchess

The Milliner Mysteries
The Killing at Kaldaire House
Murder at the Marlowe Club

The Mystery at Chadwick House

Deadly Manor

Kate Parker

JDP Press

Deadly Manor

ISBN: 979-8-9860225-8-1 [print]
ISBN: 979-8-9860225-7-4 [ebook]

Published by JDP Press
Cover Design by Lyndsey Lewellen of Llewellen Designs

Dedication

To my beloved children who know their own minds and are usually right.
To John, forever

Late October, 1940

Chapter One

When we alighted from the train in Lancaster, I found a porter to handle our luggage while Adam had all he could manage to get off the train and cross the platform on his canes. Everyone, including the doctors and Adam, had told me not to make a big deal of it or help him in any way. It was hard, but I was trying.

Rosalie Billingsthorpe, our hostess and my friend from my days at Bletchley, had said she was sending her chauffeur to pick us up at the station. I breathed a great sigh of relief when I saw him come toward us in his livery. "Mrs. Redmond? Captain Redmond?"

"Yes." I gave him a smile. "It's Miles, isn't it? The porter has our luggage."

Miles and the porter nodded to each other. I felt certain the porter was familiar with the earl's automobile.

"Can I help, sir?" Miles asked Adam.

"Just lead the way. I can make it." He managed, just, not

to grumble. The trip had taken us all day. Between the dust and fatigue, I was barely staying civil myself.

Rail travel more than a year into the war was slow, crowded, and smoky from decrepit engines and carriages being kept in service far too long with too little maintenance.

Fortunately, Miles had parked the big, black car close to the entrance and I was glad to get inside, letting him sort out the luggage. Adam had already developed the knack of getting in and out of cars with his canes and once inside, he collapsed onto the back seat next to me.

I gave him an encouraging smile. After the first terrifying days when I hadn't wanted to leave his side in the hospital, there wasn't much else I could do.

With luggage in the boot and in the front by Miles, we took off through the darkening streets of the city and into the countryside. Adam looked around for a couple of minutes and then let his head roll back against the smooth leather seat, shutting his eyes.

Again, I wondered if this trip was too much for him physically. German bombing in London had begun more than a month before, causing incredible damage. I'd accepted Rosalie's offer because Adam needed rest to regain his strength and there was plenty of room around her mansion for him to walk in an effort to practice moving on damaged legs. Plenty of peace and quiet for healing.

Her husband, Thorpe, Earl of Briarcliffe, had been in a wheeled chair for about five years since a skiing accident robbed him of the use of his legs. It would be interesting to see how his relationship with my wounded Adam developed. I hoped it wouldn't be fraught with difficulties.

Adam had at least the hope of improvement.

There was less traffic out than the last time I'd ridden along these lanes with Rosalie, and compared to our train journey, it wasn't long before we reached their home. Miles pulled up out front and opened the back door of the car for us, standing with one arm positioned so we could brace ourselves on him to get out or not, depending on our wish. I wasn't too proud. I was glad of the help. Adam struggled out alone.

"I'll see to the luggage," Miles said.

"Thank you," I told him.

A maid opened the door, light spilling into the gloom, and we slowly entered the massive two-story front hall. Two steps in, Adam stopped and stared all around him. Paneling, shields, swords, even a suit of armor. It gave me the feeling that none of this had changed in hundreds of years.

Rosalie and Thorpe, with Thorpe's aide and valet Cummings pushing the wheeled chair, appeared at the far end of the hall. Adam didn't seem to notice them. After looking around him for a few moments, he uttered a single word. "Amazing."

"I'm glad you like it," Thorpe said, being rolled forward. Glancing at the canes, he said, "I'll wait to shake hands until we're both seated."

"I'm glad to meet your lordship," Adam said. "Livvy has spoken highly of you. Well, both of you."

"You're all she's ever talked about with us. I'm glad to see you back on English soil, Major." When Adam shot a look at me that said I shouldn't be boasting, Thorpe quickly added, "I'm familiar with the insignia. Congratulations on a well-deserved promotion."

"You both look exhausted from your journey. Would you care for tea before you go up to see your room? We have a lift installed for Thorpe. You're welcome to use it, Major, unless you're required to climb so many steps a day," Rosalie said.

Adam looked relieved. "That's very kind, your ladyship."

"Rosalie, please."

He nodded. "Adam."

"And I'm Thorpe," the earl said. "Now, Rosalie, if you'll lead the way?"

We went into the large but surprisingly cozy drawing room done in blues and yellow. I noticed Thorpe's lap rug, a new one no doubt knitted by Rosalie, was in the same shades with the addition of gray and cream.

"Adam, I think you'll find this chair to be the most comfortable," Rosalie said of a brown leather-covered, well-stuffed arm chair that sat a little higher than the others. There was a side table next to it for setting teacups or small plates and a spot between them to tuck Adam's canes.

Our hostess had given a lot of thought to our visit.

Thorpe wheeled his chair to the other side of the table from Adam and the two of them began conversing as if they were old friends. After everyone was served, Rosalie sat next to me on the sofa.

"You gave this a great deal of thought," I told her. "Thank you."

"It becomes habit after a while, to look at things from the point of view of those who can't get around as well. And besides, your invitation this weekend was not altruistic."

"What do you mean?"

"When I got this time off from Bletchley, I thought I could just spend some quiet time with Thorpe. However, he mentioned to a neighbor that I'd be home for a while. This neighbor, the Earl of Silverthorn, is an old man who has been kindness itself to Thorpe."

"And he's coming over here?"

"No. He's quite elderly and doesn't go out much anymore. However, he has a problem and he's dumping it on us." She made a face.

"His heir is the Viscount Norrington, an obnoxious prat who normally lives in London. With the bombing, he's decided he needs to come out here for the shooting season."

"Hasn't he heard there's enough shooting in Europe to make the idea of a shooting season absurd?" I asked, aghast at this insensitive fool.

"For the safety of our troops, the fathead has a desk job in the Ministry of Information."

"He's a censor?" I asked, still aghast.

"Well, he mustn't do much censoring, since he's invited a battalion of his friends and relatives here this weekend for shooting."

"He's invited them to your house?" I was growing more amazed by the moment.

Rosalie and I exchanged a look. "He invited them to Silverthorn's, but the old man has shut off most of the house and only keeps two servants, an old married couple. Silverthorn said they can shoot on his land but asked if we could put them up."

"Oh, dear." The Billingsthorpes didn't entertain much or keep a large staff. "Am I an extra maid for the weekend?"

"No. What you are is an excuse. You and Adam. Right now, Thorpe is probably impressing on Adam how it would be a great favor to him if Adam were to say he can't shoot or walk out with them. Then Thorpe will have to stay back with Adam, which is exactly what he wants to do. Then you and I can stay back too, but we'll have to entertain any women who don't want to go out with the men." She looked at me with a guilty face. "Sorry."

"You have nothing to be sorry about. The viscount sounds horrid."

"He is, rather. And there's no point in telling him no. He simply doesn't listen to anyone."

"In other words, he's a bully," I said. I turned to look at our host when I heard Thorpe laugh. He had heard me.

"He's a self-serving, maniacal, pompous ass, but 'bully' covers it quite nicely," he said. "Don't, whatever you do, give in to him or go along with him. Once you do, you're lost forever. I'm living proof."

Thorpe was a genuinely nice man. This bully I was

hearing about could have easily used his good nature against him.

"Perhaps this isn't a good idea," Adam said, setting down his teacup. "I'm in enough pain that I can be quite rude."

"Just what Norrington needs," Rosalie said.

"Who is coming?" I asked. "I don't want to be rude to the wrong person."

"Oh, there won't be any trouble with that. He's the only one who will immediately introduce himself as Viscount Norrington, as if you should kiss his ring," Thorpe said.

"There is also a cousin of his from the wrong side of the blanket. A few generations back, though, and Northcott is a perfectly respectable banker. They look a bit alike, but Northcott is darker and more wholesome looking," Rosalie added.

"Is he also obnoxious?" I asked.

"Oh, no. In temperament, they are night and day. In fact, the rest of the group staying here are delightful. You'll enjoy meeting them. Particularly the Northcotts and the Larimers. We know them, and they are jolly."

"If his friends are so nice, then this Norrington can't be too bad," I said.

"He surrounds himself with nice people as they are easier to bully. The people here this weekend aren't so much friends of Norrington as victims," Rosalie said.

I determined then that I would not be a victim of this odious man. Adam's expression said much the same, mixed with a desire to let his pain and frustration loose on somebody deserving.

* * *

After tea, I left Adam in our room sleeping the sleep of the utterly exhausted while I went downstairs. Partly because I wanted to talk to Rosalie on her own to learn if I could do anything to help her out this weekend. And partly because Adam hadn't had a moment completely on his own since before the shooting in France that had left him hobbling.

There was no one in the main hallway nor in the blue and yellow drawing room. I continued on to the morning room, decorated in yellow and sunny and warm even on the bleakest of days due to its south-facing position.

As I pushed open the door, I heard "Oh!" I stuck my head around the massive, dark-paneled door and found a chunky woman in perhaps her late forties wearing a tweed suit and looking at me as if she'd seen a ghost. She was leaning on a delicate-looking sideboard and must have been peering at her face in the mirror above.

"I'm sorry. I didn't mean to startle you," I said.

"No, no. I'm sorry. I shouldn't be in here." She shoved something in her pocket. A letter, perhaps, or a note of some kind?

"Why not? I'm sure Rosalie wouldn't mind." She would mind if this unknown woman was stuffing a letter of Rosalie's in her pocket.

"You're not Rosalie?" she asked, appearing baffled.

"No. Livvy Redmond." I walked forward, holding out my hand. "And you are?"

"Betsy Oswald." She grabbed hold of my hand with a painful grip.

"Is your husband here for the shooting?"

"The what?" She looked momentarily confused.

"Hunting pheasants."

"Oh. Yes. Yes."

What had she been thinking of when I said "shooting"? "Is your husband an avid hunter?"

"No. Only when the viscount says they must." She gave me a smile that looked as feeble as her handshake was athletically strong. A smile that said she wanted to disappear.

What was going on here?

"Would you care for some tea, Mrs. Oswald?" I asked, gesturing at two overstuffed chairs on either side of the unlit fire. "I don't think Rosalie will mind if we ring for tea to be brought to us here."

"Where is the countess?" She looked around as if she expected Rosalie to materialize at any moment.

"I don't know. I suspect she is spending some time alone with the earl. She works for the government, so she's away from him for weeks at a time."

"Oh. Yes. I expect you're right." Betsy Oswald was still glancing around as if she was afraid she'd been caught committing some crime.

I wondered what was on that paper. "What's the matter, Mrs. Oswald? You seem frightened."

At a distance, I could hear men's voices.

"Drat. It's the viscount." Mrs. Oswald fled past me out of

the room.

Chapter Two

By the time I reached the main hallway, Mrs. Oswald had disappeared. I had no idea where. I could hear men's voices coming closer, loud, boisterous, hectoring. I headed for the stairs.

I was at the bottom of the sweeping, red-carpeted staircase when six men came into view. I wondered which one was Mr. Oswald.

"Who are you?" one of the men demanded.

I wondered if this was the odious viscount. I had expected this bully to be young and dressed in the height of fashion. But all six men were middle-aged and wearing tweed. "Why do you want to know?"

Then I realized one of the other men was bleeding from several spots on or around his ear. "Good heavens. You've been shot."

The man I addressed gave me a smile that was at least half-grimace. "I'm afraid so." He was dark haired, dark eyed, and handsome despite being splattered with his own blood.

At that moment, Rosalie rushed into the hallway and put an arm around his back. "Robert. Oh, dear lord. You've been shot. We must get you cleaned and bandaged up. Did it hurt your eye? Should I call Dr. Hamelstein?"

The man I thought was the viscount snorted.

The man called Robert said, "My eyes are fine. Yes, let's get me cleaned up and bandaged. Do you mind?"

"Not at all. We'll take the lift up." Rosalie urged the injured man into the lift with her and shut the door on the rest of us, leaving me with five tweed-suited men, including the presumed viscount.

"Billingsthorpe didn't tell me anyone not in our party would be here this weekend." His tone said Thorpe and I were guilty in equal measure. The man I suspected of being the viscount was chunky, fair-haired, and his voice was set to echo in every corner of the manor house.

"He must have had his reasons." I marched up the stairs.

"Come back here," rang out below me.

I ignored him.

* * *

Adam, freshly awakened from his nap, laughed when I gave him a comic reenactment of my run-in downstairs without mentioning the shooting. "I'll bet he's the viscount, too. Good for you."

"I hope it wasn't anyone else," I said, thinking of how bad my manners had been. "The Billingsthorpes wouldn't have two odious people here on the same weekend, would they?"

"If they do, we're leaving." Adam didn't sound as if he

were joking.

"Poor old thing, I was hoping this would be a holiday for you. Fresh air, good cooking—"

"Not eating your cooking. Well, there is that." He tried to hide his smile.

I gave him a quelling look. My cooking skill, or lack of it, was an embarrassment for any bride without a cook. Ignoring his comment, I continued. "—plenty of room to walk, outdoor benches in the gardens, this was meant to be a rest." One that didn't involve anything that would remind him of being shot, such as what had happened to poor Robert.

"It will be. Anything I don't want to do, I'll just blame it on the doctors." He took my hand. "It will be wonderful. You'll see. Thank you, darling."

"I'm sure it will be. But if it's not, you have only to say the word and we'll go back to London." I wanted him to know it was his decision.

"And the bombing." He made a face. Spending nights in the shelter in the basement of our building would destroy any progress he'd made toward health or mobility.

There was a tap on the door. I opened it to find Rosalie. "Everything to your liking?"

"It's perfect," I said. Our room was decorated in lavender and aqua, not a combination I would have thought of, but Rosalie had a wonderful eye for color and shading. It was spacious and faced south, giving us a marvelous view of rust-colored trees in the distance.

There were two chairs and a tiny table by the window,

and an electric fire on the hearth, cheerfully glowing. The room had en suite facilities, a luxury, with plum-colored walls. "You've thought of everything."

"The bed is very comfortable. I had the best sleep I've had since I left for the continent," Adam called out.

"I'm so glad. And you found the lift all right?"

"Yes. Right outside the door. I shall think I've been declared visiting royalty," Adam told her and grinned.

"You are royalty come to call. You're Livvy's husband," Rosalie said with a laugh and a cheery, "Dinner's at eight. Do you want to wear dress uniform or civilian evening dress?"

"Civilian. I've seen nothing but uniforms for months now."

"Good. If Norrington tells you otherwise, tell him you outrank him."

"I don't, do I?" Adam said, slumping.

"It doesn't seem fair. He does all his fighting in a sitting position." Rosalie laughed and said, "See you at eight."

I shut the door and came back to where Adam was sitting. "He sounds as if he's a weasel," he grumbled.

"Just ignore him. He won't know what to make of it."

We were dressed and had left the room at a few minutes to eight when we met up with Thorpe and Rosalie. We sent the men down on the slow-moving lift while Rosalie and I walked down the stairs. "How's the man who was wounded?" I asked.

"Stung with minor cuts. Fortunately, it was at a good distance and at an angle to where Robert was standing. I can't understand it myself. They're all good shots. It was such a foolish mistake."

"Who shot him?"

At the bottom, Rosalie shrugged as she was approached by one of her staff, and she sent me in to the formal drawing room alone.

I walked in and was greeted with, "There you are." The loud, chubby man walked up to me and grabbed my arm above the wrist. "When I tell you to come back, I expect you to return."

I'd met Nazis who were much better at intimidation. And had better manners. "Remove your hand, sir."

I was aware of several pairs of eyes staring at us from around the room, but none of the men said a word. Was this normal behavior for this man?

He let go, but he stood intimidatingly close. "I expect an answer when I ask you a question."

"I haven't heard you ask a question." With a little maneuver that wasn't quite backing up, I turned and walked away from the man.

"Who are you?" he demanded.

"I'll introduce you, shall I?" Rosalie said as she hurried over to me. "Livvy, this is Viscount Norrington. Viscount, this is Mrs. Redmond."

"Has your husband come to shoot, Mrs. Redmond?" he asked in a socially normal tone.

"I think he had enough of that in France," I told him, my tone still icy.

"At Dunkirk, was he?" the viscount asked.

"Everywhere but," I replied. I'd let Adam tell them anything he wanted to and could without breaking the rules. The viscount was with the Ministry of Information. He might try to get Adam to say something so the viscount could then get him into trouble.

"Oh?" the viscount asked.

I ignored him, instead asking Rosalie to introduce me to some of the guests. She introduced me to Valerie Northcott, who she explained was married to a distant cousin of the viscount. I quickly learned the viscountess was not there and was unlikely to be found within a mile of her husband.

Valerie Northcott lived in Lancaster, where her husband managed the largest bank in town. They had three school-aged children, two boys and a girl, and they both enjoyed singing in the church choir.

They visited the Earl of Silverthorn at intervals, being distantly related and liking the old man. Then Valerie and Rosalie went on to a discussion of how the old earl's health was fading and wasn't it a shame. From the looks they were shooting in Norrington's direction, neither woman thought the viscount was the best person to succeed to the title of earl.

The man who had been hit with birdshot came up to us and was introduced as Robert Northcott, Valerie's husband. I saw a warm gaze pass between Rosalie and Robert and wondered if he was a relative or just grateful for getting his wounds bandaged up. Valerie looked past her husband, but I had no idea who or what she was looking for.

"I haven't thanked you for putting us up for this shooting party," Mr. Northcott told Rosalie.

"It's always such a pleasure having you stay."

"I'm just grateful I get to take another look at the medieval armory." He turned to me then and said, "I'm fascinated with the medieval weaponry and suits of armor that Thorpe keeps in his museum. Have you seen it? It's a wonderful collection that I have to study every time I come here, and I always learn something."

"No, I've not seen it," I told him.

"I came down here a couple of weeks ago to visit the old earl and had a chance to study the suits of armor while I was here."

"How did you think he looked, Robert?" Rosalie asked.

"I thought he looked all right. Has there been much change in the past two weeks?"

"I just got home recently, but the Smiths seem to think he's fading fast."

"That's a shame. He's a grand old man," Robert told me.

Another man I'd not noticed before came up to us. "Sorry I'm late. I was delayed at Silverthorn's. How is everyone? Robert, you look as if you've been in the wars."

Before Robert Northcott could answer, the new man was sharing a smile with Valerie Northcott. "This is Daniel Perkins, our solicitor. Well, everyone's solicitor around here," Rosalie said.

People were certainly friendly out here in the country.

"Thorpe, how are you?" a male voice boomed out from across the room. I'd soon know Norrington's voice anywhere.

Thorpe wheeled into the room, followed by Adam on his canes. "Have you met Major Redmond? And that's Mrs. Redmond."

"Yes, I've met your wife, Redmond. She says you don't shoot." He made it sound one step down from treason.

"Viscount Norrington?" Adam asked.

Thorpe did the introductions.

"I'm afraid I've had enough of shooting for the moment," Adam said. "Hardly seems to be sport if the birds aren't shooting back."

I heard a couple of chuckles. Norrington huffed and walked off. Thorpe then wheeled around with Adam following to make introductions.

Rosalie next introduced me to the Larimers. They appeared to be a rural couple, solid and capable. He was the solid squire of some village while running a large farm and she appeared capable of wrestling recalcitrant cows or whipping up five hundred jars of jam overnight for the women's institute. Or possibly both.

As soon as Rosalie left us for some other guests, I learned I was at least close to the mark. Larimer was also the magistrate for the district, and stroked his thick mustache while he listened to someone speak. They had a son'd who made it back from Dunkirk unscratched and a daughter who was expecting her first child with her RAF mechanic husband.

And it turned out that Louise Larimer was another fan of

Rosalie's knitting. We had just started praising her work when Rosalie lined us up for dinner and marched us into the dining room.

I had never seen the dining room set for a large dinner party before, since I had visited before when no one else was staying. The table was a mammoth expanse of shining dark wood, reflecting the light from the glittering chandelier and the wall sconces. I'd never seen the full silverware service set out for use or the rich cream and gold dishes in use that night. The napkins were starched and ironed to a smooth ivory perfection. The centerpiece, a large silver and china creation with animal figures on the sides and flowers on the top, was breathtaking. More than amazed, I was speechless.

I was seated between Mr. Northcott and Mr. Oswald. For the soup course, a herb-flavored broth, I was supposed to converse with Mr. Oswald. He was a London-bred friend of the viscount who could talk about nothing other than shooting game, mostly by the viscount.

Apparently, he heard his wife, the nervous creature I'd met before dressing for dinner, say something about shooting partridge and shouted across the table, "It's pheasants, Betsy. Pheasants are in October. Get it right."

When he shouted, the entire table fell silent as everyone looked in his direction. Betsy Oswald turned red and made a sort of squeaking sound.

Wanting to put her out of her misery, I said, "It hardly matters."

"How can you say that?" the viscount barked at me.

"We're at war. We have more important things to worry about. France has fallen. London is being bombed nightly. Not remembering which bird is being blown out of the sky is hardly the end of civilization," I told him.

Betsy Oswald looked pleased as she listened to me. Had she never heard a woman disagree with the viscount before?

"But if we don't keep up our traditions and customs, what will we have at the end of the war? Nothing," Viscount Norrington said.

"There are traditions. And then there are traditions. I think things such as trial by jury and free debate in Parliament are more important customs to preserve."

Two maids came in at that point to clear away the bowls and bring in the fish course. I breathed a sigh of relief as I turned to speak to my partner on the other side.

"Mr. Northcott..."

"Robert, please."

"I'm Livvy. Are you involved in the war effort?"

"No. I had several bouts of pneumonia as a child and it's left me with weak lungs. They sent me back to the bank to do my job and two others besides."

"That must keep you busy."

"I don't mind. I understand you work for one of the London daily newspapers."

"Yes. I'm sorry you were wounded today."

"It doesn't look too off-putting, does it? I don't know where that low shot came from, but it didn't leave any permanent damage. Not anything to worry about. Shall we talk about something else?" He caught the eye of Rosalie and smiled.

She smiled back and then returned to what someone else was saying.

We began a lively discussion of London newspapers and their coverage of museum exhibits that saw us through the end of the course. He said he'd been in London for a couple of days the week before last and hoped we weren't finding the Blitz to be too difficult. I found I liked Robert Northcott.

Then it was the game course and I was back with Mr. Oswald. "This is supposed to be a shooting party, but look around this table. So few of us will actually be shooting," he said and stabbed a piece of rabbit with his fork.

"Oh?"

"Yes. Only six. Norrington, Northcott, Larimer, the reverend, Downing, and myself."

"I don't believe I've met the reverend or Mr. Downing." I glanced around for a clerical collar.

"The Reverend Wilbur Shaw. The man with the shabby evening clothes by my wife. You'd never expect him to be the best shot, would you?"

"No. Do you shoot with him frequently?"

"Every chance I get to escape London and come out here to the countryside. Shaw always bags the most birds. Just as well, since his parish is a poor one, despite being ancient. A woman in the congregation cleans and dresses the birds for him, and then they split the meat. Suits them both well, I daresay."

"Who cleans and dresses the birds you shoot?"

"I give some of them to Shaw and some to Thorpe's cook. Not something I can take back to London, is it?"

"I imagine it would be difficult." I imagined anything to do with cooking to be difficult. I had finally mastered omelets and boiling potatoes and was making progress on chops and toast. Dressing fowl was not high on my list of things to learn.

Thank goodness Adam didn't shoot birds.

"And Mr. Downing?" I asked.

"Didn't know him before this weekend. Decent enough chap. Must be a friend of the viscount's from out here. What do you think of the Blitz?" he added.

"It's horrible."

"It's a terrible nuisance, that's what it is," Oswald proclaimed. "The Germans need to make up their minds. Take over Britain or forget it and return home."

I couldn't wait until the next course so I wouldn't have to talk to this dreadful man.

At that moment, Cummings, Thorpe's valet, came into the dining room and whispered in Thorpe's ear.

Thorpe gave him a sharp look and said to the table at large, "Silverthorn has had some sort of attack. The doctor asks, if you are going to shoot on his lands, to stay far away from the house so you don't disturb him. And he says, Norrington, you may want to go over there tonight."

"I'll go over after breakfast on my way to the shoot. I'm certain my uncle will be fine."

"The doctor seems to think it is serious," Thorpe said.

"You might—"

"Nonsense. He'll be fine. What I want to see are those magnificent weapons in your armory after dinner." Norrington didn't voice it as a request.

I saw the look of dismay on Thorpe's face as he glanced at Rosalie, and her expression of disgust.

Chapter Three

At Norrington's insistence, after dinner we formed a large group and headed to the old wing of the manor. I'd never been there before, and Rosalie, as she walked down the hall next to me, told me I'd find it both cold and boring.

She was right about the cold. While the rest of the manor had been modernized over the centuries, the original section, the old wing, was still unheated and the stone walls and floors were still visible. In my green evening gown with bare arms above my long gloves and bare upper chest and back, I was freezing, and my gauzy shawl did nothing to help.

Worse, the only lighting was lanterns, making the suits of armor come alive and the large weapons look even more menacing. There was enough height to the building and double rows of narrow windows to show where there had once been a second floor but had been removed, so I could see the whole way to the roof. Or would have, if the lantern light wasn't swallowed up in the gloomy, oppressive darkness above our heads.

"We keep meaning to add wiring and lights, but there's always something that is needed more," Rosalie murmured.

There were several high-ceilinged rooms, divided by one-story-high stone walls with doorways but no doors. These rooms were set up in this wing as if it were a museum, and we wandered from one area to another staring at the displays set up on stands or in glassed-in cases, each more lethal looking than the one before.

I could hear Thorpe and Robert Northcott ahead of us talking about some of the displays with a knowledge of era and design that marked them both out as historians.

"I say, Thorpe," Norrington said, "but these weapons give me an idea. How about if we have a fancy-dress dinner one night this weekend? Medieval costumes are easy enough to do. You do still have a dressing-up box in the attic? It seems as if all these old houses do."

"I was hoping this weekend would be quiet. You'd go over to Silverthorn to shoot and come back here for meals and a good night's sleep. Nothing formal. Nothing too jolly," Thorpe said.

"Oh, it would just be one evening."

"Norrington, when you take over Silverthorn, you can have all the fancy-dress dos you want. I'm not feeling up to it right now. Hope you don't mind," Thorpe said.

"That is a good idea, Viscount," the Reverend Shaw said. "I have to come up with a theme for a pageant for the school around Guy Fawkes Day, and the Gunpowder Plot is getting a little old. Perhaps a medieval tournament with broomstick horses. Yes." The vicar wandered off, lost in thought.

"Better than rifles and cannons. You have to get close to your enemy with these weapons," Adam muttered from next to me as he studied some nasty-looking pieces of fancy metalwork. "No chance of a sneak attack."

I felt certain he was thinking of the Nazi sniper he'd never seen who'd hit his legs from some distant point. "I think they'd get heavy quickly. That should shorten the battle," I replied.

"And the blood loss must have been horrific," Adam said, staring at one large metal ball on a handle with long spikes sticking out of it.

"That's a medieval mace with spikes. A very effective club," the viscount pointed out as if we'd asked. Or were interested. "You hold the handle end there," he gestured, "and swing it around. No one is going to get in your way."

"Back when hand-to-hand combat was possible," Adam said.

"When warfare was glorious," Norrington replied.

"It was never glorious," Adam snapped and hobbled off on his canes.

I started to follow him, but then I heard Norrington behind me say, "No wonder France was lost if our army has no more pride than that."

I was glad Adam had enough self-control not to strike out in anger. Especially with all these lethal weapons around.

In the light of a lantern, I saw Rosalie's eyes widen. She walked up to Adam and said, "Perhaps you'd care to see this suit of armor. The design worked into the metal is quite splendid."

She led him off as Mr. Larimer walked over to the viscount. In his magistrate voice, he said, "Never been in combat, have you, Norrington? My war was more than twenty years ago, but I can still imagine what that chap has been up against. They all deserve our respect."

"They lost the battle and now they're going to lose the war!" The viscount's tone dripped with anger.

"It's not lost yet!" Larimer snapped back at him and stalked off.

I wanted to applaud Larimer, but I knew that wouldn't help keep the weekend peaceful or make the Billingsthorpes thankful they'd invited Adam and me.

I walked into the next room along with the rest of the guests, leaving Norrington behind. One of the shooters walked along beside me. "Henry Downing," he said.

"Livvy Redmond. Are you from around here?"

"Oh, no. I'm part of the London contingent. You?"

"London."

"I think Briarcliffe Hall is fabulous." He looked around. "I'm sure none of my neighbors have anything such as this in their homes."

"Thank goodness."

He smiled then, and as I returned the smile, I realized I'd never be able to describe him. Average height, average size, average coloring. He had lovely manners, but that was hardly a description.

And then I wondered why I felt the need to describe him.

Adam, balancing on one cane, tried to take off the helmet of one of the suits of armor. Robert Northcott hurried over. "Let me help you. This stuff is old and fragile, and if you twist it that way, it'll likely... And you might fall and get hurt." He slipped the helmet off and held it with one hand inside the top of the helmet so Adam could examine it.

"Thank you. I don't want to knock anything over," Adam said, giving Northcott a nod after examining the helmet for a minute.

Northcott gingerly put the helmet back on the suit of armor.

We didn't stay in the old wing of the manor for long before the Billingsthorpes led the way in a sort of loop through the rooms back toward the exit. The Northcotts, the Larimers, Betsy Oswald, the solicitor Perkins, Adam, and I followed our hosts back to the main part of the house in a group. Robert Northcott glanced back at the entrance to the old wing longingly before going on, while the rest of us scurried out.

The Northcotts and the Larimers sat down to a game of bridge. Thorpe and Adam began a chess match. Perkins announced he was staying at the pub in the village, the Hound and Dame, thanked our hostess for dinner, said he was glad there was a moon to walk down the hill by, and said good night. That left Rosalie and me to entertain Betsy Oswald.

Rosalie asked her if she wanted a sherry or a brandy.

"Oh, no," was Betsy's reply. "George wouldn't approve."

"Tea, then?" Rosalie asked, and Betsy dithered before deciding he wouldn't mind that.

I looked at Rosalie, shrugged, and said I'd prefer tea also.

Even fueled by tea, Betsy didn't add much to the conversation, so Rosalie and I found ourselves making small talk of the most innocuous sort.

"One of our tenants was talking with one of the Duke of Marshburn's tenants and he said the duchess is in residence here. Has been for more than a week," Rosalie said after we'd exhausted the topics of the weather, rationing, and how gloomy the blackout was at that time of year with short days and long nights.

"I thought they didn't get on," I said. When I'd met the duchess before the war, she'd made it quite clear she couldn't stand her husband.

"They don't. I suppose the duchess came here because the duke wouldn't. That doesn't spare me from calling on her. Would you care to come with me tomorrow?"

"If you'd like me to, of course." Rosalie had been so nice. How could I say no?

"I appreciate it." Rosalie's expression told me how much she dreaded the meeting.

"I met the duchess once while I was doing a piece for the newspaper on her daughter and her upcoming wedding. She won't remember me," I added.

"If we're lucky, we can walk over and drop off our cards without actually having to talk to her," Rosalie said with a smile. Apparently, she wasn't impressed with the horse-faced woman, either.

When the last men returned from a study of the medieval battle implements, George Oswald decided to turn in immediately, and Betsy Oswald gulped her tea and hurried off with her husband. The Reverend Shaw thanked Rosalie as he put his bicycle clip on his trouser leg and headed out to ride down the hill to the vicarage.

Norrington ordered a brandy as if he were at his club and then sat down on a chair by the fire, adding, "Do you want one, Downing?"

"If the earl offers," Downing replied. I noticed then his accent was very ordinary southern England, too.

"Help yourself if you want," Thorpe said with a small smile for Downing.

"Thank you, your lordship."

"Thorpe, please."

"Thank you, Thorpe." Downing gave him a small smile with his nod.

Not long after that, Adam asked Thorpe if they could finish their game in the morning. I could tell by the set of his shoulders that he was tired and in pain. I set down my teacup, nodded to Rosalie, and rose to join Adam.

I saw him to the lift and then walked over to the staircase. My last view through the doorway was of the bridge players rising from the table and Rosalie joining her husband.

* * *

Noises kept waking me during the night. There was enough moonlight when I opened my eyes that I could see the outline of the furniture in the room.

I rose carefully so not to disturb Adam and walked over to the window. I pushed aside some of the drapery and looked out. Below, I could see the drive and the path heading directly toward the village. Hurrying along the path was a woman. I couldn't tell who she was, bundled up in her coat and hat, but she'd definitely come from the direction of the front door of the hall.

Just before she stepped out of sight beneath some trees, I saw a figure step out to greet her. Their two shadows melted into one and vanished.

I waited, but no one came into my section of the lawn, either coming or going. I gave up and went back to bed.

As I carefully climbed back into bed, I heard footsteps on the stairs or the upstairs hall. It was too soon to be the woman I'd seen before returning. Who else was wandering around Briarcliffe Hall?

Later, another sound woke me and I heard Adam say, "Sorry. I didn't mean to wake you." He was sitting in the dark in a chair by the window, a ghostly figure in the room.

"You didn't. Did you hear something?" I thought I had.

"Yes. I think it was indoors, but I have no idea where or what it was."

"Do you want to investigate?" I asked, half hoping he'd agree.

"No. My legs had enough of a workout on those stone

floors in the old wing. If you're awake, I don't have to worry about waking you, and I can come back to bed."

"Please do. Let's see if we can get you to relax."

* * *

We rose, still tired, when the sky was beginning to lighten on a cloudy morning. We washed and dressed and went downstairs using the lift in search of tea or coffee. Having visited the Hall before, I knew where to look.

Valerie Northcott and Rosalie were in the hall when we exited the lift. One look at their faces and I asked, "What's wrong?"

"Robert was missing from our room when I awoke this morning. I've looked around, but I can't find him anywhere," Valerie said.

"I was just in the breakfast room, and I know he wasn't in there," Rosalie said. "I've asked the servants to check the grounds and the gun room. That sort of thing. Livvy, Adam, do you have any ideas?"

"Has anyone checked the old wing?" I said before I thought about it. "Maybe he wanted another look without bothering anyone. He seemed interested in all the historical details."

"Adam, would you mind accompanying us?" Rosalie asked.

"Not at all." I thought I heard him grit his teeth at the pain that more walking on the worn stone floors would cause his legs.

I set out in the lead, hoping to save Adam at least a few

steps in the old wing. Rosalie was right behind me, and Valerie was walking with Adam, thanking him for checking this out and putting her mind at rest.

I opened up the door that led to the old wing and was immediately hit with a blast of cold air. I hadn't realized how much the fires warmed up the occupied part of the house. I wished now I'd brought a coat with me, but this was the last place I had thought I'd be that morning.

Pulling my red woolen cardigan tighter around my back and arms, I stepped into the first room without need of a lantern. The windows, glazed by some earlier earl to keep out the wind if not the cold, let in enough light we didn't need lanterns to find our way around.

Despite the cold, the air smelled stale. That made sense, since I was sure the windows couldn't be opened and had been sealed up decades or centuries ago, but I didn't remember the stale smell the night before.

Probably because of the paraffin smell of the lanterns.

Rosalie walked into the room to our right calling, "Robert? Are you in here?"

I walked straight ahead to the next room, which had a bigger window and better light. It took my brain a moment to process what my eyes were seeing, and a few moments more before I found my voice. "Don't come in here."

That brought all three people to my side. Rosalie had the sense not to look directly at the sight and take Valerie out of the old wing immediately.

"Call the police," Adam told them as he moved very close

to me. "Can you handle it?"

My breathing was jerky, but I nodded. "Yes."

He stepped forward, blocking my view of the worst of the damage. I could still see the medieval battle axe, splattered with rust-colored dried blood, on the floor. There was more blood splattered all over the stone floor. I could see the lower part of a pair of tweed trousers and heavy lace-up shoes, but nothing else.

I only had a momentary glance at the head and torso of the victim, but I knew it was enough to tell me I couldn't easily recognize Robert Northcott. He'd fallen forward toward the entrance to the wing, toward where I stood, struck down from behind.

"We have to search the rest of this wing," Adam said.

"You think the murderer is still here?"

"No. This isn't Northcott. He didn't have a mustache. This is Archie Larimer."

I didn't know how Adam could tell the victim had a mustache or could look at the wreckage that had been Larimer long enough to identify him.

And then I realized. "You think Robert Northcott could be in the same state in another of these rooms?"

"Yes. You don't have to come with me, Livvy."

"Yes. I do."

"Then stay behind me. I'll try to block you from seeing anything too bad."

Rosalie had been through the first two rooms on the right, so we skirted around the body to enter the next room.

Nothing looked disturbed there but the dust mites floating in the sunshine coming through the window.

Adam looked into the room to the side where there were a couple of suits of armor. He returned almost immediately. "Nothing there."

There was one last room to check, and I hesitated to go in there. If we found Northcott's body, that would be terrible. If we didn't, that could indicate he had murdered Larimer and fled. Perhaps he had been one of the people I'd heard walking the halls the night before.

"You can go back into the main part of the house," Adam said, no doubt seeing the fear on my face.

"You had a difficult-enough time in France. You shouldn't have to deal with a slaughter here at home. On what was supposed to be a recuperative visit. If you can do this, so can I."

With that I stepped into the last room and wished I hadn't.

Adam turned me around and leaned on me as he held my face against his chest. His canes hung uselessly, looped over his wrists.

"Is it?" I asked, swallowing hard and glad I hadn't yet eaten.

"Yes. Robert Northcott has had his skull bashed in with one of those medieval mace things with the spikes sticking out. And Livvy, I don't think you can sneak up on someone and attack them with these weapons."

Chapter Four

"You're certain it's Robert Northcott?" I asked, not wanting to gaze at the body a few feet away.

"Yes. Much easier to identify than Archie Larimer. Less damage done."

I was amazed at how detached Adam could sound in the face of what were two horrific deaths. Then I remembered what I'd heard at the newspaper about the war in France. And Norway and Belgium and Poland.

"We'll have to tell Valerie Northcott what we found. And Louise Larimer. Oh, Adam. How awful."

I knew just how awful that could be. I'd imagined hearing this sort of news about Adam daily for weeks during the fall of France.

Adam straightened, still holding me lightly for support before he put his canes down and rested his weight on them. "Can you walk back to the drawing room under your own power?"

"Now you sound the same as me," I told him,

remembering how he disliked me to ask that question in the early stages of his recovery.

"Now you know how I hated it."

I nodded. "Sorry."

Adam steered me to the connecting rooms on one side of the main rooms to avoid Larimer's body as we walked out of the old wing. Once we were out of there and the door shut, I wondered if I'd ever warm up again.

We walked directly to the blue and yellow drawing room where Adam dropped into the chair he had sat in when we arrived the day before. I felt certain he would have no desire to move again any time soon.

Rosalie came over to us. "Brandy and coffee?"

"Yes," Adam said.

"I'll take tea with lots of sugar," I told her.

"Have you called the police?" Adam asked.

"Yes. They should be here soon."

"We found both Northcott and Larimer. Murdered."

"Good Lord!" Rosalie dropped into a nearby chair.

"Where's Thorpe?" Adam asked.

"Still in bed. Yesterday was difficult for him," Rosalie said before pausing. "As it must have been for you."

"Where are Mrs. Larimer and Mrs. Northcott?" I asked.

"In the breakfast room. Shall we?" Rosalie asked me. "Adam, I'll have your coffee and brandy brought in shortly."

I decided I'd let Adam rest a little before seeing if he wanted breakfast. Rosalie rose and I followed her to find Valerie Northcott and Louise Larimer sitting side by side at the breakfast room table with coffee cups in front of them. Neither appeared to be eating.

"Archie wasn't in bed when I woke up this morning, either," Louise said, studying our faces. "He's dead, isn't he?"

"They both are. Murdered."

Louise Larimer let out a gasp while Valerie Northcott sobbed for a moment before pulling herself together.

"With all these young men dying in battle and then the deaths from the Blitz, you don't expect murder," Louise said. "Right. What do we do?"

Of the two of them, Louise Larimer seemed the one better equipped to handle tragedy. "First, we wait here for the police. They'll be here shortly," I told them.

"If you wouldn't mind heading off Norrington this morning, I'd appreciate it. I don't think I could face him," Valerie said in a breathless sort of voice.

I had a mental image of her lying on a fainting couch.

"He, Downing, and the Reverend Shaw took off for Silverthorn's at first light to check on the old earl. I don't think he'll be around to bother you for a while," Rosalie said.

"Oh, that's right. Poor Edwards. Have you heard how he is?" Valerie asked.

"'Edwards'?" I asked.

"Edwards Norrington, Earl of Silverthorn," Rosalie said. "No, we've heard nothing since last evening."

"We named our oldest after him. Edwards is an old family name. We call our son Teds." Valerie seemed to be talking just to do something. She had a grip on her cup that was likely to shatter it.

The deep tone of the front bell rang out. No doubt the police. "Do you want me to take them to the old wing?" I asked Rosalie.

"Do you mind?" she asked.

I shook my head.

We went out together to greet the police, a uniformed constable and a plainclothes officer. Rosalie said she would be in the breakfast room with the widows and I led the way down the hall and through the door into the old wing.

"You'll find Mr. Larimer straight ahead a couple of rooms, and Mr. Northcott in the last room of the row," I told them, waiting in the first room.

"Who found them?" the plainclothes officer asked.

"My husband and I. Major and Mrs. Redmond."

"Inspector Andrews," the officer said.

"I'm Sergeant Wilcox," the uniformed constable said. He glanced toward the body in the next room and then back to me. "Has anything been touched?"

"Oh, good grief." I glanced down, saw blood on the floor in the next room, looked away, and shuddered. "No. No one wanted to get close enough to check to see if they were alive."

Andrews went into the room Larimer lay in. "Looks as if he was attacked by someone behind him. Someone farther in this wing."

I heard him move deeper into the wing while I looked at the stone floor. "Looks as if this fellow, Northcott, was facing this suit of armor when he was surprised," he called out. "And then the other, Larimer, realized what happened and ran for it, but was struck down. Is that what you think happened, Mrs. Redmond?"

"You'd better ask my husband. He was more able to look at the bodies than I was. But..."

"Yes, Mrs. Redmond?"

"There is no electricity in this wing, Inspector. If the murderer was waiting in here, moving only by moonlight, and the victims came in without lanterns, and none had been left behind, it would be very easy to hide until the killer reached out to strike."

"Where are the lanterns kept?"

"I don't know. You'll have to ask the earl or countess. I just meant it would be easy for the murderer to surprise both his victims. If Mr. Northcott was struck down first, Mr. Larimer might not have been able to see much, which would give the killer a head start in reaching Mr. Larimer."

"Right. Wilcox, take a look and tell me what you think."

Andrews came to stand by me while Wilcox wandered the floor. "Yes, it looks as if Larimer was in the wrong place at the wrong time. I wonder why?" the sergeant said.

The inspector said to me, "Go join the ladies in the breakfast room, and we'll come to get your statement later. One thing, though. Why did you come in here first thing in the morning?"

"There was a general search for Mr. Northcott, requested by Mrs. Northcott. Since other places were already being searched, we offered to look in here."

He nodded and walked off, then stopped again. "The coroner and the scene of the crime men will be here soon. Will you direct them back here?"

I nodded and gladly escaped the old wing and went back to the breakfast room, hoping I could get some food without appearing too callous.

I needn't have worried. When I arrived, Adam was sitting down to breakfast and both new widows had left the room. I fixed myself a plate and joined my husband. "The police are here," I told him.

"Good. They're equipped to handle this," he said and took a bite of toast. When he finished, he added, "Thorpe's cook is a marvel. Have you tasted her preserves?"

They were good. After we enjoyed the meal in near silence, I said, "Where did everyone go?"

"Mrs. Larimer is informing the magistrate in Lancaster, Rosalie is phoning Silverthorn's place to find out how the earl is faring and to tell the vicar he's needed here, and Mrs. Northcott went to her room. I've not seen anyone else."

At that moment, the Oswalds came into the room. Mr. Oswald immediately headed for the sideboard with the heated dishes and Mrs. Oswald stood aside waiting for him. "I haven't missed the shooting, have I?" Mr. Oswald asked.

Adam and I both stared at him. Adam muttered, "No."

"Well, where is everybody?"

"The police are in the old wing with the bodies," I said. After listening to him at dinner the night before, I didn't feel any need to be kind.

"Bodies?" Mrs. Oswald said. She appeared oddly eager and not at all squeamish.

"Don't be ghoulish, Betsy," Mr. Oswald said. "What bodies?"

Adam told him what little we knew as Oswald filled up his plate.

I watched Betsy Oswald, who seemed to be listening with rapt fascination and what I thought might be a little glee. Only when her husband finished piling on his food did she pick up a plate and take small helpings.

Thorpe was then wheeled in by Cummings and a moment later Rosalie joined us. "Your usual, dear?" she asked. "I've got it, Cummings."

The servant nodded and walked out.

"Are the police still in the old wing?" Rosalie asked.

"Why would they be there?" her husband asked.

Oswald rushed to tell the earl everything he'd been told.

When he finished, Rosalie said, "Adam and Livvy went looking in the old wing for Robert Northcott and found both men."

"How dreadful for you both. And here you are for a rest," Thorpe said, looking embarrassed, as if this was his fault.

"Yes, well, the police are here now," I said. "The coroner and the evidence collection people will be here soon and are supposed to be directed to the old wing. Can you let everyone know?"

At that moment, the doorbell rang at the same time as a

loud knock. "That must be them now. I'll send Cummings to deal with them," Rosalie said and walked out of the room.

"And the police can deal with the murders," Adam said. Now that he'd had breakfast, he wasn't looking so pinched and pale with pain and exhaustion.

Rosalie returned. Everyone ate in silence for a few minutes, each lost in their own thoughts. Then Cummings came back into the room and spoke in a murmur to Thorpe.

"Of course," Thorpe said. "I'll speak to them now." Then Cummings wheeled him out of the room.

The pair returned a few minutes later and then Cummings left. "I've set them up in the study. Inspector Andrews is leading the investigation. They want to see you first, Redmond. I hope you've finished breakfast."

"Yes, I have." Adam gave me a brief smile and rose unsteadily from the table before he had both canes lined up properly. Then he was able to walk out of the room with something of his old grace.

I remained where I was at the table, waiting for my turn to be called. Only the Oswalds seemed to have hearty appetites. The rest of us ate enough to keep away hunger.

"I hope this doesn't interfere with the shooting," Mr. Oswald said.

No one replied.

Finally, Adam appeared in the doorway. "They want to see you in the study, Livvy. Thorpe, would you mind finishing the chess match we had last night? I need a distraction."

"Not at all." He wheeled himself away from the table and

out the door, with Adam following him down the hall by the time I reached the doorway.

I turned the other way toward the study and tapped on the door. Sergeant Wilcox opened it and directed me to a chair across the desk from the thin older inspector, who wore a well-pressed blue wool suit.

Wilcox returned to his chair at the end of the desk, where he opened his notebook and readied his pencil. This was the first time I'd taken a good look at Wilcox. He was younger and larger than the inspector but with less hair on the crown of his head than his boss.

"I'm Chief Inspector Andrews. Could you give me your full name for the record?" The inspector was a studious-looking man who fit in well against the background of the study, paneled in dark wood, with a typewriter in a corner of the room and a telephone on the desk between us. The draperies were a port wine color that blended well with the rest of the room. The inspector appeared to have been born to work in this study.

"Olivia Harper Denis Redmond."

The expression on his face indicated that he found my name a mouthful, but he took me through the events of that morning. When I finished what little I could tell him, he said, "Had you been in the old wing before?"

"Once. Just last night. Viscount Norrington was here for dinner and said he wanted to go through the museum. So, we all walked through afterward."

"What did you think of it?"

"That those weapons make warfare much more personal. Close up. Adam never saw the sniper who shot him in France."

"Adam? Major Redmond?"

"Yes."

"I'm sorry to hear that." The chief inspector sounded as if he meant it. He continued with, "So everyone at the dinner would know where these weapons are, how to get in there, and the general setup of the museum?"

"Yes. It's not locked. Anyone could get inside at any time. And the cases where the smaller weapons were kept weren't locked, either." I wondered if Thorpe would change that now.

"Did anyone show a particular interest in the museum or the exhibits?"

"Thorpe and Mr. Northcott. They're both amateur historians. They were discussing details about dates and construction and their use in various battles. I'm afraid I didn't listen. Mr. Northcott mentioned the museum before dinner."

"Could Mr. Northcott have gone back later to look at something?"

"He could have. I don't know."

The chief inspector then walked me through my actions for the rest of the evening, followed by, "Where did you meet the earl and countess?"

"I met Rosalie where she works and where I used to work. We became friends and I've visited her here a couple of times. When I mentioned Adam was recovering after returning from France, she invited us down for a rest for him to regain his strength." I glanced out the window at the drive. There were now an extra four automobiles outside, no doubt brought by the investigators.

"Where do you live?"

"London."

Both men looked directly at me then. "How is it?"

"Our flat hasn't been bombed yet. Well, at least not when we left."

Chief Inspector Andrews shook his head. "Anything else you can think of that might help us solve this crime?"

"No." There were people wandering around inside and outside the hall the previous night, but I couldn't give him names or times or anything useful or definite.

They released me then and asked me to send in Rosalie. I headed for the breakfast room, thinking she might still be there. Instead, I found her with Mrs. Northcott and Mrs. Larimer in a small drawing room decorated in cream and lavender. Mrs. Larimer was dressed in her coat and hat.

"Rosalie, the police want to speak to you next," I told her.

"Good," Louise Larimer said. "I'll go with you. I'll tell them I need to leave and they can contact me at the farm."

"We'll see if they'll interview you before me, because I suspect they will want to talk to you before you leave," Rosalie said.

"Nonsense. I can't tell them anything useful, and I need to get back to the farm and reorganize tasks. Whatever else happens, crops and animals need to be looked after." Mrs. Larimer stalked out of the room with her countrywoman's stride and Rosalie followed her.

I walked over and sat near Mrs. Northcott on a stuffed chair in lavender plush. "We thought we were so lucky," she told me. "Away from London, Robert not subject to being called up, and the boys are years too young. And now this. Why?" Her voice rose in a wail on the last word.

Chapter Five

"Are you also anxious to get home?" I asked.

Mrs. Northcott took a deep breath, dabbed her eyes, and said, "No. The children are at their schools. It would only mean going home to an empty house. I'll wait until Mr. Perkins finishes his work here for the earl and then I'll ride back to Lancaster with him."

She was one of those women who were still beautiful well into middle age and could cry without looking blotchy or messy. She made a striking widow.

At that moment, Viscount Norrington marched into the room, saw Mrs. Northcott, and said, "Where's your husband? We have shooting to get in before it's too late in the day."

Mrs. Northcott burst into tears, which left the viscount with his jaw hanging.

"Mr. Northcott and Mr. Larimer were both murdered last night," I told him.

"Well, that's going to mess up the numbers for shooting."

The statement was so breathtakingly insensitive that it stopped Valerie Northcott in mid-sniffle and left me glaring at Norrington.

Rather than apologize, he turned around and stalked out of the room. I thought he found their murders to be a personal affront. Valerie looked at me in amazement, and all I could do was shake my head.

The Reverend Shaw walked in then and came straight over to Valerie. "One of the policemen told me what happened as soon as I arrived. I am so sorry."

I rose so he could take my seat. "How is Silverthorn?" I asked.

"A little improved."

"Well, that is good," Mrs. Northcott said warmly. I knew she knew the old man and she appeared to be a genuinely nice woman.

I left, softly shutting the door behind me as I went in search of Adam. He was finishing a chess match, which he lost badly to Thorpe as Rosalie looked on.

As I reached them, I told them what Norrington had just said. They all looked as aghast as I had felt.

"And he said this to Mrs. Northcott?" Rosalie said. "Oh, Thorpe, that man is never coming here again."

I heard the door open behind me and turned to see Mrs. Larimer enter the room. "I've cleared my departure with the police and the car is packed. I'm going home."

"Oh, Louise, I am so sorry," Rosalie began. "Is there anything we can do?"

"Unless you murdered my husband, you have nothing to be sorry about. Now, I need to reorganize things on the farm so that everything gets done. Archie managed things so well. He'll be missed by us all."

"Oh, yes," Thorpe said. "He was a good friend and an excellent farm manager. I shall certainly miss him and his good sense on the land council."

"I want his seat on the land council," Louise Larimer told him in her no-nonsense tone.

"I don't know why not," Thorpe said. From his expression, I didn't think he had been expecting the widow to issue orders to him about a county committee. Especially when the victim wasn't even coffined yet.

"Good." She pulled on her brown leather gloves that matched her brown tweeds and sensible brown low-heeled shoes. "I'll call you later about the funeral arrangements."

Rosalie and Thorpe walked with the new widow to the front door. I said my condolences and then sat down by Adam. After they left the room, Adam said, "She is a formidable, well-organized woman. Was her husband the same?"

"I don't know. I suspect tonight when she's home she'll collapse with grief. Keeping busy might be her way to keep from breaking down in public."

He studied me for a moment. "She could be our killer. She has the size and strength and determination."

"But not the motive or the temperament. I think we can rule out both widows."

"That doesn't leave us with too many possibilities. Can you get into the old wing from outside?" he asked.

"Have you had your morning exercise yet?" I asked him, holding his gaze. I felt certain we were reading each other's minds.

"No. Let's put on boots and try to circle the house."

I went upstairs to get our coats. As I left our room, I looked down the hall where Valerie Northcott was reading a note, her skin growing paler by the second. One hand flew to her mouth and attempted to stifle a sob. Looking up, she saw me and then dashed into her room.

* * *

A half hour later, we left by the mudroom near the estate agent's office. We both had on wellies and Adam had exchanged his canes for walking sticks with pointed ends to jab the ground. We came out on the far side of a dry-stone wall separating the gardens from a field for grazing sheep.

Briarcliffe Hall was a three-story stone gothic-style building with tall arched windows. We stood back and stared at it for a minute, enjoying the sight. "And this is just the back of the house facing up the hill," I told Adam. "You need to see the front facing down toward the valley while we're here to appreciate just how beautiful this place is."

Then with our backs to the garden, we headed on a slight downhill slope toward where the old wing must be.

Once we turned the corner, we found the wind was weaker there, and one side of the old wing was in front of us. All of the window glass seemed to be intact and the windows on the ground floor were too high up to climb in without a tall ladder.

I walked along the side of the building looking for marks from the feet of ladders but finding mostly sheep droppings. The best I could say was there hadn't been any ladders there. However, there had been plenty of sheep. As a city girl, I couldn't imagine how Rosalie stood having animals so close to her nice house, grazing in her side garden.

There was no way into the old wing from this side. I looked at where Adam stood waiting and shook my head.

I walked around to the end of the wing and found a wooden door painted dark brown to match the walls. "Adam?"

It took him a couple of minutes but he finally reached my side. "Have you tried it?"

"I was waiting for you."

Adam made a face before setting down his walking sticks and lifting the latch on the door. When it didn't open immediately, he put his shoulder against the door and pushed.

After a moment, the door swung open. I caught Adam before he collapsed on the stone floor. We teetered for what felt as if it had been minutes before Adam got his legs under him. I reached for his walking sticks while he came back outside to lean against the wall.

"Can you see where this leads to?" he asked me.

I nodded and walked into the gloom. Within a few feet, I found a staircase and started up. I fumbled my way to the top and found another door. When I opened it, I found myself in the much brighter museum of horrors.

From the marks on the floor, I guessed this was the room where Robert Northcott had been found.

Before the police noticed me, since I could hear them in another nearby area talking, flashing camera bulbs, and moving something heavy, I backed out. I shut the door silently and crept downstairs to Adam, grateful that they'd moved Northcott's body so I didn't have the jolt of seeing him again in that state. I told Adam what I'd found and then added, "They keep the staircase clean for someplace that's rarely used."

"What do you mean?"

"No cobwebs."

Adam moved just inside the door and then felt along the edge with his hand. "Here it is. There's a bolt here to keep the door locked from inside. It wasn't fastened. It was only stuck since the wood had swollen from the damp."

"Do you think the killer came in this way?"

"Maybe. How many people know about it?"

"I'll have to ask Rosalie." Leaving Adam by the door, I walked to the end of the wall and then looked down the other long side of the old wing. No other doors, and everything appeared solid, including the glass in the windows.

"I've had enough of this uneven ground," Adam told me. I suspected his near-fall had jerked muscles and bones that were already sore, setting them on fire.

"And we learned what we came for." We walked slowly back, watching where we stepped, and returned to the mudroom in time to learn lunch was being served. We tidied up in the mudroom and then wandered the halls back to the magnificent entrance hall and from there to the dining room.

The soup course was just being served, and Adam and I slipped into seats across from each other. Two seats were still empty. Mrs. Larimer's was one, I guessed, and Mrs. Northcott's was the other. The viscount was on Rosalie's right, and she didn't look happy about sitting by him.

"Is Mrs. Northcott having a tray in her room?" I asked.

"No. She's meeting with the police and her solicitor in the study and then she plans to travel back to Lancaster," Rosalie told me.

"Her solicitor? Does that mean the police have decided she finally did away with Northcott?" the viscount asked.

"Really, Norrington. What a terrible thing to say," Thorpe said.

"Well, he was the most appalling stick in the mud. Couldn't shoot worth a bean. Not a gentleman."

Rosalie had an expression on her face that told me she wanted to slap him. Fortunately, I don't think anyone else saw, since it was only there for an instant.

"I've known plenty of gentlemen who couldn't shoot. Don't think that disqualifies them," Downing said. "Good soup, this."

I couldn't think of anyone who would want to kill either victim. If the viscount turned up dead, we'd have a wide choice of suspects.

And it would be a long time before someone wanted to see Thorpe's museum of medieval weapons again.

"Does anyone use the doorway going outside from the museum?" I asked.

"No. The entrance stairs get cleaned monthly the same as the rest of the old wing, but no one ever uses the door. It only leads to a pasture. We have sheep there now."

"We found the outside door unlocked just a little while ago." I held Rosalie's gaze.

"It can't be. I made certain it was bolted when I checked the cleaning. That was when I first returned home this visit." She glanced at Thorpe and then back at me. "It was only a couple of days ago, but we might be lucky we weren't all murdered in our beds."

The Reverend Shaw said, "I think this needs to be brought to the attention of the police."

"I would hope they would have noticed already," Thorpe said.

"This is the Lancashire constabulary we're talking about," the viscount said and chuckled. "They're almost as bright as your sheep."

"I'll have a word with them after lunch and make certain they know," Thorpe said, sounding formal and autocratic in his reply. Or just fed up with his guest.

The servants came in with the next course and conversation stopped for the moment. When they left, the viscount began to give us a shot-by-shot description of the pheasant hunt that morning. I couldn't help wondering if his call on the earl was merely a pretext to hold a hunting session. No one was able to get a word into the conversation, so we all ate quickly to shorten the amount of time we'd be tortured. Rosalie only toyed with her food.

Then Norrington said, "I still think it was a shame no one thought to organize a fancy-dress party."

"Hardly the time to hold a party when two of our group have been horribly murdered," Thorpe said, sounding aghast.

"If it had been planned, we could have held it last night," the viscount said, unwilling to give up the idea.

"Or we could have planned it for tonight and then not held it because of the murders," Rosalie said, "which would have been the same as not planning for a fancy-dress dinner at all."

The viscount didn't seem to have any response beyond "Not the same thing at all."

Rosalie looked heavenward, possibly asking for a lightning bolt.

Once lunch was over, Adam went with Thorpe to tell the police about our discovery that morning and the four remaining shooters went off for a longer session on Silverthorn's land. I couldn't help marvel at the sheer insensitivity, even as I was grateful to have the viscount out of the way. Then I saw Rosalie slip upstairs holding a handkerchief to her nose.

I followed her upstairs and knocked on the door she had entered. Then I walked in. "Rosalie, is everything all right?"

"Two people were murdered in my home last night. No, everything is not all right." She was sitting on the bed, tears running down her cheeks.

I glanced around at the bedroom I was in. "Is this yours?" There was a framed photograph on the bedside table of Rosalie and Thorpe at their wedding. The room was done in pinks and yellows with a lounge chair under the window across from the four-poster bed.

"Yes. Thorpe and I haven't shared a bedroom since his accident."

"But you two are so loving. Such a perfect couple." I didn't understand. "Adam and I share a bedroom despite his war injuries."

"Oh, Livvy. You don't understand the nature of Thorpe's—disabilities. From the waist up, he is a man. Forceful. Energetic. The man I married. From the waist down, he is a baby. Cummings is his nursery maid, dealing with his nappies. I can't, Livvy. I just can't." She burst into tears.

I walked over and dropped onto the bed next to her. "I'm sorry, Rosalie. I didn't realize how terrible his injuries are."

"We make sure people don't."

"You present such a united front. You aren't thinking of leaving him, are you?"

"Never. I promised him in the hospital that I would never leave him. What Robert and I had was only a bit of fun."

"Robert? Northcott?" My voice rose.

"Hush." Rosalie gestured me to lower it. "He was kind, gentle, and looking for some understanding, just as I was. It wasn't serious. We were both married."

"Why was he looking for understanding?"

"Because his wife has been carrying on with that solicitor, Perkins, for years. Robert and Valerie have nothing in common and little reason to stay together. I made it easier for Robert to stay with her."

"Gracious," I said, shaking my head. "It makes Valerie Northcott and Daniel Perkins suspects in the murders. Particularly if Northcott was killed first and Larimer stumbled upon the murder."

"That's what the police think happened." Rosalie held my gaze. "You must promise not to tell anyone. Not even Adam. It would break his heart if Thorpe found out I was looking for solace elsewhere."

"But Perkins wasn't staying here. How could he and Valerie...?"

"She left the hall and met Perkins toward the village. He would slip her in the side door to the pub. We have a publican who turns a blind eye to everything that involves outsiders renting his rooms. Locals can't visit his place for the same reason, but outsiders can."

That explained the woman I'd seen walk out the front door in the night and meet someone in the woods. I nodded and patted Rosalie's shoulder when I rose. "I can't say anything to the police, even though it points to two people having a motive for the killings?"

"No. Absolutely not. It would get back to Thorpe, and with it, my affair with Robert."

I didn't like the idea of keeping secrets from the police in a murder investigation, but I couldn't betray Rosalie. She and Thorpe had both been too kind to Adam. If Perkins and Valerie Northcott had killed her husband, there would be other evidence. Evidence I could take to the police.

"And this has come at an awkward time, too."

"Awkward? How, Rosalie?"

"We just had our last estate agent, or manager if you will, leave for a government post. I should resign from Bletchley and come home to run things here for Thorpe."

"Oh. I thought Thorpe ran all the farms and mills and things."

"He tries to, and he does run the things closer to home, but the more distant things such as the uniform factory and the munitions factory are too far for him to travel to. I could help him, but it might feel as if I was pushing him aside. Making him feel more of an invalid than he already is."

"I'm sure he wouldn't feel that way."

"Well, that's pointing out the things he can't do rather than the many things he can do, and do well. He does much better with the books and locating supplies for the mill and the factories than I do, and those are things he can do here or on the telephone. He just needs me to make the rounds of businesses. But Livvy, I don't know how to bring up the subject of leaving Bletchley. Especially since I don't know if they'll allow it."

I didn't know a good answer to that. I patted her shoulder. "I'll see you downstairs."

The first person I met downstairs was Betsy Oswald. Lucky me. I suggested we go out on the terrace since it was lovely outside. A short time later, Rosalie met us there.

Rosalie, Betsy Oswald, and I wandered into the morning room and a few minutes later Valerie Northcott came in to tell us she was leaving.

"Everything was all right with the solicitor?" Betsy Oswald asked. Knowing what I now knew, I thought she asked too eagerly.

"There's a great deal of paperwork awaiting me in Lancaster, he tells me," Valerie replied. "Some of it he says will be a shock. I don't know if I want to see it."

"Do you want some lunch before you go? Perhaps you don't want to face this shock on an empty stomach," Rosalie said.

"Thank you, but I'm not hungry. And if it's too much of a shock, it'll wait until tomorrow, I'm sure."

"Of course," Rosalie and I said in unison.

"When I left the police, your husbands went in, saying they had something important to tell them. Do they know who killed Robert?"

"Nothing as useful as that," Rosalie said. "Livvy and Adam found the door leading outside from the old wing was unlocked."

"You mean anyone from outside could have entered the weaponry museum?" Valerie asked.

"I'm afraid so," I told her.

"Then anyone could have killed my husband."

"Yes." Rosalie nodded and looked down, obviously ashamed for not keeping her guests safe.

"It's all right, Rosalie. You couldn't have known what someone had planned. And Robert did tend to tell everyone when we were coming up to see you and Silverthorn."

"Anyone you have suspicions about?" I asked.

"No, but you don't tend to look at people you know as homicidal maniacs, do you?"

Rosalie and I shook our heads, and Betsy Oswald echoed us after a moment.

"Do the police have any clues or suspects?"

"Nothing and no one." Valerie looked as if she might dissolve in tears at any moment.

"Are you over your shock from the note?" I asked her.

Any hint of tears evaporated. "What note? I didn't receive any note." Valerie shot an angry look at Betsy Oswald, who was looking at a magazine and didn't see the venom aimed at her.

Perkins, a good-looking middle-aged man who had wide shoulders and less gray at the temples than Robert Northcott had had, knocked on the door and stuck his head in. "Ready to go, Mrs. Northcott?" He had a pleasant baritone and a ready smile.

"Yes, thank you. I'm riding back with Mr. Perkins. He's headed back to Lancaster," Valerie told us, unnecessarily I thought.

Looking at them now that I knew their secret, I thought them a handsome pair. Good looking, elegant, and devious.

But were they killers?

"You're fortunate he had business with the old earl, Valerie," Rosalie said, her voice stiff with formality that I suspected hid her sorrow.

Her smile was weak. "Yes."

We gave her our condolences as we saw them out. Perkins, I discovered, drove a green saloon. We then returned to the morning room. As we sat down, Betsy Oswald said, "He's in love with her. Do you think he killed her husband to marry her? He could have come in that unlocked door."

I blinked. Or unlocked it to make it look as if there'd been an attack from outside.

Chapter Six

Rosalie and I stared at the woman. Rosalie said, "No, I don't think so," and left the sunny morning room. I wondered how many sandwiches short of a picnic Betsy Oswald was or how tactless she could be and followed Rosalie out.

"It's stupid comments such as hers that can get innocent people hanged," Rosalie muttered when I caught up with her.

"She is rather strange," I told her.

"And what about Thorpe? What if he heard her comments and started to wonder about..."

"Did you invite the Oswalds, or was it the viscount who invited him to the shooting?" I asked.

"He did. Speaking of the viscount, where is he?" Rosalie asked, looking around the great hall.

"You want to avoid having him shoot you, mistaking you for a bird?"

"I want to avoid him."

I smiled at her and whispered, "Would it be too terrible of me to picture him running from our crazed killer?"

"Only if the killer is now armed with a shotgun full of birdshot." She returned my smile.

Adam and Thorpe came back into the hall at that point and we stopped our uncharitable talk.

Betsy Oswald edged in silently until we realized she was right behind us, making me wonder how much she'd heard. "Why don't we take a walk in the garden? It's such a lovely time of day. And it's sunny," I suggested to Adam as I took his arm.

With a tight grip on his two canes, he made his way down the great hall toward the back parlor and the French doors leading to the terrace with me next to him and Rosalie behind us. From there we walked out into the garden and made our way to the first bench, a black wrought-iron backless seat.

When Adam sat down with a muffled groan, I asked, "This isn't too much for you, is it?"

He gave me a smile that was half-grimace. "I'll be fine." Then he looked out over the garden. "Rosalie, you're certainly a talented gardener. It's peaceful here."

"Thank you." Rosalie walked over to us, Betsy trailing along behind her. I glanced at the doorway where Cummings was maneuvering Thorpe's wheeled chair out onto the terrace.

"I could sit and look at this all day," Adam told her, the stress lines on his face smoothing out.

"I'm glad," Rosalie said. She sounded genuinely pleased. "Would you gentlemen care to sit out here in the sun while we ladies hike up to the ridge? I really do need to pay a call on the duchess. Much as she probably won't appreciate it."

"Fine with me," Thorpe said.

"You'll be all right?" Adam asked me.

"I'd love a good hike in the autumn air about now," I replied. I was just sorry Betsy was coming. Her whining and unfortunate remarks were getting on my nerves.

"Come on. Your shoes look stout enough. We'll follow the path up to the ridge so we won't need boots." Rosalie led the way, with Betsy and me following her.

It was a gentle climb down one side of a small valley and then up the other side. This, Rosalie pointed out, was a small side valley that fed into the main valley where the village rested. She stopped at a fence and gestured out over the valley. "Isn't it beautiful?"

The leaves were in full glorious color on the far hill and the harvest was well along below us. All around us was quiet, full of birdsong and wind through the trees. Directly below was Rosalie's glorious garden. We could see the front drive from which the extra police cars had all departed. We could have been a million miles from the bombing and rubble in London. "It's so peaceful," I told her, leaning against the fence.

"Is that one of your tenants?" Betsy asked, looking toward a substantial house down slightly from our viewpoint and at a distance from where a blonde stood staring in our direction.

"No, this is the edge of our property. Over there is the Duke of Marshburn's land and the large building there is

Marshburn Lodge. I suppose it could be one of his tenants, although she doesn't look familiar," Rosalie said.

"How can you tell at this distance? Your eyesight must be very good," I replied.

"It's a small holding for the duke, and he doesn't have many tenants. They're all related and dark haired. That woman's a blonde."

Betsy began a long, sweeping wave to the woman who returned it with a raised hand for a moment before disappearing around the side of the house. "People are so friendly in the country."

"Yes, they are," Rosalie replied. "Shall we continue?"

We climbed over and followed the path to the solid, Elizabethan stone and brick and half-timbered two-story house and then went around the building to the front door. Rosalie rang the bell and Betsy and I handed her our cards to present with hers. Standing on the steps and looking out, I could see Marshburn Lodge also faced down the slope to the village.

Perhaps a minute later, a shortish, stocky, dark-haired man in livery opened the door.

When Rosalie told him our mission, he said, "Her Grace is not at home. If you'd care to leave your cards?"

Rosalie set them on the silver tray he held in one hand. "It's Thomas, isn't it? Thomas Burke?"

"Yes, milady."

"I didn't realize you'd taken over as butler here."

"Only temporarily. If there's nothing else?"

"No. Thank you, Thomas."

We turned to leave and the man had the door shut before we were off the steps. "Thomas is one of the tenant farmers here," Rosalie said. "I didn't realize they were staffing up the house again. Ordinarily, they just have a housekeeper who does some light cooking and a maid for the heavy work."

I glanced up at the house, admiring the composition of different building materials in the Elizabethan manner, and caught sight of a fair-haired woman in a first-story window. She stepped back, but not before I got a good look at her.

Fleur Bettenard.

I was sure it was her, but what would she be doing in England caught behind enemy lines? I had to be mistaken.

Or maybe not. Leaves were partially off most of the trees, including one large old oak near the lodge where I spotted antenna wire strung across its branches.

Antenna wire that would be needed for shortwave radio communication. Something Fleur would find useful.

The walk was quicker on the way back to the house since we were following a trail down the hill toward the gardens. I stopped when we first found an unobstructed view of Briarcliffe Hall and the old wing, but Betsy continued on ahead of us. "This would make a beautiful painting," I said. All the features of the stone gothic-style country house were visible from this point.

"Surprisingly, no one ever has," Rosalie told me. "You should try it."

"I just sketch. But I brought my sketch pad and pencils, and if you don't mind…" I looked at her, excitement building. Usually I only sketched fashions, for my job at the *Daily Premier*. This would be a real challenge.

"Not at all. There's plenty of time before tea. Do you want to give it a try now?"

"Not right this moment. There's something I need to consider first. Rosalie, I think I saw a blonde watching us from a first-story window. Not the duchess. A woman named Fleur Bettenard."

"Who is she?"

"A Nazi spy and assassin who is a good friend of the Duke of Marshburn."

"What would a Nazi spy be doing in rural Lancashire?" Rosalie sounded skeptical. She had every right to. It was a crazy idea.

"She's a good friend of the duke's," I repeated.

"Who isn't here. He's locked up somewhere for his pro-German sympathies."

"It does sound silly, doesn't it?"

Rosalie shook her head. "They've rounded up all the spies by now, haven't they? We've been at war over a year."

"I imagine so." Actually, Sir Malcolm had told me they had. And that Fleur had gone back to the continent shortly after war was declared. "Let's go tell the boys about my plans for a sketch of the house."

Adam and Thorpe were still sitting in the garden, talking quietly. "I want to see your efforts, but I don't think I'll try to hike up there," Adam told me when he heard my plans.

"Will you be all right on your own for the afternoon?" I asked.

"Of course. I'm quite comfortable here." He did look comfortable, too, with his canes laid aside and his face tilted to catch the sun's rays.

Adam had been looking pale since his ordeal in France. I hoped this stay would give him some of his color back.

I dashed in and gathered up my sketching supplies. When I returned, Rosalie had blankets to spread out over the rough ground to sit on while I drew. "Do you mind if Betsy and I tag along?"

Betsy I minded, but Rosalie would be welcome company. "Not at all."

We followed the same trail we'd used to return before, and I was surprised to see how far we had to walk to get to the point with the lovely view of the house. It hadn't seemed so far when I'd hurried down to get my sketching supplies.

When we settled down on the blankets and I began to sketch, Betsy said, "I'm going to walk up and look at that other view again. I think it's even prettier."

"Don't go past the fence. Marshburn doesn't like people wandering onto his land," Rosalie warned. "We had a good excuse when I thought the duchess was in residence, or was in residence and would want company, but I don't suppose the tenants would welcome us back."

"I'll be careful. And I'm not going far," Betsy said and walked off.

Rosalie loosed a sigh. Then she looked at me and smiled. "Quiet."

I smiled. Betsy's constant chattering was starting to get on my nerves as well.

I didn't know how long I'd been sketching when we heard a car drive up the lane to the hall. Rosalie stood, trying to see who her visitors were. "I'd better go play hostess. I don't know where Betsy could have wandered off to, but she's been gone a long time."

"I'll find her and we'll walk back together," I said, also rising.

"Thanks." She grabbed up one of the blankets and headed down the path.

I gathered up my sketching supplies and walked the other way, intending to get the other blanket on the way back. I was surprised to reach the fence without any sign of Betsy. She was foolish, but surely not so foolish as to get lost in the woods. Was she?

"Betsy!" I bellowed down the hill. Some birds took flight. "Betsy!" Glancing toward the Duke of Marshburn's estate, I saw Betsy coming toward me. Why would she be coming from that direction?

"Ssh," she said when she climbed over the fence. "There are some beautiful redbirds over there. Don't disturb them."

"What kind of birds?" I asked.

"They're red and lovely. I don't know what they're called." She walked past me and down the hill, not stopping to pick up the blanket on her way.

I folded the blanket and carried it down along with my sketching supplies. This slowed me down, so I reached the hall a couple of minutes behind Betsy. The only person I found was Adam, sitting in the small green drawing room.

He greeted me with "The viscount's back."

"Oh, goodie."

"He's insisting we shoot from the garden tomorrow so Thorpe and I can join in." His expression said what he thought of that idea.

"He better not. I'm sketching the house from that direction. He'd probably shoot me." How dare he ruin my sketching when I finally had the beginnings of a really good work?

"We certainly won't let him shoot you." Adam lost his bantering tone and his shoulders sagged. "I can't stand the sound of gunfire anymore. I'll do my duty when I'm fit again, but not for some sport." He shook his head. "I can't, Liv."

"And I don't expect you to." I took his hand. "I'll talk to Rosalie."

"Thorpe told him no, but I don't think the viscount listens very well."

I sat down next to Adam and put a hand on his shoulder. "If you want to go back to London..."

"No. That's not fair to you or the Billingsthorpes."

"But what's fair to you?"

"Don't worry about me. Now, let's see your sketch."

Adam was very complimentary about my drawing of the house, probably more than it deserved.

Rosalie hurried into the room, her arms wrapped around herself. "That blasted man," she murmured before she realized we sat looking at her. "Oh, I'm sorry."

"I understand the viscount wants to shoot where I've chosen to sketch. How do you like it? It's unfinished, of course."

She studied it for a moment. "That's excellent. I don't suppose you intend to complete it?" she asked with her eyebrows raised.

"It may take my entire stay, so shooting from the garden simply won't do." I changed my haughty expression then for a smile for Adam and Rosalie.

Rosalie strode over, threw open the door into the great hall, and bellowed, "Thorpe. You must see this. Thorpe."

It was so unlike her to shout when she would be more likely to call a servant to pass on a message to her husband.

"Coming," wafted down from above us.

And even more unlike Thorpe to respond in this fashion.

A minute later, the lift opened and Thorpe and the viscount exited, Cummings coming down the stairs to meet his employer in the hall.

"What is it?" Thorpe asked Rosalie, wheeling over to her and ignoring Norrington, who was still hectoring him about shooting. "Oh, that is good," he said when Rosalie showed him my drawing.

Now I understood. Rosalie wanted to stop the viscount in mid-flow. I was certain Thorpe appreciated her shouts.

"It's not finished yet," I told him, "but I hope to have it

done by the time we leave. I'm working from the rise beyond the gardens in the woods. There's a clearing there that gives me a great view."

"Oh, you must," Thorpe said, ignoring the viscount. "We'll want to frame this when you're done. It's magnificent."

"But it will mean no shooting from the gardens. Too dangerous for Livvy," Rosalie said.

"But we agreed," the viscount shouted.

"No, you said you wanted to. I didn't agree to anything. Besides you have plenty of places to shoot over on Silverthorn's lands." Thorpe turned back to me. "Oh, it's going to be magnificent."

"Where are Mr. Oswald, Mr. Downing, and the vicar?" Rosalie asked.

"Oswald went off with his wife, and Shaw stayed with the earl. He'll walk back later," Norrington said. "I never seem to know where Downing is. I don't even know who he is."

"Well, you invited him," Thorpe said.

"No, must have been Larimer or the vicar."

"Did you see your uncle?" I asked.

"Briefly. Didn't want to tire him out. I'll let the vicar do that," the viscount said with a hearty and inappropriate chuckle. That man made my skin crawl.

A maid came up to Rosalie and whispered something, and then Rosalie bent over and whispered something in her husband's ear.

"The police want a word on the telephone. If you'll

excuse me," Thorpe said. Cummings pushed him through a doorway.

"Perhaps you can make your drawings after we have our game drives," the viscount said.

"No. I plan to spend a great deal of daylight time out there with my sketching. You have other places to hunt. Do it there." I probably sounded annoyed, because I was.

"Nonsense. You're being unreasonable."

"Try this for unreasonable," Adam said. "If you shoot from the gardens or anywhere near there in the direction of my wife, I will kill you. And thanks to this war, I've had practice."

Norrington leaned back, looking shocked. "Really, there's no reason to be rude."

"Then don't even think about it." Adam spoke quietly and lethally.

Whatever the viscount thought of replying, he decided against it.

Silence fell for a minute. Then we heard the sound of Thorpe's wheels on an uncarpeted section of floor. He came back in, pushed by Cummings, who then stepped discreetly out of sight.

"I've just had a call from the police. They're coming back out. They have a suspect helping with their inquiries and they want to check out what he's been telling them about the old wing."

Chapter Seven

"Will you have to escort them around the old wing?" Rosalie asked, concern in her tone.

"Probably. There's nothing to see there now, nothing to upset you. The bodies have been moved. I'd like you to come with me, as well as Adam and Livvy. After all, you two were the ones to find out the door to the grounds was unlocked." Thorpe sounded regal.

"I'm coming along. They'll want to speak to me," Viscount Norrington said.

"And us," Oswald said, sounding certain of his own importance.

"Why don't we have tea while we wait for them," Rosalie said and began to usher all of her guests into the blue and yellow drawing room.

Adam instinctively headed for the brown leather chair he'd sat in the day before when we arrived, but the viscount arrived there first and sat, looking smug.

Rosalie appeared annoyed. I was furious. "I didn't know

you had problems getting up and down from a seat," I said to the viscount.

"No. Of course not." He sounded insulted. Good.

"That chair is specially designed for people with trouble moving about. If you sit there, we'll all assume you have problems moving your limbs." Adam would never speak up for himself on the matter of his current limitations, but I was more than willing to champion him. I'd been living with his groans that he could not stifle.

"Nonsense."

"I'm afraid so. It was especially designed for me when they thought my paralysis might ease. But you go ahead and sit there, old boy, you're not getting any younger," Thorpe said with a bland smile.

"Nonsense." Norrington rose from the chair as if he were a rocket and stalked across the room.

"Why don't you try it, Adam?" Rosalie said. I was in the right place to see her wink at him as he reached the chair. Then she rang the bell for tea and it arrived almost immediately.

As everything else was at Briarcliffe Hall, it was delicious. When the police arrived, Rosalie offered them a cup of tea in the study they were using for their interviews.

Inspector Andrews thanked her. Sergeant Wilcox eyed the small sandwiches hopefully. When the maid appeared at Rosalie's ring, the countess gave quiet directions for tea and sandwiches to be sent to the study for them.

Downing strolled in at that moment, nodded to his hosts,

and took a chair.

When the police followed the maid out, I whispered to Rosalie, "You don't miss anything, do you?"

"His hungry stare was hard to miss." Then she smiled slightly and added, "Well done on the chair."

"Thank you." I was glad to have her and Thorpe's support. Dealing with Norrington on my own would be unbearable. And success would be unlikely.

We had a few minutes to finish our tea before a constable came in and asked Thorpe to join the detectives.

"I'll let you know if I need you," Thorpe told his wife and then Cummings rolled him out of the room.

Conversation, barely started before, came to a halt again.

A few minutes later, the constable came back and asked for me. Norrington replied, "Now see here. I demand to be interviewed next."

"Sorry, sir," the constable, a large country lad who'd grown up wrestling boulders or something, said. "I'm only to bring Mrs. Redmond this trip."

I rose and hurried from the room as quickly as I could so the viscount wouldn't make more of a scene. Instead of the study, the constable led me to the old wing. I walked into the drafty space wishing I had worn something warmer.

"I understand you entered this wing from outside," Inspector Andrews said.

I went through our entire adventure, making our arrival at the doorway more of a lucky coincidence, until he stopped my account at the point when Adam forced the door open. By then we'd walked partway through the old wing. Rosalie must have had a maid scrub up the blood on the stone floor, because there was no sign of violence now. The inspector turned to me and said, "Are you certain your husband didn't force the lock?"

"Yes. You've seen him. He doesn't have much strength, particularly in his legs. The door was stiff, but it was unbolted."

"What happened to your husband?"

"France happened, Inspector." Then I relented a little. "I believe he was on assignment south of Cherbourg when a Nazi sharpshooter took aim."

The inspector remained silent for a moment looking ill. I suspected he had lost someone at Dunkirk. "Did you see any sign of anyone using that stairway or door in the recent past?"

"No. The stairs had been swept not too long before, but Rosalie has a staff she keeps busy with sweeping and polishing."

"Has she always kept this wing cleaned?"

I shrugged. "You'll have to ask Rosalie or the maids."

Then he took me back to finding the two murders as we walked into the room where Larimer's body had been discovered. I'm certain I turned an unhealthy shade of green. I leaned on an ancient stone wall and said, "Ask someone else."

"Why did you decide to look in here?"

"It was the only area indoors no one had thought to search. Adam, my husband, would have insisted on helping with the search. He's naturally kind. I thought the old wing would be easier for him to negotiate than the outdoors. It's hilly outside and the paths are uneven."

"Then why did you walk around the old wing? It's hilly on that side of the house."

"Adam wanted to, and there was a wall for him to use for extra support if needed. And after finding the bodies, I was just as happy to be out of doors." I studied the inspector for a moment.

Shuddering, I walked out of the room where we found Larimer's body. "We didn't realize we'd find Northcott and Larimer dead. I thought maybe they'd gone in for another look at the displays before anyone else rose. Northcott seemed particularly keen on the historical aspects of the weaponry and the suits of armor."

I looked at the inspector. "When we discovered the door, we expected it to be locked. Adam never expected to go flying inside when he leaned on the door."

"Then why did you try it?" the sergeant asked.

"Because we hoped it would open so the killer hadn't necessarily slept in the house with us last night." I shook my head. "Rosalie and Thorpe are too nice to have friends or servants who go around murdering each other."

Even as I spoke those words, I knew they weren't true. They were a lovely couple, but that didn't mean no one around them could be a killer.

Inspector Andrews said, "There is one more thing you might do for us."

That sounded ominous. "Yes?"

"I wondered if you could lift and swing around, very carefully, please—we don't want any accidents—this medieval poleaxe."

"Surely, that's not..." I didn't want to touch the murder weapon. My stomach flipped over at the thought.

"No, it's not the murder weapon. This is just a display in this museum of your friends. I'd like to know if a woman of your size could handle such a weapon."

"All right."

He helped me lift the long, top-heavy implement from its stand and move to the center of the space. Then he let go, and I felt the poleaxe wobble in my hands. I lifted it straight up with my grip near the head and then carefully back down until the shaft was on the stone floor.

The instrument was about five feet long with a head that included a sharp spike at the top, an axe on one side, and a hammer head on the opposite side. The metal was decorated with curves worked into the designs.

I lifted it again and swung. By using both hands, I could control the weapon without too much difficulty. And I could see how easy it would be for someone with upper body strength to kill someone with a weapon such as this.

"I'm having no real problem handling this, Inspector. It's not heavy, but it does require two hands."

"So, anyone in the house that night could have attacked

Northcott with this." Inspector Andrews nodded as he spoke.

"I have no doubt Adam and Thorpe could both handle such a weapon. They both have upper body strength. But neither Northcott nor Larimer would have stood still and let anyone attack them, and neither Adam nor Thorpe are agile," I pointed out. "Adam would have had to balance against one of the walls, and Thorpe would have had to wheel his chair with only one hand."

"Either might have taken them by surprise. The lighting would have been poor."

"You can hear them both coming. Thorpe by his chair squeaking along the floor, and Adam by the thump of his canes."

"And Larimer had a pocket torch with him, so there would have been some light to see the attacker," the inspector said.

"Really? We didn't see it."

"Larimer was lying on it. We found it when we lifted his body. And it had been switched on."

I could imagine a thin beam of light shining on Northcott lying injured on the floor. Ghastly.

"Have you ever heard the name Dermot Young?" the inspector asked.

I blinked at the change in subject. "No."

"Thank you, Mrs. Redmond. You've been most helpful." The inspector's expression told me nothing.

I could tell when I've been dismissed. I handed him the poleaxe. Before I left, I asked, "When did they die? Was it at the same time?"

"As far as we can tell, both murders took place at the same time. Between two and four in the morning."

"Why would they have gone to the old wing at that hour? Maybe when we'd all gone to bed, or just before breakfast. But in the middle of the night? It's as if everyone was suffering from insomnia."

"We'd like the answer to that, too," the inspector said.

I shook my head and hurried out of the old wing.

Everyone was still in the blue and yellow drawing room when I arrived looking for more tea. I hadn't seen Thorpe return but he was there again. "Is there tea?" I asked Rosalie.

"You look as if you need brandy," she replied.

"Tea is fine."

While Rosalie ordered another pot of tea, the viscount kept up a steady stream of complaints, saying the police hadn't interviewed him yet.

Then the constable came in and asked Adam to accompany him.

Viscount Norrington loosed a volley of shouts at the constable, who kept a placid demeanor as he escorted Adam out and shut the door behind him. The viscount poured himself a whisky and asked Thorpe if he wanted any.

Since it was Thorpe's whisky, I thought that was rude.

Thorpe declined, and we all fell into silence.

Betsy Oswald broke into our thoughts with, "Are you going sketching tomorrow?"

"I plan to. Why?" I asked her.

"I thought I'd go along. Get in a bit of a ramble." For once, she didn't appear frightened of her husband's opinion. He must have approved of his wife wandering the countryside, as long as it was well away from him.

"I'll let you know when I'm ready to go up there," I told her, not thrilled with the company.

"It will have to be after we shoot over there," the viscount said.

"You are here to shoot on Silverthorn's land, not ours," Rosalie said.

"Thorpe doesn't mind," the viscount told her without a glance at Thorpe.

"Thorpe minds."

We all turned to look at the quiet man sitting motionless in his wheeled chair. "I don't want to listen to the noise. And it is my land, after all."

Rosalie gazed on her husband with a smile.

I mouthed a silent *Thank you.*

The viscount spluttered, "But you have such nice birds."

"No."

It was nice to hear Thorpe stick up for himself. Particularly since he was making it possible for me to go sketching again in the same locale as I had that day.

"Silverthorn hasn't put any restrictions on your shooting on his land, has he?" Rosalie asked in what I thought was a deceptively innocent tone.

"My uncle has been very generous in letting us shoot over there. I thought your husband would show us the same hospitality." Viscount Norrington was sounding a bit huffy. "It is only four of us now, unless Briarcliffe or Redmond want to join us."

"I certainly don't, and Redmond has expressed a desire to be far from the shooting. So, stick to Silverthorn lands, Norrington," Thorpe said, annoyance beginning to creep into his voice and his expression.

I'd never seen him express anything but cheerful good humor. The viscount must really be angering him. For Adam's sake, I hoped Thorpe's determination would stick.

"There's plenty of birds for the four of us," Downing said. Unlike the rest of the viscount's group, Downing seemed willing to stand up to the bully.

A few minutes later, the constable came in with Adam and asked the viscount to join him in speaking to the inspector. Norrington puffed up with importance as he strode out and the rest of us exhaled and relaxed a little, just enough that I could notice this change in the rest of our party.

"I hope it wasn't too awful," Thorpe said.

"No. Andrews seems to be an intelligent man," Adam told him.

"Thorpe told the viscount he can't shoot here," I told Adam.

"Thank you. I've had enough of gunfire for a while. It makes my legs ache."

"It makes my ears ache," Thorpe replied, sounding cheerful once again.

"Who is Dermot Young?" I asked the room at large.

I could tell everyone heard me by the way they all seemed to freeze for a moment. It was so quiet I could hear breathing. Then Betsy Oswald said, "Who?"

"Dermot Young," I said.

At the same moment, George Oswald said to his wife, "Hush."

I glanced at Rosalie, but she had turned her head away from me.

Chapter Eight

"He lives in the village now," Thorpe said, "although he used to be Silverthorn's estate agent. He practically ran Silverthorn's life."

"He was, but he isn't anymore?" I asked.

"Norrington found evidence of Young stealing from his employer. Young said he didn't do it, but the evidence was pretty clear. Northcott undertook the legal side of things, the prosecution, for Silverthorn, since they are relatives after a fashion. Larimer was the magistrate who initially heard the charges against Young."

Rosalie picked up her husband's narrative. "Dermot Young spent two years in prison and came out a bitter man. His wife died of shame while he was in there." She looked at me then with sad eyes. "I should have done more for her. I should have done something."

"You had your hands full with my care at the time," Thorpe told her. "But yes, we should have done something."

"I feel as if I failed the family, too," the Reverend Shaw

said. "I knew they shouldn't have suffered for Young's mistakes, but I failed to act with Christian charity."

"If his wife is dead, why did he come back here after he was released from prison?" It didn't sound as if it was the action of a wise man.

"His children stayed here with his sister and her husband. Young works for his brother-in-law and he and his children live with them. He's too old for conscription, but no one will hire him with a conviction," Rosalie told me.

"What does his brother-in-law do?"

"He runs the tobacconist and newspaper shop. He has Dermot do the heavy lifting, the cleaning, open first thing in the morning and close last thing at night. It's a job..." The reverend's voice trailed off.

"But hardly what Young was used to as Silverthorn's estate agent and head of his household," Thorpe finished.

"Is his bitterness aimed at anyone?"

"Silverthorn, Northcott, Norrington, Larimer, the judge at his trial, his defense barrister, his brother-in-law. Almost anyone he's had dealings with in the last few years," Thorpe said. "I suspect it includes me, but I think he finds me almost too easy a target."

"Poor man," Rosalie said.

"It's of his own making," George Oswald said with the righteous indignation of the unaffected ringing in every syllable.

"Even so, he's lost everything," Downing said.

"Do you know him?" I asked Downing, who was sitting

somewhat aloof from the rest of the group.

"Just what everyone's been saying."

"I can't help feeling sorry for him. Now, if you'll excuse me, I'll see whether it's time to dress for dinner," Rosalie said.

She had no more than risen from her seat when Cummings came in. "Do you wish me to ring the gong for dressing?" he asked. I wondered if he'd been listening in to our conversations. And where else might he listen?

"No," she told him, "we're all here except for the viscount. If you'll tell him it's time to dress once he finishes with the police?" Then she glanced around. "Shall we go up?"

We all rose and headed into the great hall, where Adam struggled to the lift and waited for Thorpe to be wheeled over. I'd hoped this time in the countryside would give Adam an opportunity to heal his legs and his nerves, but so far, this had not been a restful stay.

I walked up the stairs and met him outside our room, where I opened the door and walked in. He followed me in and shut the door before slowly, painfully crossing the room and dropping into a chair.

"Today's been hard on you."

"I'm not a piece of china. Don't treat me as if I'm fragile."

I looked at his angry expression and my heart sank. "I'm not. I was making a statement of fact. Today's been hard on all of us, but the rest of us aren't fresh from the hospital."

He looked away. "You're right. I'm sorry."

"Don't apologize. I'm sure I've not been helpful."

"Don't tell me what to do."

I could tell Adam was in a foul mood, probably due to the pain in his legs. "I'm sorry. It seems to be what I do best."

He shook his head. "I shouldn't snap at you because my legs hurt. But if Norrington keeps up being such a prig, I may have to snap at him."

"He was obnoxious while I was out of the room?"

"Setting records." Then Adam grinned.

"If it's too much, we can go back to London and take our chances there."

"No. Norrington and two murders aren't as difficult as the Blitz. We both need a few days' rest." He reached out and took my hand. Suddenly, the problems melted away because Adam was there.

We started dressing for dinner while Adam asked about my sketching. I offered to take him with me, but I warned him it would be a longer, steeper hike than he'd attempted lately.

He assured me he was content walking the paths through the garden, which were flat and relatively smooth. I suspected they were designed that way to handle Thorpe's wheeled chair.

"You're looking very handsome," I told Adam when he finished dressing in his evening clothes. "I think you have more color in your cheeks." And that color showed up particularly well against the perfect black and white of his evening wear.

"I was outside morning and afternoon today, and I think it agreed with me. You appear to have been out in the fresh air, too." He was smiling and looking more relaxed than he had lately, which made me glow on the inside.

"How do I look?" I twirled around in my elegant, pre-war midnight blue gown. I wore few jewels with this, but my ornaments sparkled with diamonds, low-grade chips, really, including a tiny tiara, more of a comb, in my upswept auburn hair.

"You'll be the belle of the ball." Adam took me in his arms and gave me a possessive kiss that said he was feeling better.

We left the room in time to see Thorpe get into the lift. He held the door and said to Adam, "Will you join me?"

"Gladly."

The two men were chatting amiably before the door shut and I headed down the stairs. I was nearly on the ground floor when I heard the viscount's overly loud voice demand something of the vicar in the hall above me. I hurried on to avoid him, joining Adam and Thorpe by the lower door of the lift.

"Why are you in such a rush? You're not late," Thorpe said. A moment later, the viscount's voice reached us and Thorpe cringed. "Oh."

Adam raised his eyebrows.

I shook my head slightly to let him know nothing had happened. So far.

"Are we early for dinner?" I asked a little too brightly.

"Oh, no. I'm sure Cummings will ring the gong any minute," Thorpe said. "Rosalie said we should gather in the large drawing room."

We started that way as Rosalie came out of a doorway in one direction and Inspector Andrews and Sergeant Wilcox came toward us from near the front door.

"We're leaving now, and we may not have to return," Andrews said as he reached Thorpe.

"Have you solved the murders?" Thorpe asked.

"We have a strong lead, and someone helping with our inquiries in town."

"Who?" Rosalie asked as she reached us.

"Dermot Young."

"No. He absolutely couldn't have done it. People have been misjudging him." Rosalie sounded certain.

"Nonsense," Viscount Norrington said as he joined us. "Everyone's heard him threaten me, among others. The man has a foul temper."

"I think it's more a case of not suffering fools gladly," Thorpe murmured.

Downing, who'd just walked over to join us, heard him and smiled.

"What was that?" the viscount said in tones that echoed in the high-ceilinged great hall.

"I think it's time we let the inspector get on with his work," Thorpe said.

I trusted Rosalie's judgment of people. That trust propelled me to say, "Do you have evidence that Mr. Young was here last night? And why, if the viscount was the one who discovered that Mr. Young was cheating Lord Silverthorn, didn't Mr. Young kill him?"

The viscount was so arrogant, I couldn't imagine why no one had murdered him before then.

"Those points are being considered," Inspector Andrews said in a neutral tone of voice.

I read his answer to mean either they knew the reasons, or they didn't have any evidence at all.

Rosalie lifted her chin and used her best countess tone to say, "I want to visit Mr. Young."

"For pity's sake, let the police do their job," the viscount snapped.

Rosalie turned partway away from the viscount. "Inspector?"

The inspector appeared as if he were trapped between the two aristocrats and didn't like it. "Tomorrow morning. Ten o'clock." With a nod to Thorpe, he walked away, the sergeant in his wake.

"I suppose you're satisfied, having involved yourself in police business," the viscount said to Rosalie.

"For the moment. Shall we proceed into dinner?" With her head held high, she led us to the dining room, knowing without a glance behind her that we would follow her.

She was every inch a countess.

I noticed Cummings was immediately at the earl's chair to wheel him in behind the countess. Either the man had perfect timing or he heard every word spoken in the manor.

Adam and I strolled in behind the viscount, the vicar, and Downing to discover the Oswalds were already at their places, having closely followed the Billingsthorpes.

Norrington took the seat to the right of Rosalie before she could object, with Mrs. Oswald on his other side. I sat across from her, with the Reverend Shaw on one side and Mr. Oswald on the other. Adam sat across from Mr. Oswald and between Mrs. Oswald and Thorpe. Downing took the extra seat on the one side.

Since there were only nine of us, Rosalie made it clear from the outset that the conversation would be free to spread across the table. We had no more than started on the soup course, mushrooms in broth, when she said, "I don't believe Mr. Young killed two men in our home."

"Why not? He's a violent, brutish thief," the viscount said in his usual loud tone.

"He's taciturn and bitter. But can you blame him, after losing his wife while in prison? From all reports, he was very fond of her," Rosalie said.

"Poor man," I said. I didn't think I'd want the viscount hounding me, either.

"Poor man! There was absolutely no need for him to steal from my uncle. He brought this on himself." The viscount made his pronouncement and then turned his attention back to his soup.

"Will we be shooting tomorrow? My larder is low, and so is that of some of my parishioners," the Reverend Shaw said in a quiet tone.

"Of course," the viscount said.

"Your parishioners have the best-stocked larders in England," George Oswald said, "with all the birds you shoot."

"Many of them are in great need," the reverend told him.

"Not that it matters to our host, who won't allow us to shoot on his land." The viscount set his spoon in his empty bowl with a clatter.

"Is that how you see it?" Thorpe asked the reverend in a mild voice.

"No. No, not at all. You've always been most generous to the poor of the parish. You and your lady wife," Shaw immediately replied.

"As I'm sure they'll be to the family of Dermot Young. I'm certain there isn't a sinner in the parish that the Billingsthorpes won't aid." Norrington was scoffing now and Rosalie was glaring at him.

"Of course we help the unfortunate, as does your uncle," Thorpe told him.

"You won't see me wasting my money on murderers and thieves such as Young," the viscount said. "If you want to throw away your family inheritance, I won't stop you."

"Christ tells us to be generous to the weak and afflicted," the reverend said.

"He didn't say we should waste money on killers. Pray for them, surely, but not waste money on them. Northcott was my relative of sorts and a good man. Young deserves to be hanged."

"Given the right circumstances, aren't we all murderers?" Downing said in a mild tone.

We fell silent as the soup bowls were taken away and the

fish course was served.

"I'm going into town in the morning to visit Dermot Young in the jail. Livvy, I'd like you to go with me," Rosalie said.

"Of course. You won't miss me for a while, will you, Adam?" I asked, allowing Adam to object if he wanted to.

"No. I'll keep Thorpe company if he wants."

"You'd let your wife visit a strange man, a murderer, in prison?" the viscount said. "Who runs your house?"

I saw daggers flash in Adam's eyes, but I wasn't certain if he was angry at Viscount Norrington or at me. Then it was clear the daggers were aimed at the viscount. Despite his needing his canes, I feared Adam would invite Norrington to step outside.

Chapter Nine

Then I saw Adam relax a little. "I trust my wife. As you must, Norrington, since your wife isn't here."

Bland expressions faced us around the table. Rosalie's eyes gave away her appreciation of Adam's refusal to put up with the viscount's insults. A stand her own husband couldn't adopt, since Norrington would become his neighbor and his aristocratic equal when Silverthorn died. Something that would happen in the near future, I'd been hearing. Thorpe kept a bland expression, as if this had nothing to do with him.

Norrington said nothing as he stabbed his fish with his fork.

The Reverend Shaw leaped in to change the subject, mentioning how he'd read in the newspapers that the Germans had left it too late to invade the northern shores of England or anywhere in Scotland due to weather, and that the RAF were holding their own against the Luftwaffe over the southern coast.

"Do you think the war will be over soon, Major?" Betsy

Oswald said to Adam.

"No, but I think Hitler has run out of chances to invade us. If we're smart about this, we'll be all right in the short term."

"And in the long term?" the viscount asked.

I hoped Adam remembered the viscount worked for the Ministry of Information.

"I'm waiting for the Ministry of Information to tell us."

Well done, Adam. I gave him a warm smile.

Thorpe chuckled at Adam's response. "It would be nice if someone could tell us what to expect."

"Wars are rarely predictable. We just have to keep working and fighting and praying," Adam told us as he gave me a weak smile.

"With the continent lost, no thanks to the army, and the U-boats controlling the seas, the Germans will try to bomb and starve us out. If the combined strength of the British and French armies couldn't hold off the German military, I don't see how they can stop an invasion," Norrington said. "Useless. It's being left to old men and children to save our country."

For a moment, I thought Adam would leap up and strangle the viscount with his bare hands. From my position across the table, I didn't see how I could stop him. Everyone else seemed frozen in place.

"Remind me of your military experience again, Norrington," Adam said.

"I'm in a command position," the viscount replied.

"In an office. Not many battles in an office." Adam stared at Norrington until the other man dropped his gaze.

"I'm too old to be of any use on a battlefield. Headquarters has put me where I can do the most good." The viscount lifted his chin then and looked down his nose at Adam.

"And too young for the Great War," Adam continued. "Am I right in thinking the Germans have never shot at you?"

Norrington spluttered.

At a nod from Rosalie, the fish plates were taken away and the game course was brought in.

"We were told the Duchess of Marshburn was in residence, so we walked over to see her today, but she was out," Rosalie said to the group in general. She was no doubt hoping to deflect the simmering resentment at her dinner table.

"Did you leave your card, dear?" Thorpe asked as he cut his game bird.

"We all did."

"Then I'm sure she'll get in touch with you if the gossip is to be believed and she truly is here. How long has it been since she set foot in Marshburn's hunting lodge?"

"Three years? No, four. But Thorpe, Thomas Burke is acting as butler at the house," Rosalie said.

"Really? Then someone is in residence. Otherwise, it would just be old Crofty and whatever maids are working there now." Thorpe shook his head. "I'm sure we'll find out soon enough."

"Crofty?" Betsy Oswald asked.

"Mrs. Croft, their housekeeper and cook," Rosalie said.

"And a very good cook she is," Thorpe added.

"But Thorpe, I can't imagine the duchess using Thomas Burke as a butler. He's an adequate farmer, but a butler? He doesn't seem her style."

Thorpe smiled down the table at his wife. "You complain about how hard it is to get servants since the war began. Perhaps the duchess couldn't find anyone to come out here."

The room fell silent for a minute before Betsy Oswald said, "All this talk of invasion and murder is frightening me. I'll lock our door tonight, George. You'd better be in bed when I lock the door, or you can sleep in the hall."

"Yes, dear."

Considering her bloodthirsty comments earlier in the day, I was surprised at her change of heart. Perhaps that was what staying in an ancient manor house surrounded by the dark countryside did to some people.

You couldn't get me outside in the cold and dark of night in the countryside, either. The city, even with the bombing, seemed safer. There were always people around in London.

And the same as me, Betsy Oswald was a resident of London.

Still, I couldn't help but wonder about this convenient murderer. "Did anyone see Dermot Young near the house last night?"

"That's the business of the police," the viscount said.

"If no one saw him around the hall, he wouldn't be a

likely suspect, would he?" I pressed.

"He's threatened all of us often enough. Isn't that right, Thorpe?"

Our host barely kept from glaring at the viscount. "Nothing anyone ever took seriously."

"Maybe if we had, Northcott would still be alive."

Rosalie gave a loud sniff. "Excuse me. I seem to have swallowed some of this meat wrong."

It didn't sound as if it was a choke to me. She must have really cared for Northcott. Or how he filled a void in her life. "What time did the murders take place?" I asked to cover my thoughts.

"Middle of the night. No wonder none of us saw him," Viscount Norrington said.

"Northcott and Larimer did," Betsy Oswald said brightly, leaving the rest of us speechless. "Strange place to meet someone in the middle of the night. Everyone having to carry lanterns."

Lanterns. There hadn't been any lanterns in the old wing. There were windows, and no clouds, and a moon, but why go into the old wing to look at the museum pieces without a lantern?

The rest of the meal was eaten in silence with even Norrington behaving. I felt myself relaxing by the time cheese and fruit and coffee were served.

As we rose from the table, Adam told me, "I'm going up to our room now. I think I overdid today."

"Then you need a good long rest. Would you mind if I

stayed behind to talk to Rosalie for a few minutes before I come up?"

"Stay as long as you like. I can manage."

I gave him a smile, hoping I didn't show how I worried about him when he was on his own. "I'll see you upstairs later."

Adam spoke to Thorpe on his way out of the room and I lingered, joining everyone else in the drawing room. Downing also wished our hosts a good night and left the room. Norrington, the Reverend Shaw, and the Oswalds began to play bridge, leaving Rosalie, Thorpe, and me to entertain ourselves.

"I think Adam and Henry Downing had the right idea. Would you mind if I went up early?" Thorpe asked his wife.

"Tired?" she asked.

"A little. And I've worn Adam out, too. I think I'll have Cummings give both of us massages tomorrow. I imagine Adam needs it more than I do." He gave me a smile.

"That is most generous," I told Thorpe, hoping Adam would accept the offer and that it would help him.

"Go on up, dear. Livvy and I will see to our guests."

Thorpe had no more than turned his wheeled chair when Cummings appeared to push him out of the room.

"What? Is everyone quitting early?" Norrington asked.

"No. We're here with you," Rosalie said with a faintly audible sigh.

The bridge players turned their attention to a spirited hand, and I murmured to Rosalie, "You're certain you didn't notice the woman in the first-floor window looking down at us as we left Marshburn's hunting lodge?"

"No. I'm certain."

"The more I think about it, the more I think it was Fleur Bettenard."

"The friend of the duke's you mentioned?" Rosalie lowered her voice. "The spy?"

"Yes."

Rosalie didn't make a sound, but I could tell from her expression that she wanted to shout a demand for me to explain.

"I came across her a couple of times before the war. She was never captured, enjoying the duke's protection as she did, but everyone thought she'd gone back to Germany when the war started. It would have been the sensible thing to do. Now I think everyone was wrong." I kept my voice low, not wanting any of this to come to Norrington's attention.

He'd never believe who I sometimes worked for.

"Why would she stay?" Rosalie whispered.

"I don't know. Maybe she and the duke are better friends than anyone thought." I raised my eyebrows and Rosalie swallowed her laughter.

Then I had a sobering thought. "Perhaps she's still carrying on her old trade for the Germans."

"Are you certain it was her?"

"At an angle through an upstairs window? No. I can't be certain. But it's worrying me."

* * *

After the bridge game finally ended with the Oswalds in command and the viscount complaining about the lack of skill of his partner, we all went upstairs to bed. I said good night and went into our darkened room, one dim lamp lighting my path. Gentle snores told me Adam had gone to sleep, and I definitely didn't want to awaken him.

One of Rosalie's maids had laid out my nightgown. I changed in the near darkness, put out the lamp, and crawled into bed beside Adam. His snores told me I hadn't wakened him. I quickly dropped off to sleep as well.

Hours later, I awoke and lay in the darkness, unable to think of what might have disturbed my sleep. Adam slept on. Thank goodness for that. He must have been exhausted.

I listened but didn't hear anything. No air raid sirens. No bombs. No loud engines droning overhead. No children crying in the basement shelter of our building. No wonder Adam was sleeping peacefully. He needed to make up over a month and a half's worth of sleep missed since the Blitz began.

Before that, he'd been sleeping in a noisy ward in the hospital or doing without sleep in battle-torn France. Exhaustion was wearing him down. This stay in rural Lancashire was a blessing.

I said a mental thank-you to Rosalie and snuggled down into the covers.

And heard a board creak.

I lifted my head and tried to tell from where the sound was coming. Nothing. Probably the old house settling in the cold night. I lay awake listening for a time, but eventually, I fell back to sleep.

* * *

Adam was shaved and halfway dressed by the time I woke up. I sat up and smiled at him. "You're up with the dawn today. Feeling better?"

"It's a wonder what a good night's sleep on a comfortable bed will do for someone."

I rose and went past him to clean up, leaving the door open so we could talk. "What do you and Thorpe have planned for today?"

"No idea, but I'm sure it will be pleasant. Thorpe is an interesting man. Kind, understanding, well read, but I think there's a backbone of steel underneath."

"Too bad he doesn't show that side of himself to the viscount."

Adam grinned at me. "He does when he needs to. He'd just prefer not to need to." I was back to doing my face when he added, "What time are you and Rosalie supposed to visit that man in jail?"

"Ten." I came out with my brush and sat at the dressing table to stare in the mirror to style my hair. "Did you notice any lanterns in the old wing yesterday morning?"

"No, but if you were having a clandestine meeting, you wouldn't want a lantern to call attention to it."

"Then how could you tell who you were killing?"

"The light coming in the windows from the moon, the sound of voices. Once your eyes adapt to the dark, it shouldn't be hard."

"Who would Northcott be having a clandestine meeting with?"

"Someone who wanted to kill him, apparently."

"How very droll," I grumbled.

"Someone he was blackmailing, someone who was blackmailing him, a woman he shouldn't be seen with, someone who had something he wanted, something black market." He looked at me with a shrug.

I nodded at his logic, not willing to say I knew it wasn't a woman. "If you were to talk to this man who the police think may have killed Northcott and Larimer, what would you ask him?"

"How often had he been here at the manor house? Had he ever seen the museum? Who had told him Northcott and Larimer would be here? How did Norrington discover his theft?"

"All good points. I wonder, can anyone in his family give him an alibi? There are, what, five people living in a small cottage? Might be hard to sneak out. And why wait so long to seek revenge?"

Adam thought for a moment before he said, "Norrington was here, too, and he's the one I would have wanted revenge on, were I in that man's shoes."

I nodded. "Keep your ears open. I think there must have been another motive for the murders."

"Maybe only one motive. Larimer looked as if he was trying to escape when he was struck down from behind."

"So, it's who wanted Northcott dead." I walked over to the wardrobe. "What should I wear to jail? My navy suit, do you think?"

Adam agreed that I should look as business-like as possible. We finished dressing and went down to breakfast to find the Reverend Shaw and Rosalie already at the table.

"Do I introduce you as a reporter for the *Daily Premier?*" Rosalie asked.

"Probably not, unless we need to threaten someone with national exposure," I replied as I began to fill my plate. "Is Thorpe sleeping in this morning?"

"He had a bad night last night," Rosalie said. "Reverend, please make sure the viscount doesn't try to shoot anywhere near here while we're gone. The noise…"

"I understand," Shaw replied. "How are you doing, Major?"

"Thorpe and Rosalie have been lifesavers. Their home is so restful," Adam said and gave Rosalie a grateful smile.

Norrington's booming voice came to us from the great hall, and a moment later, he strolled into the breakfast room, Oswald following him. The viscount walked straight to the server, reaching around Adam and his canes to pile eggs and sausages onto his plate and then moving on as if Adam wasn't there.

I was glad he hadn't knocked Adam over. If he had, I might have struck out at the viscount myself.

Adam picked up the serving spoon and took a small amount of food before balancing plate and canes to cross over to sit next to me. I rose to get him his coffee, dodging the viscount on the way.

The viscount settled himself in at the head of the table and said, "When do you see the jailbird this morning?"

Rosalie drew herself up to her full countess posture and stared with loathing at the viscount.

Chapter Ten

"You've never explained why you began an investigation into your uncle's finances," I said to the viscount.

"Isn't it obvious?" His face wore the sneer I often saw on him.

"No, it's not. Perhaps once you began, but not why you started. What made you suspicious?"

"Young had too free a rein over my uncle's affairs and my uncle was no longer paying as much attention to his finances as he should. Someone needed to. Someone from the family."

"So originally, you were just checking things out, as they say." I wondered how determined the viscount had been to find something, anything, against Mr. Young.

But would Mr. Northcott go along with a financial witch hunt? He didn't seem as if he was the type.

Norrington swallowed his bite and then answered, "If you wish to be so crass."

"Have you always been so protective of your uncle?"

"Until the last few years, I didn't need to be." He ate another bite and then said, "I don't know why you're wasting your time. Young is a violent thief and we're lucky he didn't murder all of us that night."

"Odd how he attacked the two people in the old wing but didn't come into the rest of the manor. There was nothing to stop him," Rosalie said.

"There. See? We've all had a lucky escape. So why visit him in prison?"

"To hear his side of the story," I said and turned back to my breakfast.

Out of the corner of my eye, I saw Adam give me a grin.

"Surely you're not allowing these two women, one of whom is your wife, to go to that cesspool alone," the viscount demanded of Adam.

"They are both much more capable than you realize," Adam said and raised his eyebrows.

"If she were my wife…" the viscount began.

"I wouldn't be here," I finished.

Rosalie choked on her tea.

Viscount Norrington glared at me. "There are plenty of wives who don't enjoy shooting parties," he said before focusing his interest on his breakfast. Since Rosalie had finished eating, I sped up eating mine so we could get moving.

And escape dealing with the viscount.

Adam finished eating when I did and spent time with me until Rosalie and I met up in the great hall. We set off with

Miles driving us into Lancaster. He dropped us off in front of the police station at Rosalie's direction and drove off to park the car.

We walked in and were met a few minutes later by Inspector Andrews. He took us down dingy hallways until he opened a wooden door that a constable sat outside.

Dermot Young sat slumped over a scarred table, an empty mug between his large hands. He looked up when we entered, sharp eyes taking in all three of us before he lowered his gaze to the table again.

I had the impression of a big man used to manual labor. Massive shoulders and biceps, a thick neck, deep scowl marks etching his face. I sensed an angry man who felt justified in being angry.

"Young, her ladyship and her friend wanted to see you," Andrews began.

"They've seen me. Now they can go," came out in a rusty voice.

"How often have you been in the Earl of Briarcliffe's medieval museum?" I asked.

"Who are you and why should I tell you?" was said in his untrusting growl.

"This is my friend, Livvy Redmond. I've seen her puzzle out problems much the same as yours before," Rosalie told him, her voice the gentle sound one would use on young children. "Give her a chance."

Young shot her a questioning look and she responded with a nod.

He shot me a dark look before he said, "Once. Silverthorn wanted to see it, so I brought him. Must have been four or five years ago. Check with the earl."

"You live in the village with your family. I don't see how you could have slipped past everyone in your house to come out to the hall, or how you could have reached the hall, killed two people, cleaned off their blood, and gone back to the village before you were missed. You don't have access to an auto, do you?"

"No auto, no petrol. No need for either. I'd have to walk the whole way, in the dark, in the cold, to maybe find someone away from their homes who these fools think I wanted to kill." He banged the cup once, flat onto the table-top.

"You threatened to," Rosalie said.

"I was angry, wasn't I? Thrown in prison for something I didn't do, my wife dyin' of a broken heart, losing my home and job. But that was then. I've got my kids to think of now. Can't afford to let them down again."

"How much do you talk to your neighbors in the village?" I asked.

"Not at all. They all think I'm a jailbird, I'm a thief, and they don't want to talk to me."

"And your family?"

"My kids will speak to me if it's just us, but my sister and her husband won't talk to me unless it's to give me orders or to tell me I'm a disappointment."

"Who told you Northcott, the viscount, and the

magistrate would all be at Briarcliffe Hall this weekend?"

"Nobody."

"Nobody?"

"People would have to talk to me to tell me something about people the same as that. And none of them will."

"You must have something to show your innocence that night," I said. "A child with an earache. A trip to the pub."

The big man shook his head. "It wouldn't do any good. There was nothing wrong with those books before the viscount wanted to get me out of the way. Nobody believed me then, nobody believes me now that Mr. Northcott and the magistrate's been murdered."

"But Northcott was the one who audited the books and found the discrepancies, and I believe he was an honest man," Rosalie said.

"And now he's been murdered," Inspector Andrews added.

"I can't explain what happened, but I never took a penny that wasn't mine." Young looked at Rosalie. "You have to believe me."

"I want to," Rosalie said. "And I don't believe you murdered those two men. There can't be any evidence that you did."

"There was blood on his shirt. A lot of blood," Andrews said.

"I told you. I had a nosebleed. I get them."

"Were you at home all night?" I asked.

"My sister's husband was expecting a delivery at his

shop, and he made me stay to take it in when it came. They were late, and I didn't get home to my bed until three."

"Who were they, this delivery company?"

"Dunno. Not the usual truck, but it was the usual driver. Whoever my brother-in-law does business with." He shrugged. "They brought two boxes, I put them inside the shop, locked up, and then I left."

"Two boxes of what?"

"Fags. Bagged tobacco for pipes."

"Delivered at nearly three in the morning?" Inspector Andrews said. "On top of everything else, you're dealing with black market goods."

"No. I just waited for our regular delivery to arrive. Truck must have broken down. That's what they said. It broke down, and they were hours late on their regular route."

"Does your brother-in-law know you're dealing in black market goods?" Andrews said. His tone was aggressive, and the prisoner leaned back slightly even as he glanced up defiantly.

"No, and neither do I. You won't get me saying something that isn't true."

"It can be easily checked with the wholesalers around here."

"Then do it. You'll see it's the truth."

"And you still don't have an alibi."

"How was I to know I'd need one? My sister's husband saw me when I arrived back at the house. He was angry I had wakened him coming in."

"If Mr. Young did have to wait until three in the morning to bring in the boxes of goods, then he might have been seen by the milk truck or anyone who had to get into Lancaster early," I told the inspector.

"If the delivery did arrive at three in the morning, he'd still have had time to get to the old wing of the hall and kill both men," the policeman reminded us.

"Late in the window of the time the police surgeon said the killings could have taken place," I said. "Have you asked his brother-in-law what time he arrived home, Inspector? Or spoken to their usual delivery company about a truck breaking down?"

"I will be," Inspector Andrews said, glaring at me.

"Did you hand the Silverthorn accounts directly over to Northcott?" I asked Mr. Young. Something was nagging at me.

"No. I handed them over to the viscount, and he gave them to Northcott. There was nothing wrong with those books before I gave them to the viscount, but there was by the time Northcott took them to the magistrate."

"You think Norrington changed entries in the ledgers?" I asked.

"Yes. Him or Northcott. But no one believed me. He's a viscount. I'm a nobody." Young's shoulders slumped.

"I think you've spent enough time with the prisoner. Let's go," the inspector replied, ushering us out of the small room.

"Inspector Andrews, have you made up your mind Mr.

Young is guilty and you don't need to look any further for the killer?" Rosalie asked as soon as we reached the hall with the door shut.

"That could be a big mistake," I added.

Andrews shook his head. "We're still looking for any other possibilities, but we're not finding them. We also haven't found out how Young could have known where Northcott was that night," he continued, sounding glum.

"You believe Northcott was the main target of the murderer?" I asked.

"Yes. Larimer was apparently trying to flee when he was cut down. Northcott was struck down quickly, by surprise. His was the first death. Larimer must have walked in on the killing, although we don't know why."

I shuddered at the mental image I now had. "Tell me, inspector, did you see any sign of lanterns? There is no electricity in the old wing."

"No sign of lanterns, but the moon was out and bright that night. With the large windows in the old wing, anyone could have seen what they wanted. And Larimer had an electric torch to help him see."

"And be seen by the killer," I added.

Andrews nodded.

"Was anyone seen outside the hall that night?" Rosalie asked.

"We keep asking everyone in the area, but so far, no one saw a thing at the right time."

"Are you being pressured to make a speedy arrest?"

Rosalie asked.

"Yes, but not by his lordship."

"The viscount," I said with a theatrical shudder, and Rosalie nodded.

"How is the old earl?" Andrews asked.

"Not well," Rosalie said.

"Inspector, can you find out if the viscount's finances have improved noticeably in the past three years?" I asked.

"You think the viscount is robbing the old earl and got Young out of the way so he could do it?" the inspector sounded shocked.

"Yes. The viscount already thinks of the title and estate as his. If the old earl dies soon, no one will ever be able to prove it was the viscount who did the thieving," I told him. "He'll have control over the accounts, his own, the estates, the old earl's, all of it."

"I'll make some inquiries. It should have been done when the case was first brought to trial, but I wasn't here then," Inspector Andrews told me.

"The old earl should probably be our next call. Ready, Livvy?" Rosalie said.

"I'd like to meet him," I told her.

Miles picked us up under more clouds, but no rain. Rosalie gave him directions to take us to Silverthorn Manor. Then we sat back and Rosalie said, "What do you think?"

"It seems unlikely that Mr. Young is the killer. Much more likely to be someone who was already in or around the house that night. Someone who could arrange for one or both men to meet him in the old wing."

"I can't believe any of the servants were involved."

"There's no reason to think so unless we find one of them had a motive. And we need to look, just to prove there isn't any. You realize that, Rosalie."

"Yes. Miles, you're my witness. I've given Livvy permission to ask questions and look around in the servants' area to make sure there isn't any reason why any of you would want to murder my guests."

"We wouldn't, your ladyship," he said quickly. Then he took a deep breath and said, "Yes, your ladyship."

"What I want to do is clear all of you so I can go on to more likely candidates. All right, Miles?" I asked.

"Yes, ma'am." He didn't sound pleased.

"For starters, do you have an alibi for part or all of that night?"

I didn't think at first that he'd answer me. Then he breathed out heavily and said "No. I'd done a bit of work on the car and driven to the station and back twice in the afternoon, and I knew I had repairs to make on the boiler the next morning. After dinner—we had a late dinner in the servants' hall because of the dinner party upstairs—I went to my room over the garage and went to bed."

"And you didn't see anyone until morning?"

"No."

Was that a hesitation? "What time did dinner end downstairs?"

"A little after nine. I lingered over my coffee and headed

out to the garage before ten."

"Did you ever have any dealings with Mr. Northcott?"

"I may have driven him once or twice, but nothing other than that."

"Do you use his bank?"

"Don't have much use for banks."

I glanced at Rosalie, who shrugged a little. That seemed to be all I could do for the moment.

As we pulled up to an old manor house and stopped, I could hear shooting in the fields. "Well, that's restful for an invalid," Rosalie said shaking her head as she climbed out of the automobile.

Climbing out after her, I gazed at the magnificent front of Silverthorn Manor. It was made of a buff sandstone with simple lines and large symmetrical windows. Graceful pillars held up the two-story porch roof. Here was a traditional Georgian-styled manor house.

I followed Rosalie to the front door and watched her tug on the bell pull. After a minute or two, a thin middle-aged man in a black suit opened the door.

"Smith, is his lordship up to seeing visitors?"

"I know he'd want to see you, milady." He led us to a ground-floor room at the side of the house. "We've moved him down here since he gave up climbing the stairs. The room is warm and sunny, if there's any sun to be had." He glared at the closest window as we walked, as if daring the sun to show itself.

A fire was burning brightly and quite warmly in a large

fireplace as we walked into the room that had been turned into the Earl of Silverthorn's bedroom. A four-poster bed had been assembled in here, taking up most of the room. The heavy velvet curtains and the thick patterned carpets were left over, I felt certain, from when this room had been a drawing room or perhaps the morning room.

"Ah, Rosalie," the old man in the bed called out before coughing, "how good to see you."

"I'd like you to meet my friend, Livvy Redmond."

"Come closer. I want to get a good look at you. I don't often get to see anyone as young and pretty as you two." His voice was gaspy but his words were clear.

I looked at Rosalie, eyebrows raised, but she was already walking toward the bed. "I've heard you've not been a good patient."

"Nonsense. Where did you hear that? From my nephew? I'm not dying fast enough for him, that's his problem. Oh my, a redhead. Where did you find her, Rosalie?"

"We used to work together. This is Livvy. I'm hoping she can figure out what happened to Robert Northcott."

"You're certainly pretty enough, but do you have brains, girl?"

"I hope so," I told him.

"You'd better do more than hope to get to the bottom of this tangle." The old man began to cough until he was out of breath.

The middle-aged butler and a woman about the same age in a black dress hurried in. "You need to stop talking. You know what the doctor said," the woman told him as she poured out a spoonful of a brown liquid from a dark bottle.

"We'll come back later when you're feeling better," Rosalie said, backing up.

"Robert told me," the old man wheezed out. "Is that why he was killed?" Then he began to cough again and we were hurried out of the room by his manservant.

Chapter Eleven

Neither of us spoke until we reached the automobile. "He looks awful," Rosalie said and sniffed.

"I wonder what Robert told him," I replied.

"Certainly nothing that would get either him or Larimer killed in our medieval museum," Rosalie said. "I shouldn't have waited so long before going over to see him. He's always been so lively. Now he's fading before our eyes."

"When did Robert Northcott last see the earl?"

"I don't know. I only arrived here from Bletchley two days before you arrived." Rosalie glared at me. "If you think it's that important, we'll go back tomorrow and ask him what Robert said and when."

I nodded, letting the conversation drop. She was obviously worried about her old friend.

When we reached Briarcliffe Hall, we wandered the ground floor before finally finding Thorpe and Adam sitting on a bench in the garden. "Cummings works wonders," Adam greeted me. "He massaged my legs and they feel oh, so much better."

"Or they did," Thorpe said, laughing, "until he walked the whole way around the paths twice and overdid it."

"I'd hoped you wouldn't tattle on me," Adam said, but he grinned and Thorpe chuckled.

"I wonder if he'd teach me some of his techniques so I could try to give you massages when we get home," I said.

"I'm sure he would," Thorpe said. "He works miracles."

"I'd be indebted if he would. You can't believe how much better I feel after he's pounded on my muscles, and not just my leg muscles. My shoulders ache from relying on my canes all the time," Adam said and held out a hand to me. I walked up to him and clutched his fingers. I'd be glad to learn anything if it would help Adam.

"Silverthorn looks terrible," Rosalie told Thorpe.

Thorpe's shoulders slumped. "I'm sorry. He's always been a good neighbor and a good friend. I'll miss him."

"I will too," Rosalie replied.

"Viscount Norrington inherits the title from him?" Adam asked.

"The title, the estate, the house. And he won't let you forget it, either," Thorpe said.

"Does he have any children?" I asked.

Rosalie shook her head. "He and the viscountess have not been blessed. Perhaps because that would require them to spend time under the same roof."

"An arranged marriage?" I asked.

"By people who took much too much for granted."

Rosalie gave me a smile.

I smiled back. The viscountess had my sympathies.

Loud voices headed in our direction warned us the shooting party had returned. "We've stocked the reverend's larder and some of his unfortunates," Norrington boomed. "When's lunch?"

"We've been waiting for you," Rosalie said. "Mr. Oswald, if you could tell your wife lunch will soon be served?"

"She didn't go with us," George Oswald replied.

"We haven't seen her, either. If you could think of where she is, I'd appreciate it," Rosalie said.

I saw movement on the hill coming down from my sketching spot. "There she is."

"Good," Rosalie said. "I'll see about having lunch brought in now." She rose and walked into the house. The rest of us traipsed in after her, the four hunters moving quickly on her heels while talking about the birds they'd shot that morning. Adam and I moved slower while waiting for Thorpe.

We assembled ten minutes later in the dining room, Betsy Oswald having reached the house and brushed herself off before she came to the table.

"Where did you walk to?" I asked her.

"Up and down hills and around by the path that takes the far side of the stream away from the village. It was quite a long walk."

"I'm surprised we didn't see you," the Reverend Shaw said. "That route would have taken you close to the field where we were shooting."

"I heard some shooting in the distance," she replied, "but I turned and went another way so I wouldn't disturb you. I know better than to disturb hunters." Betsy gave her husband an unreadable look.

Was this something the couple fought about? Had Betsy blundered into a bird shooting session before? That could have proved painful.

"We took the birds to a couple of my parishioners. I hope you don't mind, Lady Briarcliffe," the reverend said.

"Not at all. I'm glad you're seeing to their needs," Rosalie replied.

"The young and fit have joined the military or are working in the factories. It seems as if it is only the very young or old who are left out here in the countryside with the war going on and they're in need of our support," the Reverend Shaw continued.

"But there are a couple of factories here in the countryside belonging to Thorpe that employ some of the locals," Norrington said.

"Wish they were closer. They're too far for me to visit either of them with any frequency. And we lost our last manager to a government job. Can't seem to find a replacement," Thorpe grumbled. He wasn't usually one to complain about his limitations, Rosalie had told me.

I glanced at Rosalie, who looked worried. Oswald and Downing looked interested. I wondered what their government ministries were.

"Do the Duke of Marshburn's tenants attend your parish

church?" I asked to change the subject. Fleur Bettenard's possible presence worried me. Had I seen her, and had the vicar met her as part of his duties?

"They're a part of the parish, but they don't attend regularly. Not something the duke fosters."

"So, you don't know if the duchess is in residence."

He looked at me, scowling. "I wouldn't think so. But if she's there, and she hasn't been here in a year or two—no, it's been nearly four years—she'll be in church tomorrow, as will her tenants."

"Speaking of which, Livvy, will you attend church with me tomorrow? Adam?" Rosalie asked.

We both agreed. I didn't think Fleur would be a guest of the duchess. The Duke of Marshburn was more her political ally and possible lover, but I hoped Fleur for some reason, for any reason, would come into the village tomorrow so I would know if I was right.

Or the person I'd mistaken for Fleur would appear so I'd know I was wrong.

"Will you be going back to the Silverthorn estate to shoot this afternoon?" Rosalie asked.

"Since your husband refuses to let us shoot here, we'll have to," Norrington said. "No shooting tomorrow. The vicar won't allow it."

I gave Shaw a grateful smile, and then glanced over to see Rosalie do the same.

The rest of the lunch went quickly, being just three courses followed by cheese and coffee. The hunters finished and then readied for their afternoon shoot while Thorpe, Adam, and we three women lingered until we heard them leave out the front door, boots clattering on the stone steps.

"I'm going to continue with my sketch, if no one minds," I said.

"I'm going to hike around the village," Betsy Oswald said.

"I'm going to visit one of the factories, if I'm not needed here. We need to keep an eye on these things, otherwise something is always falling apart," Rosalie said.

"I have work to do in the estate office," Thorpe said. "You won't be too bored on your own, will you, Adam?"

"I'll choose a book out of your library and go into the garden and read," Adam told him. "I could do with an easy afternoon after all the walking I did this morning."

We split up then. When I left by the French doors to the garden, Adam was seated reading. No one else was about.

"Will you be all right, darling?" I asked.

"Of course. Enjoy your sketching." Adam turned his attention back to his book.

After an hour or two, I'd finished my outline of the sketch of the house and some of the details were roughed in. The only person I'd seen in that time was Adam and he seemed immersed in his book, so I was certain I wasn't missed.

I decided to indulge my curiosity and see if I could find Fleur Bettenard or another woman with blonde hair at the Duke of Marshburn's lodge. Even as I rose and left my sketching materials where they were, I knew it was a foolish thing to do. Particularly if the woman I'd seen was Fleur.

I hiked the short distance up the hill to the fence and climbed over the stile. From there it was a short distance to Marshburn Lodge. I expected I would be met by a man toting a shotgun, but I saw no one.

Fleur had threatened to kill me every time I'd met up with her. No doubt because I'd been trying to capture her as part of a Nazi plot to harm Britain, but she found me easy to evade and so never tried too hard to harm me.

I knew it was a stupid thing to do, but my curiosity drove me on. I promised myself to be careful. I walked up to the front door of the Elizabethan-era hunting lodge, rang the bell, and when the glowering, stocky, middle-aged man answered the door, I said, "Mr. Burke? Livvy Redmond. I'd like to see Fleur Bettenard."

"No one here by that name." He began to shut the door in my face.

I leaned on the heavy wooden door with my left arm and shoulder. "The blonde who's staying here? I'm sure it's Fleur. We're old friends. Please tell her I'm here."

Burke began to push on the door, shoving me out of his way, when a slightly accented voice behind him said, "Let her in."

The butler jerked open the door and, since I was still pushing on the door, I nearly fell onto the marble floor. When I caught my balance, I looked up to see Fleur Bettenard looking at me from the third step from the top of the massive dark wooden staircase leading to the first floor.

"I'm surprised you're still here, Fleur, if you knew you'd

been spotted." She looked exactly as I remembered her. Had so little time passed that neither of us had changed? I hadn't seen her since before the war began. Well over a year, and such a stressful year.

"I'm surprised you're brave enough to show your face here." Fleur, menace in her tone, took two steps down the stairs and I backed up to the door. Somewhere, deep in the lodge, I heard a door shut. A back door leading outside.

"Why aren't you at home, aiding the war effort?" If she were caught here, she could be hanged as a foreign agent.

"I'm not everyone's favorite patriot, so I'm staying here for the time being, out of the way. Besides, do you know how hard it is to get out of England in one piece these days?" She gave me a smile that made me wonder if hawks smiled.

"Does anyone know you're here?"

"Very few. The duke has vouched for his good behavior and mine, and we have pledged to stay silent and well-behaved, out of the public eye. I am essentially under house arrest. Mr. Burke is one of my jailers."

"Is the duke here, too?"

"No. They have separated us for the good of the country and the duchess's peace of mind." The corners of her mouth lifted in a little smirk. "The duke is also under house arrest. He is paying for his confinement, and mine, saving the British government the cost of imprisoning us."

"So, Mr. Burke, you are working for the British government but on the duke's payroll?" I asked, turning to look at the glum man.

"Aye."

"And my being here will appear on some government record sooner or later."

"Consorting with a known traitor." Fleur laughed. "That won't do you any good."

I'd have to report this to Sir Malcolm as soon as I returned to London before he discovered it on his own. Sir Henry wouldn't care unless I could write an article on Fleur and her exclusive prison for the *Daily Premier,* and Sir Malcolm would never allow that.

But Sir Malcolm would be livid if I didn't tell him immediately that a German assassin was still in England. He might lock me up for a while until his temper cooled if I didn't let him know quickly enough.

Fleur's presence here shouldn't hurt Adam's army career as long as I kept him well away from the Duke of Marshburn's estate, and he could never walk up the hill on his canes. I'd better warn Rosalie, since she'd left her calling card and mine at the lodge for the duchess. Rosalie was still working at Bletchley Park, and they were not a group who cared for nasty surprises in their employees' contacts.

I crossed my arms. "I don't think my visiting you during your incarceration would do you any good with some of your friends, either."

We stared at each other for a moment before Fleur came the rest of the way down the stairs. She stopped in front of me and smiled, with a smile that caused me to press my back into the door. "But it would do you less good. I don't let people stand in my way. I am a killer. You've said so yourself."

She was, as I knew from experience. My knees began to give out so I stiffened them and edged toward the door handle. "If you were going to kill me, you'd have done it by now." I hoped.

"Don't be too sure of that."

Blast. She could not only kill me, but also spread lies about me that would hurt not only me, but also Adam, my father, Rosalie, and who knew who else. "Is there anything either of us can do to improve the situation, now that I've found you here? There's no denying our meeting." I looked over at Burke.

Fleur gave Burke a momentary glance. "We could ask Mr. Burke not to record your visit."

"I doubt he would listen to either of us." He kept glowering at me.

"You can at least take your calling cards and remove proof of your visit for yourself and your friends." She held out the three embossed cards. Until that moment, I had forgotten Betsy Oswald had been with us.

"They were meant for the duchess, not you. Is the duchess due here soon?"

"Not with such an unwelcome guest as me. Besides, she prefers London society to hunting parties."

I took the cards from Fleur's outstretched hand and put them in my jacket pocket. At least that preserved Rosalie's situation. "I should be leaving. I don't want to ruin any reputations more than they already are. And this way, Mr.

Burke can report that I only stayed a few minutes and never left the entrance hall."

"Oh, Olivia, you are such a slave to propriety. Don't you know that if people want to lie about you, the truth is such flimsy protection?"

"I'm not going to lie about you, Fleur, and I don't think you would lie about me. You're a woman of integrity, no matter that we are on opposite sides of this war."

"How does it help my integrity if I've promised to kill you and then let you leave here alive?" There was that frightening smile again.

"Wisdom should increase your reputation. Now, I'm going to leave before anyone decides to make this accidental meeting lethal." I gave her a smile and a nod before edging into the door opening.

Mr. Burke opened it long enough for me to leave and then shut it against my back. I left and hurried along the path I had followed, not looking back until I reached the stile in the boundary fence.

There was no one behind me.

Chapter Twelve

I walked down the path to where I'd left my sketch and supplies. Immediately, I saw something was wrong, but my brain couldn't register what I was looking at. My pencils had been snapped in two and the sketch I'd worked on was crumpled and dragged along the ground. My sketchpad was tossed several yards away, dented where it had hit the tree trunk it lay below.

Either someone didn't care for my sketching, or they didn't like me. The person I'd heard leave Marshburn Lodge?

I picked up the ruin of my efforts and trudged back to the hall, my shoulders slumped. When I reached the garden, I realized Adam had already gone inside. I was glad I didn't have to explain any of this to him yet.

This was all my fault. If I hadn't had to satisfy my curiosity, no one would have had an opportunity to destroy my artwork.

And I still had to tell Rosalie and Adam whom I'd met while someone carried out this attack.

Sitting on the bench, I tried to straighten out the crumpled sketchpad, which would be much improved after I weighed it down with books for a while. The pencils would be short, but once I sharpened the points, they would be usable. But the sketch itself, a single sheet without a backing to protect it, was beyond salvation.

"Livvy. We're in the small drawing room. Would you care to join us?"

At the sound of Rosalie's voice, I held up the ruined sketch.

She walked over to see the damage close up. "Good grief. What happened?"

"I went to Marshburn Lodge to see if I had been right about Fleur Bettenard. I was." I handed her back the calling cards. "The duchess will not be here as long as Fleur is in residence."

Rosalie sat next to me on the bench and began to try to flatten and brush the sketch. "Why don't you tell me about it?"

I did, but I didn't feel any better about my mistake afterward.

"You will have plenty of opportunities to draw Briarcliffe Hall. It's doing Adam a world of good, and Thorpe and I will want you to visit time and again. The problem, as I see it, is you calling on this woman Fleur Bettenard."

"As soon as I get back to London, I'll call on the 'spymaster,' shall we call him, and tell him what I found. He's the reason I know Fleur and can recognize her."

"Will this get you into trouble?"

"I wouldn't think so, as long as I report it as soon as I can. I suppose we'll have to return to London tomorrow." I really didn't want to.

"Do you want to telephone him? Would that help?"

A boulder lifted off my chest. There was no way I could put enough in a telegram to explain my meeting Fleur at Marshburn Lodge. And this way Adam and I could stay here in Lancashire. "Yes. Could we do it now? Before we go into the drawing room?"

Rosalie nodded. "Come into the office."

I followed her inside and down a corridor to the estate manager's office. Servants were busy in the kitchen, so no one paid us any attention. While Rosalie stood guard at the door, I made my call to the memorized number.

"Olivia. What do you want?" came Sir Malcolm's familiar grumble.

I hoped no one was listening at one of the other two phones in the house or the switchboard in the nearest town before I said, "Did you know Fleur Bettenard is still in England?"

There was silence for a moment before he quietly said, "No. I did not."

"She's under some sort of house arrest at the Duke of Marshburn's lodge near Lancaster, while he's under house arrest at another of his manor houses."

"I knew about him. We couldn't just lock up a duke. He gets touchy about his rights as a peer. Thinks some King

Henry from long ago is still on the throne."

"You managed to lock up Mosley." Sir Oswald Mosley was a former member of the House of Commons who became the head of the British Union of Fascists and was imprisoned the previous May after his hero, Hitler, invaded the Netherlands, Belgium, and France.

"Mosley's only a baronet. They're ten a penny. So, Marshburn is locked up on one of his estates, has been since last May when Churchill became PM, paying for his guards and his upkeep and saving the British taxpayers the cost of dealing with a duke's expensive taste." Sir Malcolm sounded grimly satisfied with the result.

"My hostess heard a rumor that the duchess was in residence, so we went over to pay a social call. The duchess wasn't there, but I looked through a window and saw a woman I thought could be Fleur. I went back on my own later to see if it was Fleur, and she made an appearance."

"I thought she threatened to kill you the next time she saw you."

Yes, but it had been a long time ago, and I hoped she had forgotten. "I stood just inside the door, and while she threatened me again, she didn't make any effort to attack."

"How long did you speak to her?"

"Five minutes at most. More likely three or four. I didn't want to compromise Adam or my hosts by staying longer, or give her time to change her mind and attack me. A local man named Burke is supposed to be her jailer."

"I'll follow this up and make sure everything is according

to regulations." As was often the case, Sir Malcolm hung up without saying goodbye.

I walked over and opened the door to find Rosalie talking to the cook. When they finished, she asked me, "Are we covered?"

"Yes, it's reported to the proper people."

"Good. Let's go back up to the drawing room and see what Thorpe and Adam are up to."

"I'll need to tell Adam whom I've found, and I don't like the idea of keeping Thorpe in the dark unless you think I should." With Thorpe confined to a wheeled chair, I never knew if I should coddle him or keep him involved in everything. I wasn't certain how fragile his health might be.

"We'll tell Thorpe and Adam together. Not in the drawing room," Rosalie said. "We'll meet you in your room after the dressing gong has sounded."

I nodded, hoping Adam wouldn't be able to tell I was holding something back from him until then. When I walked in to the drawing room to join them, he was playing chess with Thorpe again and trying to hold his own despite our host having a great deal more experience. And the time to practice.

"How did your sketch turn out?" he asked me after moving a knight.

"I set it down when I finished and went for a walk. When I returned, someone had destroyed my sketch and broken my pencils." I spoke quietly, but both men looked shocked as they stared at me.

"Why would anyone do that?" Betsy Oswald asked as she stepped in directly behind me.

"They don't like me or my sketching," I said with a shrug. I didn't like Betsy sneaking up behind me that way.

"Or they don't like Rosalie and me and our house," Thorpe said.

"That I can't believe. You're two of the nicest people I've ever met," I said immediately and with some heat.

"Thank you for your endorsement, Livvy, but I can't believe we're universally loved," Thorpe said with a grin. He obviously wasn't worried about it, but I was. It was mean-spirited and sneaky. Much the same as the murders that had taken place in the old wing of the hall just days before. The similarity worried me.

"Oh, Rosalie, I forgot to mention Constable Cole came by to share Dermot Young's thanks for sending that solicitor Perkins to defend him. But we didn't, did we?" As Thorpe spoke, I turned to see Rosalie walk around the other side of the chessboard table.

"No, we didn't. So, who did?" she answered.

Who indeed? "Where is Cummings? I'd like to ask him if he can give people alibis or if he saw anything strange. You don't mind, do you, Thorpe?"

"Not at all. He should be around here—oh, there you are, Cummings. Would you answer Mrs. Redmond's questions? She has experience solving mysteries, and I want her help in solving this one before anyone else gets hurt."

Betsy Oswald backed up a step or two while Thorpe was

speaking. I didn't believe she had anything to do with these tragedies. Was she frightened I might suspect her, or did she find my employment not suitable for a woman?

"Shall we speak in the study, madam?"

"Please. Lead the way." I followed him down the great hall and into a door near the entrance. We both paused in the doorway when we found Henry Downing sitting behind the desk, writing something on a piece of paper.

"Oh, Cummings, I hope you don't mind. I came in to get a piece of paper to write a letter, and then I stayed to write it. You're going to think I learned my manners from Norrington."

"I'm sure his lordship won't mind, sir," Cummings said stiffly, pointedly holding the door open.

"I hope her ladyship had a good journey to the factory? She and his lordship appear to make a terrific team," Downing said to me as he stood up.

"They work in complete harmony," I replied, stepping out of his way.

"I'll just finish this in my room," Downing said, blushing a light red as he walked out of the room. "Mrs. Redmond," he said, nodding to me.

Once I'd settled into a well-padded leather chair and found Cummings insisted on standing in my presence, I asked, "The night Mr. Larimer and Mr. Northcott were killed, can you go through your movements for me?"

"The servants' dinner was late that night on account of all the guests at dinner."

"We must be a great inconvenience for the servants." I felt guilty.

"Not at all. There was confusion over the numbers and Cook prepared too little of one course. It meant she had to spend more time on the upstairs dinner and couldn't start ours until late."

"So, you were all together eating until what time?"

"Well after nine. It was close to ten before I finished my coffee, since I knew I wouldn't be needed until the tour of the armaments was finished."

"How did you know about that?"

"It was spoken of at dinner and overheard by the servers. We keep each other informed. Makes life easier for the family and for the servants."

"A good arrangement," I said and realized I sounded stuffy. "What did you do next?"

"I made his lordship's room ready for him. It's a complicated task, due to his condition, and took until he was ready to come upstairs."

"And then?"

"I readied him for bed and left when her ladyship came in to say good night before going to her room."

"How long have they had separate rooms?"

"The earl insisted on it after his accident. After he left hospital and the extent of his injuries were known. There are things about his condition..."

Oh. I nodded and held up one hand, not wanting to hear more. "And what time did her ladyship come in?"

"Well after midnight. Then I went down to the kitchen, had a cup of tea, and checked the supplies for his lordship's medications and salves. There was one I was getting low on, and so I made up another batch. That took until after two."

"Did you see anyone, either on your way to the kitchen or in the kitchen?"

"Cook came out about one and had a cup of tea with me. She was still fussing over the mistake at dinner and couldn't sleep. She stayed with me until I finished."

"And then?"

"We both went to bed."

"Alone?"

Cummings drew himself up to his full height. "I will not have aspersions cast on this house."

"I'm sorry. That sounded wrong." I held in my giggle from embarrassment. "I was just making sure I understood the timeline, and that you and Cook were each other's alibis for a small part of the crucial time. What I'm trying to do is similar to setting out chess pieces, not making a judgment."

He made a quiet grumble but no other reply.

"Did you see anyone else at any time after dinner?"

"Not once Miles and Mary went out to the stables, no."

"I didn't realize Mary's quarters were in the stables." I tilted my head and stared at Cummings.

He shut his eyes for a moment. When he opened them, he looked at me and said, "I hope that doesn't need to be repeated. They're both saving up to pay for a wedding and start a home."

"I suspect Thorpe and Rosalie know."

"I don't think they do."

"If they were against it, they'd know, and you would know they know, which makes me think they are—accepting of the situation."

"Turning a blind eye?"

"Yes, which means I don't need to mention anything." And it explained Miles's discomfort in answering my questions in the automobile in front of Rosalie. "Any other servants?"

"Another housemaid and a scullery maid, both of whom fall into bed exhausted as soon as dinner is over. They're young and local and wouldn't notice anything unless they slipped on the blood."

"Are they excited to be so close to a real murder?"

Cummings made a face. "Yes. Silly girls, both of them."

"Being local, they must know the dead men."

"And are as baffled as the rest of us. Mr. Northcott, unlike his cousin, was a true gentleman. Considerate. Polite. And Mr. Larimer, while brusque, was a good farmer and a good landlord. Well-liked by all."

"Both men had good reputations?"

"Yes."

"Are you local, Cummings?"

"Yes, ma'am. All of the servants in the hall are."

That explained Cummings's familiarity with the reputations of the dead men. "Does anyone have half an idea why these men were murdered, here, now?"

Cummings shook his head.

"Being local and well regarded, there can't be too many choices for suspects."

"None, really."

"If I told you Mr. Northcott was the intended victim and Mr. Larimer was in the wrong place at the wrong time, would people have any suggestions then?"

"I've heard that from Constable Cole. If I hear any suggestions, I will tell you." As Cummings was local, he should be a good source of information, but he was hesitant to trust me.

"Any suggestions on who hired a solicitor for Dermot Young?"

"Defending him will be an expensive task. It would have to be someone wealthy."

It was my turn to nod. "And that doesn't leave us with too many choices. Not locally."

"And this has to be a local murder."

Interesting that he would say that. "What do you mean, Cummings?"

"The killer knew where those men, at least Mr. Northcott, were in the middle of the night, they knew how to get into the old wing, they knew weapons were close at hand. Knowledge that outsiders wouldn't have."

"So, Dermot Young would know all about the old wing?"

"Yes. He's a villager. He'd know who was visiting, how to get into the old wing, everything. There are no secrets in a village."

"Even though he claims no one will speak to him?"

"He could still overhear conversations, particularly in his brother-in-law's shop."

Blast. Dermot Young could still be in the running for chief suspect. "Have there been many visitors here lately? Outsiders such as my husband and me, who would have learned about the medieval weapons only while visiting here?"

"His lordship doesn't have visitors when her ladyship isn't at home, and she's not been here in the past couple of months."

"But I thought I heard Mr. Northcott was here within the last two weeks."

"It was just him. He was company in the evenings for his lordship, insisted Cook not do anything differently from when it was just his lordship, and went about his business during the day."

"His business?"

"He visited the old earl, talked to Mrs. Cole and Mrs. Petrie—the current church secretary and the previous one—about some old church records and no doubt caught up on the latest gossip, since he knows everyone in the village. Oh, and of course he checked out some details in the old wing. He really was fascinated by those old suits of armor."

"Would the church records have anything to do with the armaments in the old wing?"

"I don't see how. They might." Cummings stared at the far wall. "Mr. Northcott didn't spend much time in the old wing during his last visit. Just a few minutes each time he went in there." He gave me a fierce look. "This business, the shooting party, the murders, has upset her ladyship. She'd been saving her leave to spend a fortnight here at the hall. Then the viscount announced he was coming here to shoot."

Chapter Thirteen

"Norrington wrote to the Earl of Briarcliffe and announced himself and his shooting party as Thorpe's guests?" It sounded as if the viscount had years of practice at being obnoxious. "Surely the old earl hadn't meant you to put the viscount up on demand with no notice."

"His lordship wrote back and said her ladyship wouldn't be here and there was no way he could host them on his own. The viscount said they wouldn't be any trouble as they'd be out all day and gave the date of their arrival. That was when her ladyship changed the dates of her holiday."

"Leave is very hard to get where she works. And then to have to spend it dealing with the viscount. That's awful. I'm sorry Adam and I came. We must be adding to her problems."

Cummings shook his head. "We've all been enjoying watching you thwart the viscount's plans. We're hoping he'll leave early due to you."

"If I manage that, I'll be glad I came here. Thank you for answering my questions. You can tell the staff everyone appears to be in the clear." I rose and headed to the door. "One more thing. When did Thorpe receive the original letter from Norrington inviting himself here?"

"Is it important?"

"I don't know what's important yet."

"I'll look for it and let you know."

"Thank you." I went back to the green drawing room in search of Rosalie or Thorpe and Adam. When I got there, Thorpe had just put Adam in checkmate and the two were laughing about it. Rosalie was nowhere to be seen.

Thorpe must have seen me looking around because he said, "Rosalie is talking to the cook about dinner."

"I don't want to interrupt that conversation," I said with a smile. "I'm going to sit in the garden if anyone wants to join me."

"Now that Thorpe has soundly defeated me, I think I shall go with you and lick my wounds." Adam grinned at his chess partner and then rose and struggled to get his canes under him.

"A rematch later?" Thorpe asked, picking up the intricately carved pieces and putting them in their case.

"Absolutely. Although I think I need a handicap."

"Not at all. Your playing has improved to the point you seem to be my equal."

"Not at all," Adam replied.

"While Rosalie isn't here, I want to tell you something." Thorpe looked somber and a little guilty, gesturing us both to come closer. "Before she came home on holiday, I'd asked through some contacts I have that Rosalie be relieved of duty so she can stay home and help me run our various enterprises. We've had so many employees, managers even, go into the military or government positions that I can't manage without her assistance."

He stared into my eyes. "I know it sounds selfish, but the farm and the mill and the factories are needed for war production. And I can only travel so far and not often. Rosalie's going to have to manage things for me."

"Have you told her how much you need her help?" I asked.

"No. I didn't want her to feel guilty if they don't release her and she has to go back."

"I think you need to trust her. Her travels today to a factory show she understands how much you need her. She'll help you get her back here full time if you'll be honest with her." I raised my eyebrows.

"Honesty is the best policy when dealing with wives?" Thorpe asked and then smiled.

"You aren't joking," Adam said. "Come out to the garden with us?"

"Not at the present time. I need to get in some exercises with Cummings. Do you know where he is, Livvy?"

"He was in the study just a—and here he is," I added, startled. I was beginning to think the man could read minds.

Cummings came in and wheeled Thorpe out to the lift while Adam and I headed for the French doors to the garden.

We settled ourselves on a bench at a distance from the

doors, sitting close together so our shoulders touched. "What's going on?" Adam asked in a low voice without turning his head to look at me.

"I have some explaining to do, to you and to Rosalie and Thorpe. After the dressing gong sounds, we'll meet in our room."

"What have you done?" He looked at me then.

I turned my head to face forward. "Later."

"Does it have anything to do with France?"

I stared hard at him then. "What happened in France that still has you worried? Did you get your targets out?" I had learned inadvertently while Adam was in the hospital that his mission during the fall of France was to get a scientist and a cryptographer to England from their perilous locations west of Paris.

"Yes, Miles and I got them out, and a few more besides."

"Miles? Remington Miles?" I'd met him over the New Year holiday during the Phony War. He was the younger son of an earl, and I didn't trust him to save anyone but his own skin in a battle.

"Miles saved my life after I was shot up and got us to Cherbourg in time to catch the last ship out. I owe him, Livvy."

"How did you get shot and Miles didn't?" I was suspicious.

"We had picked up our targets in a borrowed car"—I knew he meant stolen—"and were rushing to Cherbourg when we had to skirt a German patrol to pick up the cryptographer's next of kin. The patrol had just fired on a farmhouse and killed the occupants, but when we arrived we heard crying. It turned out the next of kin was the pregnant wife of our target. She was hiding in an outbuilding with a young boy from the farmhouse. We couldn't leave him, but we couldn't risk our targets either. And we were running out of room in the car."

"You were braver than I would be."

"No, Liv, you'd do just what I did. Miles guarded the car and our passengers while I brought these two out. We had just about reached cover, the boy was already at the car, when we were spotted by a German sniper. I never even saw him."

"And then?"

"The pregnant woman made it to the car on her own, Miles came back and carried me from where I'd hidden in some bushes back to the car, and then drove as if he were crazy the whole way to the Cherbourg docks. The scientist's wife stopped the bleeding as best she could on the way, and once we were on the ship, the medics patched me up enough to make it to the hospital."

"No wonder you had nightmares in the hospital." I leaned my head on his shoulder for a moment. "But why would you think anything here has to do with what happened in France?"

"Just a funny feeling. Probably nothing. But when you won't tell me something..."

"I'll tell you and Thorpe when we dress for dinner. And it has nothing to do with France." I took his hand and held it, rubbing my thumb along his skin.

"Oh, Livvy, I don't think I'll ever be whole again." There was a sob in his voice. He sounded broken.

"You've been making good strides. And honestly, right now, I'm just glad to have you here with me." I clutched his hand as if I'd never let it go. The doctors had warned me not to be clingy, but it was hard to hide my feelings all the time.

"You'll take what you can get." He stared into my eyes.

I gazed into his. "When it comes to you, I'll take anything. Any time we can have together."

"You'll have to take any old thing. I feel as if I'm a failure. So useless."

The doctors had warned me about the frustrated feelings of uselessness. "You're not. But you do have to work hard to get to the next level. And you'll succeed."

"Oh, I thought everyone must have left," came from behind us. Betsy Oswald walked down the path to stand in front of our bench.

Our magic moment was ruined. I took a deep breath. How much had she overheard? "Have the hunters returned?"

"Not that I know of. And I haven't seen Rosalie anywhere."

"She's probably busy running the household. It is a big job."

"And still she works for the war effort. She is amazing."

"Yes, she is," Adam said, glancing at me with a look that said, Where is this *going*?

"You used to work with her, didn't you?"

"Yes."

"And yet, you were able to leave and Rosalie is still stuck there when her husband obviously needs her to take care of him and the house."

"I'm working elsewhere. Happens all the time," I told her. What was she fishing for? "Why?"

"I feel badly for her and for the earl. I thought maybe you were released from duty because of your husband's injuries."

I felt Adam stiffen beside me and grew angry. No one else had referred to his canes or his limping gait so blatantly. "You thought wrong."

"Then no wonder she works so hard." Betsy smiled at us without any warmth and walked off into the garden.

Adam murmured, "I don't trust her."

"Remember that for tonight," I whispered back.

He raised his eyebrows but didn't continue that conversation. "I'm going upstairs to lie down."

"I'll come with you."

We went inside and went up to our room without running into anyone. Adam lay down on his back and said, "It feels so good to relax. No aircraft sirens. No snipers. I did a great deal of exercising this morning, and now I think I deserve a rest."

"Definitely." I grinned at him as I set aside his canes before I untied his shoes and slipped them off. "I wonder what Betsy Oswald was really after."

Adam wiggled his toes with a look of bliss on his face. "Probably wanted to know how you could shirk your duty and

Rosalie is still slaving away for king and country."

I nodded. "I've become suspicious of everyone since I began to work for Sir Malcolm."

"Maybe Mrs. Oswald wanted to blackmail you to keep her from turning you in to the labor board or Norrington or something. Oswald keeps some expensive company if he's shooting with a viscount. Maybe they need money to keep up their lifestyle."

Blackmail. Valerie Northcott crying over a note. Could Betsy be a blackmailer? I saw Adam staring at me and decided I didn't want to share that thought.

Instead, I said, "It could well be, but it doesn't tell us who killed those two men." If no one figured out who the killer was, Rosalie might be forced to leave Bletchley Park because of the question about her character. That might be helpful for Thorpe, but I doubted either of them would care for Rosalie to be free of her commitment due to a stain on their record.

"You're sure it's not Young? That man who was imprisoned after Northcott found the discrepancies in the books and pressed charges for Silverthorn?"

"Why would he wait for so long to have his revenge?" I asked.

"This might have been his first chance. Neither of these men live nearby. He wouldn't have had the opportunity to go out and murder without his absence being noted."

"Why didn't he kill Norrington? He was the one who first found the missing funds."

"Maybe Young broke in through the old wing and found two of his targets there. After he killed them, something frightened him off or he found he didn't have the stomach for bloodshed. Or perhaps he didn't know Norrington was staying here." Adam shrugged.

"How did he find out any of them were staying here? And get them into the old wing in the middle of the night?"

Adam scowled at me. "How would I know? That's something for the police to discover. But Young is a local, and everyone's presence here might have been the talk of the village."

I shook my head. "It doesn't feel right. He's a sourpuss. He hates everyone. But Dermot Young doesn't seem as if he's the type to do more than complain. Full of ideas, but no action."

"I've met the type." He shifted and grimaced as if he was in pain. "Officers who spend all their time at HQ."

"Except Dermot Young has no power to order anyone around." I shook my head. "It wasn't him."

"So, who was it?"

"It wasn't the servants. They all more or less have alibis. So, we're back to the guests, who have no motive." I dropped onto the bed on my back next to Adam and sighed.

"May I cheer for Viscount Norrington as the killer? I don't like him." Adam twisted his neck to look at me and grinned.

"Courts like some actual evidence."

"I can give plenty of evidence of him being a swine."

"But not a killer."

It was Adam's turn to sigh. "True."

"I think we'll need to find a motive for someone before we'll know who the killer is in our midst." And that would take a while.

"Which makes being here much less pleasant." He gave me a look. "Well, it could be anybody."

"Why do you think Valerie Northcott told Rosalie she was sorry the morning after the murders?"

Surprise crossed Adam's face. "Did she?"

"Yes. You'd think it would have been the other way around. Of course, Rosalie was visibly upset. Or Valerie killed her husband."

"Were Rosalie and Robert relatives? Childhood friends?"

"I don't know." That would explain the sympathy going the wrong way. I knew the real answer, but I had promised not to tell anyone, including Adam. I needed to change the direction of the conversation.

I didn't have to worry about it. Adam relaxed on the bed as his eyes drifted shut. I slipped out of bed and picked up the book I was reading while I waited for the dressing gong and Rosalie and Thorpe's appearance.

A while later they happened almost simultaneously, as Rosalie pushed Thorpe into our room. "Rosie says you have something important to tell us."

I explained Fleur Bettenard's presence at Marshburn Lodge and skirted around the details of our prior meetings. I also explained Sir Malcolm's interest in her while Adam frowned.

"I wouldn't be surprised if Sir Malcolm and his lackeys show up tomorrow," Adam said.

"I hardly think Fleur warrants his arrival," I replied.

"He shows up where you least expect him and stirs things up," Adam grumbled. Adam and I disagreed about everything relating to Sir Malcolm.

"If she's an assassin, and she's staying nearby, could she have broken in here looking for you and found Northcott and Larimer instead and killed them so she could escape?" Thorpe asked.

"How would she have known I was here? She doesn't keep track of me, and she doesn't see me as that big a threat." In any struggle with her, I was bound to lose, and lose quickly. She didn't need to seek me out.

Whatever the reason Fleur was here, I was certain I wasn't it.

Rosalie said, "Why was this Fleur at Marshburn Lodge? And you say she's a German spy? Does that mean Marshburn is a traitor?"

"Quite possibly."

"Does Sir Malcolm know about the murders here?" Thorpe asked.

"Now that he knows Fleur is here, he'll know about everything else happening in the area. You can count on that," Adam said.

Now that was something Adam and I did agree on.

Chapter Fourteen

Rosalie, ever the practical one, said, "Will this Sir Malcolm expect to stay here? He and his lackeys?"

"I have no idea," I told her. "I hope not."

"I'd better have a couple of rooms prepared, just in case."

"Maybe they could stay in the old wing," Adam suggested. "It would suit Sir Malcolm perfectly."

"He's a little feudal?" Thorpe asked.

"More than a little. Sorry. I'm uncomfortable, and it's making me grumpy," Adam replied.

"Do you feel up to dressing for dinner?" Rosalie asked.

"Yes. Yes. I'll be fine," Adam told her, giving her a weak smile.

I hoped he would be. Adam was doing more and resting better than he'd been able to do in London, but his pain and ill temper didn't seem to be diminishing.

"Thank you for your good advice. I spoke to Rosalie, and

we're in accord. As soon as she can be released, she'll be coming home," Thorpe told us, taking his wife's hand.

"And working just as hard for victory as I have at Bletchley," Rosalie said to me.

Rosalie and Thorpe left to dress, and we did the same. If anything, the pain lines beginning to etch into Adam's face made him even more handsome in his evening wear.

I put on my shimmery gray evening gown with a shawl so I wouldn't freeze in the dining room or anywhere else we might end up after dinner.

Adam went down in the lift with Thorpe and I walked down the stairs with Rosalie. "We rang the dressing gong just as soon as the hunters arrived back, but we won't have to wait on them hunting tomorrow, thank goodness."

"How much longer are they going to be hunting?" I asked, hoping they'd leave soon.

"Who knows? The viscount doesn't tell me anything."

"But he's a guest in your home." The words came out before I could stop them, I was so surprised. Then I realized I shouldn't have been.

"The viscount makes himself at home wherever."

"When would you like us to leave?"

"Oh, Livvy. I want you to stay as long as this is doing Adam some good and Thorpe is enjoying having both of you around. You two are no trouble. And," she added quietly, "I want you to sort out our double murder."

"Especially Northcott's?"

Rosalie stopped on the stairs and looked at me.

"I'm still wondering why Valerie Northcott gave you sympathy when her husband was killed. Especially since she seems very friendly with her solicitor. Does she know?"

Rosalie gave me a steely gaze and then whispered, "Later."

I heard someone nearby and continued down the stairs. "I still think the killer is one of your guests, but I'm no farther forward than I was a day ago. Maybe Sir Malcolm will bring some light to the problem."

"I hope someone or something does. Thorpe is growing more anxious."

The dinner gong rang.

"About what specifically?" I asked.

"Me going away from here for days at a time managing our holdings. Silverthorn's declining health. Two people being murdered in our house while he slept. So, you see, Livvy, you have to solve the murders. Thorpe needs you to. I need you to."

How would I do that? I felt as if there was a tight-knit circle around the two murders, and I was on the outside. But Adam needed the quiet and comfort of Briarcliffe Hall, and Rosalie needed me to solve the killings so Adam could enjoy his stay here.

I nodded, seeing the necessity of finding a killer for everyone's sakes.

Rosalie gave me a smile and walked over to join Thorpe. I followed, slipping my arm around Adam's and walking into the dining room.

During the soup course, the vicar put in a plea for all of us to attend services tomorrow at his local church. The three women at the table promised. The men kept their expressions wooden.

"Since you're going to be at church, I don't see why we don't do a little shooting while you're gone," Viscount Norrington said to the table at large.

"Because it will be Sunday and there are laws against it," Thorpe said with a smile to take the bite out of his words.

"If we can't shoot on Sunday, maybe we should go to church and pray for—I don't know—peace?" Downing said.

"If we're on Silverthorn's lands, no one will notice. No one will hear us," the viscount replied. "We're going back to London on Monday, so this will be our last chance to bag some birds for the reverend's larder."

Thank goodness, I thought. *And this must be a relief for Rosalie, but if I were the police I'd be suspicious.*

"Not on the Sabbath. I couldn't possibly eat them," the Reverend Shaw said.

"They'll taste just the same. Why be so silly?" the viscount replied.

"Because it's not right. Some things should not be compromised on," Shaw said.

Norrington looked at Oswald, who shrugged.

"Oh no. You'll be in church," Betsy Oswald told her husband.

"You won't all fit in Thorpe's automobile," Norrington said.

"If you don't mind taking Adam to the church, I'll be glad to walk," I told Thorpe.

"I'll of course walk with you," Rosalie said.

I gave her a smile. "And introduce me to the village, I hope." Actually, it was the last thing I wanted, but it made a nice social pleasantry.

"Constable Cole's mother is the church secretary. A most admirable woman," the vicar said.

"I look forward to meeting her," I said. What else could I say?

We all fell silent as the soup dishes were taken out and the fish course brought in. During that course, everyone expressed an opinion on who had destroyed my sketch of Briarcliffe Hall. The viscount felt it was only right since I had interfered with him shooting birds on Thorpe's land. He completely ignored the fact that Thorpe didn't want him shooting on his land.

I wondered if he'd been spiteful enough to find my drawing and ruin it.

During the main course, the viscount asked when Adam and I were leaving.

"In a few days, if that's all right with Thorpe," Adam said.

"I'd think he'd be tired of you by now," Norrington said.

"Not at all," Rosalie said. "Thorpe likes company who spends time with him."

That would have silenced a less self-centered man. Viscount Norrington said, "If I ever find myself in a plaster cast, I'll be sure to look you up."

Adam opened his mouth to blast Norrington when the telephone rang in the hall. "I hope it's not the police again," Thorpe said, probably just to say something.

Cummings entered and said, "It's Mrs. Northcott, milady."

"Excuse me." Rosalie gracefully rose and left the room, the men half-rising from their chairs as she did so.

No one spoke until she returned. "Valerie is coming down to see Silverthorn and wants to stop by to see us while she's here," Rosalie said.

"Of course. How is she? Is she driving herself?" Thorpe asked.

"No. The solicitor, Perkins, is driving her. I invited them to luncheon."

"Oh, goody," Norrington said, quietly for a change.

Everyone ignored him.

"Perhaps we can visit him after church and before luncheon. He did invite us," I said, glancing at Rosalie. Surely, she remembered how insistent the old man had been.

"Yes. I think that sounds as if it's a good idea," Rosalie replied, and then asked the Oswalds about their home in London and the effect the Blitz had had on their street.

* * *

Adam went to sleep quickly that night, tired out by the exercise and fresh air and relaxed by the peace and quiet of our surroundings. I lay awake, my mind a jumble of murder, Fleur, Billingsthorpe's anxiety, and Sir Malcolm.

Finally, I went to sleep, only to be awakened by the

sound of Adam's canes on the floor. I sat straight up, able to see him standing by the door in the faint light coming in the window.

"Ssh!" He moved to open the door.

I silently slid out of bed, worked my feet into my slippers, looked at the clock, which read nearly four in the morning, and stood behind Adam as he stuck his head out into the hallway. He retreated into the room and shook his head as he looked at me.

We heard something at the same instant. A door on this floor, a bedroom door, shut. I slipped around Adam and hurried down the hallway on silent feet, shivering as I went. Even after I turned the corner, I could see all the doors were shut and no one was walking about but us. No one was on the stairs, either.

I went back to Adam, who was standing in our doorway, and shrugged. We went back into our room and shut the door. "What did you hear?" I asked when we were back under the warm covers.

"I was lying here awake, trying not to disturb you, when I heard footsteps in the hallway or on the stairs. I'm not sure which. I rose and walked as far as to where you saw me when I awakened you."

"Were the steps going toward the bedrooms or downstairs?"

"The bedrooms. Definitely the bedrooms down the hallway. I don't know where they were returning from."

"I wish we'd seen them," I said. "Maybe someone here

was warning Fleur to get away before Sir Malcolm arrives."

"Or the killer was roaming the old wing again, looking for more victims," Adam said.

"Why?"

"How would I know why? I was just throwing out a theory. One that doesn't feature Fleur."

"She has to be involved in these murders."

Now it was Adam's turn to ask "Why?"

"She's the only known killer in the area."

"Oh, that sounds as if it's a good reason to take to the police."

I don't know if I were angrier at Adam because he scoffed at me or because he was right. "Go to sleep. I'm sure things will be clearer in the morning."

* * *

By the time we went down the next morning, our disagreement in the middle of the night was forgotten. We went into the breakfast room to find everyone else was also dressed for church, even the viscount.

"I thought it the least I could do to drive a carful to church to hear Shaw preach," he told the room in general. Personally, I'd rather walk several miles than ride with him.

And with Thorpe and his wheeled chair traveling in his car, I feared there would not be room for me in the Billingsthorpe vehicle.

My escape came when the Reverend Shaw said as I finished breakfast, "I'm off for church now. I'll see you there."

"I'll go with you," I said, trying to sound bright and

agreeable.

"It's a long walk," he warned me.

"It's a lovely morning for it." I said goodbye to Adam and the Billingsthorpes and left a minute later with the reverend.

"I appreciate the company," Shaw told me.

"So do I. And I look forward to meeting your church secretary. You mentioned she knows everyone and everything about the area."

"She does, going back generations."

"That must be handy for the police."

"We don't usually have murders in the village." He sounded annoyed.

In the lengthening silence, I said, "I didn't mean to offend you. But at a time such as this, her knowledge must be invaluable to make sure no innocent people get accused."

"I know what you meant, Mrs. Redmond. I'm just horrified murder could take place in such a tranquil parish."

"Why, vicar? There's always a reason for murder. If we knew that, we'd know everything."

"I wish I knew, but I'm afraid that's in God's province."

"Wouldn't it be nice if your church secretary knew."

"She would be much more likely to know than I would, but I think that would be quite a stretch, even for Mrs. Cole."

"Do Thorpe's servants all attend church every Sunday?"

"Oh, yes. It makes a break for them and a time to catch up with friends and family." Shaw smiled at me. "I don't delude myself into thinking they find my sermons fascinating."

We talked about the beauty of nature the rest of the way to the village. When we reached the church, we went from the cold air into the only slightly warmer temperature of the sanctuary. The church building was medieval and constructed of stone carved by artisans, which meant it was guaranteed not to ever warm up. The stained-glass windows gave off a prism of light between the exterior boards partially protecting those treasures from bomb damage.

A short, middle-aged woman in a dark cloth coat and hat was waiting to one side.

"Vicar. You need—"

"Mrs. Cole. This is Mrs. Redmond. She'd like to talk to you about—"

"Vicar. The Earl of Silverthorn is dead. There was a break-in a little while ago. My Andrew—"

"Constable Cole," the vicar told me.

"Was called for because things didn't look right to his servants or his doctor."

The vicar wrung his hands. "Not another murder. And that is why Mrs. Redmond wants to speak to you. Because of the other murders."

"Yes. I think we should," the woman said in a business-like tone, nodding to me. "But first, we need to see what we should do for the earl."

The two bustled off, leaving me standing in the center aisle of the church, not certain what I could do to help. Or how to find out what was going on. I tapped on the dark pews worn smooth from hundreds of years of use.

Or perhaps I could find out what his servants knew about the break-in and what it had to do with the death of a sick old man. The whole business, in light of two previous murders, was highly alarming.

And if it was murder, I'd need to find a different motive for Valerie Northcott and Daniel Perkins other than bumping off her husband and then needing to kill Mr. Larimer to hide their deed so they could be together.

Chapter Fifteen

I wasn't going to learn anything standing in the sanctuary. I hurried after the vicar and the secretary, who had left the medieval stone church by a side door. They took a path through the graveyard that led to a gate in the wall. On the other side was the garden of a large Victorian house.

Following them onto the porch and then in the front door of the house, I discovered they had entered a parlor that was set up as an office, complete with a telephone that the vicar was now using.

Behind me, a herd of horses came down the stairs, sorting themselves into three little boys when they came into view. A moment later, a woman I guessed was their mother rushed after them, saying "Good morning" as she passed.

I turned to face the vicar in the office, a smile still on my face.

"Some of the refugees from London staying here. You'd think they'd learn to be quieter," Mrs. Cole muttered.

Her attention was quickly focused on the vicar as he said

into the telephone, "I see. So, there's no doubt the earl was murdered. Poor man. I'll have prayers said for his soul at services today." Another pause and then, "Mrs. Cole is right here. I'll tell her."

When the Reverend Shaw hung up the phone, I said, "What happened?"

"Mr. Smith heard a noise about three in the morning and went to check on the earl. He found a figure standing over the bed, holding a pillow over the earl's face. He grabbed at the person's arm and was roughly shoved aside. He said he came back a second time and grabbed the pillow away, but the person shoved him to the floor. By the time he clutched on to the person again, Mrs. Smith heard the commotion and called out as she came into the room. The person ran into Mrs. Smith as they left."

"And the earl?" Mrs. Cole asked.

"He wasn't breathing. Mr. Smith did what he could while Mrs. Smith called the doctor and Constable Cole. They're expecting Inspector Andrews and Sergeant Wilcox to arrive shortly. They tried to reach Viscount Norrington at Briarcliffe Hall, but he'd already left to come to the church. We'll have to tell him when he arrives."

"Was it a man or a woman?" I asked.

"They think a man, but neither servant got a good look at the figure. It could have been a strong woman. With this war on, we have plenty of those."

"So the earl is dead," Mrs. Cole said, shaking her head. "Mrs. Redmond, I wonder if you and Lady Billingsthorpe could visit me after church."

"I'm sure we'd be glad to," I told her for both Rosalie and me. "We visited Silverthorn yesterday. He was trying to tell us something when he started coughing badly. He looked so frail."

"He'd been going downhill for a while, but worse since Robert Northcott was killed. Even before that, when Robert visited him, you could see he didn't have long." Mrs. Cole studied my face. "You will come for tea after the service?"

I was curious to find out what Mrs. Cole could tell us. "Yes. When did Mr. Northcott visit the old earl?"

"Two weeks ago, or perhaps three. No, it must have been two."

"We'd better get back to the church or they'll wonder if we're having service this morning," the vicar said. He ushered us outside again and then led the way over to the church.

While Shaw went into the sacristy to dress for service, Mrs. Cole walked over to Rosalie, who had entered the church and was walking to her pew. Cummings was pushing Thorpe in his wheeled chair over the uneven flagstones and Adam was carefully following, watching his steps.

I caught up to the church secretary in time to hear her say, "In light of his death, I'd like you and Mrs. Redmond to come to tea at my house immediately after service."

"As much as I'd like to, I have Thorpe with me, and we'll have to go to Silverthorn's to pay our respects."

"Something's happened to Silverthorn?" Thorpe asked as he reached us.

"He was murdered in the night. Smith heard a disturbance and found a figure suffocating him with a pillow," Rosalie answered.

Thorpe frowned. "Have the police been called?"

"Yes."

"Good."

Once again, I was surprised to hear Rosalie's husband put on his in-charge tone. I thought of him as mild-mannered Thorpe, but even in his wheeled chair he was the Earl of Briarcliffe.

"This is why it's important you come to tea after service. We'll need the earl's advice too, if you wouldn't mind joining us, your lordship." Mrs. Cole nodded to Thorpe.

"I'm sure we can spare a few minutes if it's important, Mrs. Cole. May the Redmonds come with us?" Thorpe gave the woman a faint smile.

"Yes, please."

"Morning," Norrington said as he ushered the Oswalds into his family's pew across from the Billingsthorpes. I saw Henry Downing in the side aisle near the back of the church. Perhaps he wasn't Church of England.

"Oh, Viscount. The earl is dead," Mrs. Cole said in a quiet tone. "Murdered."

"Nonsense. Impossible." Norrington looked around him at all the grave faces.

"I'm afraid it's true," Thorpe said.

"Good grief." Norrington sprinted out of the church. In a moment, we heard a car's engine start up just outside the door.

"What's going on?" Betsy Oswald asked.

Mrs. Cole told her in a matter-of-fact tone.

"What should we do now?" Betsy was looking around wildly at all of us with just a touch of glee in her tone.

"Get into the pew and find the first hymn in the hymnal," the church secretary said.

I was growing to appreciate Mrs. Cole's attitude.

We all did as she suggested and a minute or so later the organ began to play the first hymn.

I suppose the service was no longer than any other, but it felt as if it went on for hours. As soon as the sermon began, I saw Betsy and George Oswald slide out of the pew on the far side and hurry out of the sanctuary.

I spent the entire sermon wondering what Mrs. Cole was so anxious to tell us and when Sir Malcolm would arrive to speak to Fleur Bettenard and how Valerie Northcott would take the murder of a beloved relative so soon after the killing of her husband.

There would be raised voices and anxiety somewhere after the service and I was ready to get it over with.

Glancing over, I realized Valerie Northcott and her solicitor were now in the Silverthorn pew.

As soon as the last hymn finished, I was ready to run out of the church. Unfortunately, Mrs. Cole now acted as if this were any other Sunday service. Thorpe sped her up by offering her a ride to her cottage in his automobile. He told her Cummings was acting as chauffeur. Rosalie and I would need to walk to her cottage, and when Rosalie's guests, Valerie Northcott and Daniel Perkins, met the countess outside the church, that meant she had to find something for them to do.

Rosalie suggested they help the vicar with preparations for the earl's funeral. As we walked off, I heard Perkins say to Valerie Northcott, "I'm going to walk over to Silverthorn Manor. I'm sure there's something I'll need to do. Come with me."

I wasn't sure where Perkins had parked his car, but I could understand him not wanting to use any more petrol than necessary once he reached the village, since petrol was currently expensive and rationed.

I glanced around but I saw no sign of the Oswalds or Downing.

We reached Mrs. Cole's cottage with her small front garden with late-blooming roses a moment before Thorpe's car pulled up in front. Mrs. Cole went up the walk first and opened her door. She couldn't have taken more than three steps inside before we heard her shriek.

Rosalie and I ran inside and came to a halt just inside the door. The drawing room was destroyed. Books, papers, china, and chair cushions were scattered on the rug and the wooden floor. Pictures had been taken down from the walls. I saw Mrs. Cole rush through a doorway and followed her.

I stopped behind the woman in her bedroom. Pillows and bedding had been dumped on the floor and the contents of the wardrobe were strewn across the bed. Pictures were removed from the walls and stacked on top of the bed.

"At least the dining room wasn't too badly upset," Rosalie called out. A moment later she said, "Golly. The kitchen."

All of the pots and pans were piled up on the floor, and the dishes were out of the china cupboard and spread out on the table. Canisters had their tops off, having obviously been searched, but there was little spillage.

Mrs. Cole dropped into a chair. "I can't even offer you a cup of tea."

"But they were careful not to destroy anything. It wasn't someone who wanted to get revenge against you," I pointed out. "They were careful as they searched your home."

"Who would do such a thing?" Rosalie asked, gazing around at the mess.

"I don't know. It may have something to do with the reason I asked you here," Mrs. Coles said.

"Why was that?"

"It was the evidence, you see."

"What evidence?" I asked the church secretary, trying to sound calm when I wanted to shake her. People hadn't told the police or me everything they knew, and now another person had been murdered.

"It doesn't matter anymore. I never found out. And now the old earl's dead." She sounded despondent. "It concerned him, you see."

I lifted a chair and sat it across from Mrs. Cole. "What doesn't matter?" I would get it out of her if it took all day.

"Mr. Northcott had asked me to hide something for him. Something he said was important to the old earl. Something he didn't want to leave at the bank."

"Something to do with the funds stolen from the old earl? From the Silverthorn estate?" Rosalie asked.

"I don't know. But then Mr. Northcott never brought me this thing, whatever it was, so I didn't find out. I thought he'd bring it to me this past weekend during the shooting, but he was killed first."

"Is this what he talked to the old earl about?" I asked, looking at Rosalie.

"It's possible. I don't know."

"But why would anyone turn your home upside down?"

"Maybe they knew Mr. Northcott meant to give me whatever it was to keep for him?" Mrs. Cole said.

"But how?" Rosalie asked. "And how did anyone break in here to do this without even one of your neighbors noticing?"

"Everyone else was in church, but...he left. The viscount left," Mrs. Cole reminded us.

"We need to find out when he reached Silverthorn Manor. And where the Oswalds went in the middle of the sermon," I said. "Your son should have a record of when any of them arrived at the manor. Could Cummings check with the neighbors to discover if anyone saw the viscount's car?" I asked Rosalie. "Cummings is considered a local, isn't he?"

"Yes, he is. A good idea. Cummings?" Rosalie went outside to talk to him.

"Will you be all right?" I asked the older woman.

"As soon as Mr. Cummings talks to my neighbors, they'll be around to help me clean up the mess. We look out for each other here."

"And you're sure you don't know what he wanted to hide here?"

"No. He mentioned something he thought was in London, but I never saw him again. I don't know if he ever found it." She gripped my arm. "He may have left it at the hall, not having had time to bring it to me before he was killed."

The one time I spoke to him, he had mentioned a recent trip to London. Had he found something there?

I nodded to her and went outside to check on Adam. He was leaning on the car's closed back door next to Thorpe, who was sitting on the front seat. Both of them were listening to Rosalie talking to Cummings. I reached them just as Cummings walked off.

"While Cummings talks to the villagers, I'll drive us up to Silverthorn Manor to pay our respects. You don't mind, do you, Adam?" Rosalie said.

"Not at all." My husband started the slow, painful process of getting into the car.

I climbed in the back seat after him. "Do you think Cummings will succeed in finding out about any stray autos?"

"Oh, yes. Much better than anything you or I could do," Rosalie assured me.

She drove us to Silverthorn Manor with more skill and

assurance than I expected. When we arrived, Thorpe said, "If anyone wants to talk to me, I'll be here in the automobile."

"I'll be glad to wait with you if you'd like," Adam said.

"Yes. I may need assistance with Norrington. Or a witness." Thorpe turned to Rosalie then. "Tell Smith if he needs anything, to just ask. Or to come out here to talk to me."

"Of course." Rosalie gave him a big smile and climbed out of the driver's seat. I patted Adam's hand and hopped out of the back seat to join Rosalie in going inside.

Smith opened the door when Rosalie used the bell pull. "I'm so sorry," she told him.

"Who'd murder a dying man? Makes no sense. Seems cruel," he replied, starting to shut the door behind us.

Rosalie gave him the message from her husband. He nodded and said, "Cole is in with his lordship. He who was earl." With that, the servant went outside. We followed.

I trailed Rosalie to the ground-floor room the old earl had used for a bedroom to find Cole standing by the body, Viscount Norrington in front of him, lecturing him.

"I'm so sorry about Edwards's death," Rosalie said.

"Have you called Inspector Andrews?" I asked.

"There's no reason," the viscount shouted at me.

"I understand he was suffocated. Another murder here. A burglary in the village. I think there's plenty of reason to call in the inspector." I regarded him coolly.

"Who was burgled?" Constable Cole asked.

"Your mother. She's fine, she wasn't at home, but the

house was overturned."

Chapter Sixteen

Constable Cole turned and hurried out of the room with a thunderous look on his face.

"Come back here," Viscount Norrington shouted.

Rosalie and I stood at the foot of the bed, staring at Norrington.

"And what are you two doing here?" he growled at us.

"Paying our respects to your uncle," Rosalie told him. "He was a dear old man."

I could hear Cole in the hallway, talking to someone on the telephone. The old earl was tucked up in bed with the covers to his chin and appeared to be sleeping, his thin, white hair neatly combed.

"I can't imagine why anyone would want to kill him," I added.

"Nonsense. He was an old man. He was due to die at any time."

"But someone couldn't wait that long. And so they were seen suffocating that dear old man and attacking his servants," I told him.

"Nonsense."

"Don't you listen to what anyone tells you?" I demanded.

Rosalie lowered her hand, signaling me to lower my voice. And my temper.

She was right. I didn't want to be heard shouting by whoever was on the other end of the line. I'd let Norrington do that.

He was so insufferable I couldn't imagine anyone else killing the old man or burgling Mrs. Cole's home. I was blaming him without any evidence.

The constable came back into the room. "Inspector Andrews and Sergeant Wilcox will be here within the hour. Mr. and Mrs. Smith, if you could please stand watch with the body for the time being, I need to interview these people."

As soon as Cole took the viscount into the study, since the viscount insisted on going first as he was a busy man, I said to Rosalie, "How did the old earl get on with the viscount?"

"He couldn't stand the sight of him, but he blamed himself that Norrington ever became his heir. He said he should have married as a young man and had lots of children instead of leaving it to his younger brother, who was a self-centered wastrel."

"And Northcott?"

"He and the old earl rubbed along together quite well. The earl was kind to Northcott as a boy, and Northcott tried to repay him by looking out for his interests when the earl grew old and unwell."

"Has anyone seen that solicitor Perkins? Or Mrs. Northcott? I thought they were coming here," I asked.

The Smiths both shook their heads.

Doctor Hamelstein came in, greeted us with a distracted air and began to examine the old earl's face and neck, lowering the covers slightly. "Yes, there's still signs of it."

"What?" I asked.

"Suffocation. The inspector called me to return here and make certain of my earlier diagnosis."

"And you're certain he was suffocated?" Rosalie asked.

"Oh, yes." The doctor readjusted the covers to cover the earl's face and went out in search of Constable Cole.

While it was just Rosalie and the Smiths with me in the room, I asked, "Is that how Northcott found out about the estate manager stealing from the old earl? By examining the books?"

"No. The viscount found the original evidence, which he took to Northcott to look into. Said he was too busy himself." Rosalie shook her head. "Dermot Young told us the truth when he said it was Norrington who took the accounts to Northcott."

We heard Norrington coming toward us before we saw him and we both fell silent.

"Your ladyship, if you'd come this way," Constable Cole said.

As Rosalie walked off, Norrington headed back into the old earl's bedroom. I waited where I was at the foot of the bed.

"Out," he ordered the Smiths.

"We've been told to stay here by Constable Cole," Mr. Smith said.

"You work for me now. If you want to continue working here, leave."

"The law says I stay here, I stay here. All you can do is fire me. The law can put me in prison."

Then Norrington turned on me. "You. Out."

"I'm paying my respects to your uncle." If I could get him talking, perhaps I could distract the viscount into admitting something. "I'd only met him the once, but he was welcoming. Very bright. Very alert. I liked him."

"Fine. You've had your say. Get out."

"Who do you think killed him?"

"Nobody. He was an old man and he died." Norrington was nearly screaming.

"Odd how someone broke in here and attacked Mr. and Mrs. Smith at just that moment."

"Oh, really…" With a snarl of frustration, the viscount stormed out, and a moment later, we heard the front door slam.

"I guess it's his lordship's turn to deal with the," Smith raised his eyebrows, "heir."

It took me a minute to realize "his lordship" referred to Thorpe. "Were you here when Robert Northcott spoke to the old earl a couple of weeks ago? When exactly was he here? And did you hear what they said?"

"I was here," Mrs. Smith said. "Smith was seeing to a coal delivery. It was Saturday two weeks ago. Mr. Northcott didn't want me to hear, so the old earl sent me to the kitchen. After a few minutes, I began to worry about the old man and came back to the doorway."

"Did you hear what they were talking about?"

"Mr. Northcott said that old records were proof, and the earl said to guard them carefully. Then the earl started coughing and Mr. Northcott rang for me."

"What old records?" I asked.

"Dunno," Smith said. He gave his wife a look that told me they shared a secret. "But the old earl seemed pleased with them."

"And then Mr. Northcott and the earl were murdered."

They both nodded, looking glum.

"What time was the old earl attacked?"

"Early in the morning. After three," Mr. Smith said.

Mrs. Smith nodded.

"Did Mr. Northcott give either you or the old earl anything to keep secret for him?"

"No," Mr. Smith said in a tone that told me this was his final word on the subject.

"You heard Mrs. Cole's house was burgled during church, and she hadn't hidden anything for him either," I told him.

"Yes. Someone wants that evidence. We just want it found."

"Who knows the history of this village and the Norrington family the best?" I asked, trying another tack. If this was about village secrets, we might have a chance at figuring out these murders if we knew what had happened in the past.

"Mrs. Cole," Mr. Smith said.

"Old Mrs. Petrie," Mrs. Smith corrected him.

"You're right. I'd plum forgotten about her."

"Who is Mrs. Petrie?"

"Mrs. Cole's aunt. Was the church secretary before Mrs. Cole."

"Where does she live?"

"With her granddaughter, Mrs. Ivy. Old Mrs. Petrie doesn't get out much on account of her rheumatism, but I'm sure she'd welcome a visit from the countess."

Rosalie. Of course. She'd be the best one to begin the questioning.

I heard voices and realized Inspector Andrews and Sergeant Wilcox had arrived. "Thank you," I said in a low tone. "You've been most helpful."

As soon as Rosalie and Constable Cole reappeared, she and I went out to the car to drive Thorpe and Adam back to Briarcliffe Hall. "I asked Constable Cole when the viscount arrived. It was just a few minutes after the church service started," Rosalie said. "The viscount couldn't have burgled Mrs. Cole's cottage."

As we rode along, I asked, "Rosalie, how do you feel about paying a call on old Mrs. Petrie?"

"I hadn't thought about her. That's a good idea." Rosalie neatly shifted gears and asked, "Thorpe, Adam, can you find a way to entertain yourselves this afternoon after luncheon?"

"We'll be fine. Won't we, Adam?"

"I'm sure we will." Adam gave me a smile. "It sounds as if you two have some sleuthing to do."

"If Inspector Andrews comes around, don't tell him what we're doing," Rosalie said. "He just arrived at Silverthorn Manor to investigate the death of the old earl."

"Three murders in the area in the past few days. This place is deadlier than London. Do be careful, Rosie," Thorpe said. He reached over and patted her shoulder.

In the back seat, Adam squeezed my hand, but he didn't warn me to be careful. He knew he would be wasting his breath.

When we arrived at Briarcliffe Hall, we discovered a green automobile parked in front of the house. "Oh, Lord, I forgot Valerie Northcott and her solicitor friend had planned to come to lunch before calling on the old earl. I wonder if they've managed to get to Silverthorn Manor yet," Rosalie said. "I'll send someone out to help you, Thorpe. Is that all right?"

"Of course. Be a good hostess."

She dashed into the house. I slid out of the car and waited for Adam to climb out and get his legs underneath him. It was a good thing I did because he rushed and nearly went sprawling. I reached out a hand to steady him and he was then able to save himself.

He grumbled a little, took a deep breath, and said,

"Thank you."

I knew how much his thanks had cost him, to admit he was still unable to get around as he had. I gave a curt nod, not knowing what else to do. "I wonder when Valerie Northcott and her friend reached the village this morning."

"When Cummings finishes talking to the villagers, I'm sure we'll have the answer," Thorpe said.

"He knows all the villagers?" I asked.

Thorpe nodded. "He truly is a local. He grew up in the village. They'll speak freely with him about who was seen and where with all sorts of details on automobiles."

"Good. Then all we need to do at the moment is say hello to your guests." At that moment, Miles came out to help Thorpe and I started toward the house, slowly, waiting for Adam to join me.

We entered the main hall in time to hear a woman's voice say, "But that's terrible. And very unfair."

When we walked into the large blue and yellow drawing room, we found Valerie Northcott facing Rosalie with her solicitor friend, Perkins, standing a step behind her, ready to catch her if she collapsed.

Where had that thought come from? I looked at them more closely, and decided, yes, that was exactly how their postures appeared. And then she leaned back into him, obviously confident he would be there. He helped her to the nearest chair, and when she was seated, she said, "Thank you, Daniel."

I could imagine what Betsy Oswald would make of the

first-name familiarity between the pair.

Where were the Oswalds? I'd last seen them in church that morning and then promptly forgotten about them. They hadn't been at Silverthorn Manor when we had been. And where were they since the sermon? I hoped they were all right.

Downing was now patiently standing by where he'd been talking to the new arrivals. He was easy to overlook. Easy to forget. I guessed he'd walked back as soon as church was over.

Or at least that would be what he'd tell us.

Adam and I said hello to the solicitor. "It was lucky you drove Mrs. Northcott out here, since she must be shattered and wouldn't want to travel back alone," I said.

"It's true, then, that the old earl was murdered? How extraordinary," Perkins said. "Were there many killings before Northcott's and Larimer's in the area?"

"Not since the last battle between the Roundheads and the Cavaliers," Rosalie told him, annoyance in her tone. "And now three in a few days."

"But why kill a man who was from all accounts on his deathbed?" Perkins asked, shaking his head. "His affairs are in order, though. I checked through his papers before we came back here. There was nothing else for me to do there."

"I heard this from Mrs. Smith, the old earl's housekeeper," Valerie Northcott said. "She told me to get here as soon as I could since the old earl wouldn't see out this year." She looked at Rosalie. "And I wanted to know what

Robert told him when they last met."

"Why?" I asked.

She looked at each of us in turn. "Robert told me that he found evidence he, not Charles Norrington, should be the next Earl of Silverthorn."

We all looked back at her, astounded. That horrible man Norrington might not be the new earl? I was surprised there wasn't cheering.

"What do you know of this evidence?" Rosalie asked.

"Only that it proved his ancestor, the oldest son, was legally wed and that his great-grandfather was legitimate. They should have been the earls all along."

"Why was Robert's surname Northcott and not Norrington?"

"That was the maiden name of the baby's mother. The younger brother did it, I suppose, to strengthen the impression the child was illegitimate. I guess everyone was just glad the younger brother was paying for the education and upbringing of his dead brother's child."

"Does anyone know what this evidence is? Or have they seen it?" Perkins asked in his courtroom voice.

We all shook our heads.

"Then it's good that you and Teds weren't counting on anything from the old earl," the solicitor told Valerie Northcott.

"Teds?" I asked.

"Short for Edwards. My eldest has the same Christian name as the old earl," Valerie said. Then I recalled her mentioning this, right after we discovered the first two murders.

The crunch of tires on gravel alerted us to another automobile pulling up in front of the house. I looked out the window, expecting to see the viscount's motor.

Instead, it was a large black automobile driven by a uniformed soldier. The back door was opened by the driver, and Sir Malcolm emerged. His stride and the forward tilt of his shoulders as he approached the front door told me I should hide. Quickly.

Chapter Seventeen

Instead, I waited, wondering what calamity had struck that brought Sir Malcolm to Rosalie's door. Surely he'd have gone to Marshburn's hunting lodge to verify Fleur's detention, not come here. I heard him enter, speak to Thorpe, and then march down the hall with heavy steps to the drawing room.

"Olivia. Fleur's gone. Vanished. Did you tell her I was coming?" he asked as he walked in.

Everyone in the room turned to stare at him, which I was quite sure never bothered him.

"She told me a tale I believed, and she could see I believed it. I take it the story wasn't true? She couldn't have guessed you'd be out here so soon. What about her jailer, Burke?"

"Claims he's a caretaker and any guests of the duke can stay in the house and bring their own servants. He has nothing to do with them."

"I didn't see any servants other than Burke, but Fleur has

always been self-sufficient. When she said he was her jailer, he didn't deny it. Are you sure she's gone?"

"All her clothes and wigs and makeup, all of her belongings, are gone, as are her cases. Where would she have gone, Olivia?"

"I don't know. I'm sure she didn't kill any of our victims, so she must be running from you."

"What?" Sir Malcolm, Rosalie—everyone in the room stared at me now, and unlike Sir Malcolm, I found it unnerving.

I clasped my hands together before I spoke. "We've had three murders here in the last few days. Two by medieval weapons in the armament museum here, and one this morning at Silverthorn Manor. The earl was suffocated with a pillow. The murderer this morning was almost caught. Not Fleur's style at all. She'd have used a knife or her bare hands. And she wouldn't have made a sound or be seen by anyone who would live to tell the tale."

"I have men scouring the area looking for her, but I want you to come with me. You've seen her most recently."

"Any chance of luncheon first? I'm starving," I told him.

"You're welcome to stay, Sir Malcolm, and leave immediately after," Rosalie said in her most welcoming voice.

After a moment's hesitation, Sir Malcolm asked, "Is it ready now?"

"Any moment now." A maid came in and nodded. "Yes. Shall we go in?"

There were eight of us, including Sir Malcolm, at a table

set for ten when the soup course was served. It was a spicy potato soup, warm and filling.

"Shall I have a maid take your driver to the kitchen for some lunch?" Rosalie asked Sir Malcolm.

"That would be very kind of you."

With a nod from Rosalie, the maid left the dining room to see to the driver.

"Is this Fleur person suspected in the death of my husband?" Valerie Northcott asked.

"No," I told her. "She was probably at Marshburn Lodge at the correct time, but she'd have no reason to come over here to kill anyone. She's a Nazi assassin and a spy, but your husband and Mr. Larimer had no knowledge of Britain's war plans and held no power in the government. That's the sort of person she'd be interested in. And there's no one here that Mr. Northcott or Mr. Larimer could be mistaken for that hold any power."

Mrs. Northcott shook her head. "I'm sure Robert would have been of no use to her. He ran a bank. Mr. Larimer was a farmer with a large holding, but no different than many other farmers in England."

We both turned to look at Sir Malcolm.

"I see no reason why she would. She was in hiding. No reason for her to call attention to herself. When we find her, we'll ask her, but I expect the answer to be no."

"Where are the Oswalds?" Mrs. Northcott asked next.

"They left church before the sermon, and what with the break-in at Mrs. Cole's cottage and the old earl's murder, I'm afraid they've been left to their own devices. I'm sure they'll find their way back here," Rosalie said.

As soon as we finished the soup, the bowls were removed and a fish course was brought in with vegetable marrows and field greens. We set on it as if we hadn't seen food in days, which was how I felt.

A moment later, the Oswalds entered and took their seats. "It looks delicious," Betsy Oswald said before Rosalie could signal a maid to bring two more plates.

"How did you find the walk from the village?" I asked.

"Long and mostly uphill," George Oswald said. "Where's the viscount, well, the new earl, well, Norrington?"

"I don't know," Rosalie said.

"I thought you were with him," Thorpe said to Oswald.

"No. We never saw him again after he left the church," George Oswald said. "That's a nice village you have down there. Very pretty."

"I'm Betsy Oswald," she said to Sir Malcolm, sitting to her right. "Who are you?"

"Sir Malcolm Freemantle."

"Are you another neighbor?"

"No." Sir Malcolm continued eating without any further explanation.

"Did you hear about the break-in at Mrs. Cole's? Right before or during service," Rosalie said.

"Oh, dear. Was anything taken?"

"No, but they made a mess, whoever they were."

While Rosalie and Betsy talked, Sir Malcolm looked at me

and raised an eyebrow. I shrugged in reply. I had no answers for him about anyone. Only a lot of questions.

I could sense Adam looking from me to Sir Malcolm and back. I turned to him and murmured in his ear, "You can't go with us this afternoon, I'm afraid."

"Be careful. If I were Fleur, I wouldn't have gone far."

"What was that?" Sir Malcolm asked him.

Adam shook his head and kept eating.

We all continued with this course in silence and soon our empty plates were taken away and the main course brought in its place. A Sunday beef roast with potatoes and carrots and cabbage, gravy and roast pudding, the meat already carved in the kitchen. I was going to miss these wonderful meals when I went back to London and the bombing.

From the way Sir Malcolm was digging in to his meal, I guessed this was better than even what he was accustomed to.

"Are you going to try to see the Duchess of Marshburn again?" Betsy Oswald asked. "I'd love to meet a real duchess."

"It was a misunderstanding. She's not at the lodge. She's at their place in the home counties, isn't she, Sir Malcolm," Rosalie said.

"I thought I'd heard she was in London," Sir Malcolm replied.

I suspected that was a piece of misdirection courtesy of Sir Malcolm in his role as spymaster. I wondered why.

"Are you finished with your lunch, Olivia?"

"Nearly. If you're finished, you could get your chauffeur and by the time you two are ready, I should be finished with this excellent luncheon. Thank you, Rosalie. It has been a feast."

"Not staying for pudding and coffee?" Rosalie asked.

"Alas, no, madam. But this luncheon has been a treat. Thank you."

I looked at Sir Malcolm in surprise. He seldom thanked anyone. Perhaps he had a different set of manners when dealing with the aristocracy.

He rose, gave a nod to Rosalie and to Thorpe, and then left the room. Thorpe gave a bemused glance at his wife.

After hurrying to finish the meal, I reached over to squeeze Adam's hand. "Rosalie, Thorpe, thank you. I'm sorry to have brought such confusion to your door. I hope I can help Sir Malcolm find what he's looking for, and then he won't bother you anymore."

"What's he looking for?" Betsy asked.

I ignored her as I kissed Adam on the cheek and left the room. I hoped no one told her. She didn't seem to be discreet.

Shoving my arms into my coat sleeves and then pinning on my hat, I hurried out the front door to find Sir Malcolm and his driver waiting for me. "Where are we looking first?" I asked as I climbed into the back seat of the automobile, my gloves still in one hand.

"Back to Marshburn Lodge. I want you to go over it with a feminine perspective. See if she left any hints as to where she was going."

"Have you questioned Thomas Burke?"

"Yes."

"Have someone keep an eye on him. Once he sees me, I think he'll make a run for it. When he does, you'll have an easier time getting the truth out of him." If anyone knew where Fleur had gone, it would be Burke.

When I got out of the car at Marshburn Lodge, I saw Burke in the doorway of one of the cottages. He immediately faded into the shadows. "And there he goes," I said quietly.

Sir Malcolm gave a nod to a man standing near him who also slipped into the shadows.

I led the way into the lodge, followed by Sir Malcolm, where we were met by two of his men. Sir Malcolm gestured for them to let me go wherever I wanted, and I began to walk from room to room, pulling out books, rearranging pillows, looking behind and under furniture.

There was nothing on the ground floor. Nothing on the first floor. It was too tidy. Dusted and swept clean in preparation for our visit.

Now I was even more certain there was something to be found. In the basement, in the attic, in the stables.

I found the stairs going up to the attic and started up. "Anyone have a torch?"

Sir Malcolm handed me one and I led the way. Disappointingly, it was small, low ceilinged, and bare, as well as swept clean of cobwebs. The roof beams met in a peak in the center and then sloped down at each end.

We went down to the cellars, which were built of stone with even lower ceilings. Sir Malcolm hit his head on a beam and cursing, he stomped back upstairs. I continued to study the area. It was swept and tidy. I couldn't find a single footprint anywhere.

And that was probably the point.

I studied the cellars and the ground floor, but couldn't find another entrance. Then I went outside where Sir Malcolm sat in his car. "Let's go," he told the driver.

"Are you joking? This is just getting interesting." Fleur couldn't hide the dusting and sweeping, but she could hide hidden entrances that way. And I liked puzzles.

When I walked away, I was aware Sir Malcolm still sat in the car, but that he'd not had his driver start the engine. He was giving me a chance to find Fleur's hiding place.

I circled the house, but the only entrances I found took me to the cellars I had already found. Had Fleur ordered the entire house swept so I would waste my time looking for a hidden entrance that wasn't there?

That would be a trick she'd play, but it could also be a safeguard she would use so I couldn't find a secret room or passage.

I began to study the roof line and the attic area, remembering how it looked when we were inside. I was beginning to feel we'd not seen all of the attic, particularly on the far side of the house. I walked around that side of the lodge, looking up the entire time.

Yes, there was space for one more room, even with the

peaks and troughs of the ornate roof covering the angled shape of the Elizabethan-era lodge.

"Come on," I told Sir Malcolm when I reached him. "We haven't seen all of the attic yet."

He got out of the auto and followed me into the house. Once we were on the first floor, we looked all over for another staircase up. Our footsteps echoed on the bare wooden floors as we wandered from room to room, checking ceilings for opening panels and knocking on wardrobe backs for hidden doors.

Finally, in an airing cupboard, I found a door behind some shelves. As I was about to move the shelves, Sir Malcolm restrained me with one large hand. "It could be booby-trapped. It could blow up the whole house."

"How can we tell?"

"Short of trying it out? I don't know. I don't see a tripwire. Doesn't mean it's not hidden. This is Fleur, after all."

"And Fleur might want to return here."

I studied the door latch. It was an old-fashioned drop-and-catch type. I didn't see any strings or wires around the shelves or the door. Before Sir Malcolm could remind me the wires might be on the other side of the door, I pulled the shelves away and dropped the catch. The door opened slightly.

Around me, I heard short gasps. I felt with my hand for any wires or strings on the far side of the door around the frame and couldn't find any, so I shoved a little. The door opened, revealing a staircase in the gloom.

Using a torch, I led the way upstairs, testing each step to make sure it could take my weight. I was very glad they weren't sawn through or wired with explosives. The small room at the top of the stairs had one window and appeared to be as clean as the rest of the attic.

I started to check a few cases piled in a corner. Women's clothes and wigs and hats were inside. Fleur's?

Then the torchlight fell on some wire rolled up beneath the window. "Isn't that antenna wire?" I asked.

Chapter Eighteen

Sir Malcolm loosed a string of curses, followed by "Has anyone patrolled this area searching for illegal shortwave transmissions?"

"Out here, sir?" a male voice responded from somewhere down the stairs.

"With the antenna wire they have here, they could have broadcast the whole way to Berlin."

"Should we start, sir?"

Sir Malcolm groaned. "As if shutting the barn door now does any good."

"I see what she was doing here, sir, but I don't see anything that tells me where she or the radio have gone," I told him.

"Were they sending her instructions, or was she sending them information?" Sir Malcolm muttered as he paced the small space, carefully avoiding low beams.

"Where would she get her information? There's nothing around here to report on, and there's no news in the papers that would do Berlin any good," I said. "But then, perhaps questioning Burke now would give you the answers."

Sir Malcolm, wearing the smile of a snake, went back downstairs.

"I'm going back to Briarcliffe Hall," I called out, "if you don't need me."

"Yes. Go. Go," Sir Malcolm called back.

* * *

I walked over the hill and back onto Briarcliffe land, reaching the house in time for tea. When I walked in to the small drawing room, I found Thorpe and Adam at another game of chess.

"Are Mrs. Northcott and Mr. Perkins still here?" I asked.

"They went to Silverthorn's to pay their respects again, and to make certain the Smiths are provided for in the short term. They've been invited back here for tea," Thorpe told me as Adam studied the board with intense concentration.

I went upstairs and brought down my sketch pad, newly straightened, and a few short pencils to practice copying the frieze that circled the drawing room below the ornate ceiling. It was too late in the day to attempt to begin sketching Briarcliffe Hall from the spot I'd found on the hill.

The Oswalds came in and Betsy leaned over the back of my chair to ask, "Did your friend find what he was looking for?"

"Not this time." I kept sketching, trying to hide my annoyance at having someone watch over my shoulder.

When I didn't say any more, Betsy walked over to study

the chess match for a moment before wandering out of the room.

"Did you know the Duke of Marshburn is a neighboring landowner?" George asked Thorpe.

Thorpe only nodded, since it was his turn to make a move on the board.

"I wonder how the shooting is on his land," George Oswald continued.

"How did you learn the names of all the landowners around here?" I asked George.

"Betsy told me after we talked to one of the women in the village."

Betsy knew someone in this village? "Oh? Who?"

"Don't know. Didn't get her name."

Could Fleur be hiding in the village until Sir Malcolm left? She had no obvious means of transportation to get to the train station in Lancaster or anywhere else. I hoped the spymaster would either call or come to dinner.

George sat on a sofa and thumbed through a magazine, although I had the feeling he was watching all three of us. I wondered where Rosalie was as I kept sketching.

Downing didn't say a word, which was perhaps why I didn't notice him at first. He was reading a book, but he didn't turn pages consistently to note what he was reading.

Eventually, Rosalie came into the drawing room with Valerie Northcott and Mr. Perkins. I noticed Valerie had an intimate hold on the man's coat sleeve as she leaned in and called him "Daniel." I also noticed Betsy had followed them in, watching Valerie's every move.

Rosalie rang for tea as Thorpe suggested to Adam they pause their game. Adam, who I felt certain was losing, readily agreed.

As we gathered our tea and found seats, we kept up an uneven stream of social chitchat. Adam came over and sat next to me. "Sir Malcolm have any luck?"

Betsy sat behind him with her back to us.

"Later." I nodded in her direction. "How is your chess match going?"

"I'm putting up a better fight, but Thorpe will win, I'm sure."

"You shouldn't let him beat you all the time," Betsy said without turning to look at us.

"I'm not letting him. He's a very skilled player. I'm lucky he's willing to teach me."

"I hear you have a friend in the village," I said to Betsy.

"Where did you hear that?" She turned to look at me.

"Your husband."

Her posture relaxed. "Not a friend. Just someone I've run into a couple of times, so I've been asking her questions about the village."

Betsy would ask anyone anything. "What have you learned?"

"The names of some of the charming cottages. Whether the stream ever floods into the houses along its banks. It doesn't, by the way. That the Billingsthorpes don't own the village, Silverthorn does."

"Did you hear any mention of Marshburn?" I asked. That was what I really wanted to know.

"No. He doesn't seem to have much to do with the village. Just that lodge we went to." As Rosalie walked past, Betsy Oswald continued with, "I've really enjoyed my stay here, my lady. George and I will need to head back to London in the morning, but I don't know if Norrington will be able to take us to the station now that his uncle is dead."

"If it's cleared with Inspector Andrews, Miles can give you a lift back to the train station." Rosalie didn't sound upset to have two more of her houseguests leave.

Had the viscount already moved into Silverthorn House? I suspected Rosalie would be glad to see the back of him, too.

"Have you heard when the funeral is to be held?" Rosalie asked.

We all shook our heads.

"And whether Sir Malcolm is coming back tonight?"

"I imagine he'll be back for dinner if his reaction to lunch was anything to judge by," I told her. "But if he doesn't arrive on time, don't hold the meal for him."

Rosalie nodded.

"You seem free to speak for him. Who is he?" Betsy asked.

"Someone I've worked with in London from time to time. A government type. The same as your husband," I said.

"He hardly seems the type to shuffle documents all day."

"Who knows what any of these government men do? And of course, no one can tell us. Official secrets and all that,"

I told her.

"It's all so secretive. Doesn't that make you curious?" Betsy asked, looking from me to Rosalie.

We both looked at her wide-eyed and shook our heads. Rosalie and I knew our own little parts of the official secrets and definitely didn't want a gossip such as Betsy Oswald spreading them around.

"It's as if someone has a hatred of the Silverthorn estate. First Robert is killed, and then the old earl," Valerie Northcott said as she joined us.

"Surely they weren't more than distant relations," Betsy said.

"Actually, they were quite close relations as well as good friends," Valerie replied. "I'll be coming back for the funeral, if you wouldn't mind putting me up again, Rosalie."

"Of course. Is Mr. Perkins coming for the funeral as well?"

Valerie Northcott smiled. "Yes. He'd done a lot of legal work for the old earl over the years."

"We'll have a place for him too." Rosalie held out a hand to rest on Valerie's arm.

That left me to wonder what secret these two women shared. And there was a secret there. Did it only involve who was sleeping with whom?

Valerie smiled her fragile, "Thank you" smile. I was beginning to think there was a core of steel under the fragility, just as I was suspecting a reason beyond curiosity behind all the questions and comments Betsy was peppering us with. Being around Sir Malcolm over time had made me suspicious about everything.

Valerie Northcott turned down dinner, claiming she and Mr. Perkins needed to get back to Lancaster for business meetings to be held the next morning.

"Has the date been set for Robert's funeral yet?" Rosalie asked.

"I'm planning a small private funeral with his interment, as soon as possible. We'll have a larger memorial service later when his killer is captured." As she spoke, Valerie Northcott sounded quite fierce.

"I doubt Thorpe will be able to attend, but I would like to be there with you," Rosalie said, reaching out to take one of Valerie's hands.

"And I'll want you there. I'll let you know." Since Perkins had already stepped out the front door, Valerie had to hurry to catch up.

As soon as they were out on the front drive, Betsy followed them. I rushed to a window in the study overlooking the drive, not certain what I was expecting to witness.

Betsy didn't approach the solicitor's automobile, but stood at the side, waiting. Perkins and Valerie Northcott talked animatedly for half a minute and then the solicitor climbed out.

He walked over to Betsy Oswald and appeared to berate her. The fiendish light in her eyes made her smile frightening. With a final blast, gesturing and turning red, Perkins stormed back to the car, climbed in, started it up and roared down the drive.

Blackmail over their relationship? Or something to do with the murders?

Betsy came back inside, met me in the hallway and said, "I bet they want to get back tonight to spend time as a couple."

"Oh, Betsy," Rosalie said with exasperation as she came back into the hall.

When we reached the drawing room, Betsy said, "Daniel Perkins is rather good looking. I wonder if she killed her husband."

"Betsy!" her husband said, looking scandalized.

"So was Robert Northcott. Good looking, that is," I said. "So that makes it a poor motive."

"I still think there's something going on there."

"Could be, but it's none of our business," Thorpe said. "Now, I don't know how much longer our good weather will hold out, so I suggest, Adam, we take the chess board out into the garden tomorrow. Enjoy the sunshine while we can."

The peal of the front-door bell stopped Adam before he could answer. A maid came in a minute later, followed by Inspector Andrews and Sergeant Wilcox.

"As you know, the Earl of Silverthorn was murdered last night. I'd like to interview everyone in your house, Earl, to learn who was where at the appropriate times."

"What are the appropriate times?" Thorpe asked, using his lord of the manor voice.

"Between two and four this morning, your lordship."

"Very good, Inspector. It would be everyone in this room, and also Viscount Norrington, who's been staying here, the Reverend Shaw, who stayed here last night, and the servants. Mrs. Northcott and Mr. Perkins were here for luncheon, but they weren't here last night and have already gone back to Lancaster. Who would you care to start with, Inspector?" Thorpe asked.

The inspector started with Thorpe. He couldn't have done anything without help, but there was nothing wrong with his eyes and ears.

By the time they called me into the study, I guessed they would have heard everything already. Nevertheless, I told them about hearing someone in the hallway in the night and what Mrs. Cole told us about Robert Northcott's request to keep something hidden in her cottage, which was subsequently burgled.

Apparently, Adam or Rosalie or Mrs. Cole had already told them about everything I'd heard. "Do you think the burgling of Mrs. Cole's home is related to any of these murders?" Andrews asked me when I'd finished.

"Well, don't you?"

"They were done at different times."

"Robert Northcott mentions to Mrs. Cole that he wanted her to hide something for him. Then he is killed, the old earl is killed, and no one knows what this item is and whether it is missing. One event after another, all possibly linked."

"And no one has any idea who the killer is or what this thing that may or may not exist is?" the inspector asked.

I shook my head. "Any idea of how you would find the evidence you need?"

"No. The murder weapons were all on hand at the scene. No fingerprints. We think Larimer was a witness to the first murder, so he was also killed. The Smiths' testimony does us no good in finding the old earl's murderer, and a good barrister would argue the Smiths have made it up to cover their own careless or violent actions against a helpless old man. And now we have a traffic incident to investigate."

"Good grief, they're dumping everything on you. What traffic incident?"

"Freddy Croft, a young farm worker, was riding his bicycle a little before four this morning to go out to milk the cows on the Travis farm when he had to veer off the road when an automobile came racing out of the dark and nearly ran him over. He was on the stretch of lane between Silverthorn Manor and the village."

"Could he tell you anything about the auto?"

"Only that it was a big black saloon. Of course, in the middle of the night with no light out there, every car is black."

"Plate number?"

"Of course not."

Another dead end.

Chapter Nineteen

"Do you think it could have been the old earl's killer escaping the scene of his crime?" I asked with a little more enthusiasm than was proper.

"We have no idea," Inspector Andrews said stiffly. "Could have been someone passing through. Or someone out for some business they wouldn't want anyone to notice."

"Did you learn anything about the viscount's financial status and whether it changed about the time that Mr. Young was arrested and tried for theft?" I asked, feeling a definite need to change the subject.

"I have a friend in the metropolitan police who looked into it for me," Inspector Andrews said. "I've been told the viscount was practically bankrupt until about three years ago, when he received a cash infusion. Since then, he's had money at regular intervals that he didn't have before. And no one has inquired as to where his funds have come from."

"With Mr. Young out of the way, the viscount could raid the earl's funds with impunity. What an awful man," I said and walked out of the room, shaking my head.

I went back to the drawing room and George Oswald was called in. The others had already gone up to dress for dinner and the room was now empty.

A minute later, I heard Sir Malcolm acknowledge someone before he came in. He greeted me with "Well?"

I led him into the breakfast room. "Keep your voice down, but I think we're less likely to be overheard here."

He raised his eyebrows.

"Who were you speaking to just now?"

"I don't know him. He was just heading upstairs to dress for dinner, I suppose."

Whoever he was, he was late, I noted. "Fleur, walking anywhere carrying a shortwave radio, would have been commented on. This is a village and everything anyone does is commented on. The radio is probably hidden in a cottage or barn at the lodge. But if Fleur went into the village while we were searching the lodge, we wouldn't have seen her and she may have been marked down as a stranger here to pay her respects to the old earl who just died."

"You think she's still nearby."

"Yes, and she'll be broadcasting tonight. Will you have someone on the roads close by to listen in if she tries to reach Berlin tonight?"

He nodded. "You suspect someone here of being involved with her, don't you?"

It was my turn to nod.

He stared at me, waiting.

"Betsy Oswald has been too curious. And she keeps disappearing."

"And she's here now?" Sir Malcolm asked me.

"Only until tomorrow morning. She's asked Rosalie for a ride to the train station to return to London. Of course, that had always been their plan. Her husband has some sort of government wartime position." I needed to be fair and not jump to conclusions. That way had led me in the past to miss clues to the identity of the culprit.

I didn't want to make that mistake again.

"Does she have access to official secrets?"

"Not that I know of. I don't know what her husband's job is in the government."

"He's going back to London in the morning also for his job?"

"Yes."

"And you?"

"Adam and I have leave to stay here a few more days for his health."

"Did you know that Rosalie has been granted indefinite leave to take care of her husband?"

"No, but I'm glad. He's lost without her." Maybe that was what she meant about us coming out here more often. It would be for Thorpe's sake as well as Adam's since they seemed to enjoy each other's company, and with Rosalie here full time, it would be easier for us to make the arrangements.

Perhaps Rosalie needed me to come out to Lancashire as

a buffer, since Valerie Northcott and Daniel Perkins wouldn't need to come out as often. I was beginning to think Rosalie needed a houseful of guests as entertainment for Thorpe. People to stimulate his intellect, give him a reason to get up in the morning.

"I want you to watch the front hall for us tonight to see if anyone leaves," Sir Malcolm said. I knew it wasn't a request.

"If you suspect the servants, I'll have to watch from somewhere else. They wouldn't go out that way. And the closest way for anyone to get to Marshburn Lodge is by foot from the French doors and then follow the path over the hill."

"Then stand guard by the French doors."

"Inside, thank you." I stared at him.

He threw his hands in the air and took a few steps away from me. "Wherever makes the most sense. Use your head."

"Do you want me to follow them?"

"No. I want you to come get me."

"You'll be upstairs asleep?"

"Of course. Then you'll be able to go to bed and I'll be up the rest of the night trying to catch the traitor." He hissed out the last word.

"And if no one comes by, I'll be up all night."

"You're young, Olivia. You can handle it."

Before I had a chance to point out I wasn't as young as I used to be, Rosalie slipped into the room.

"My dear lady," Sir Malcolm said, "I need to impose on your hospitality for dinner and a bed."

"And for your driver?"

"Dinner in the kitchen would be wonderful for him. He'll be comfortable in the automobile for the night."

"And right at hand if needed?" Rosalie stared at the big man.

Sir Malcolm smiled. He had a smile that lowered the temperature of any room by at least ten degrees.

"We're dressing for dinner now," Rosalie told us. "Livvy, you need to get upstairs. Sir Malcolm, you might send your driver to the kitchen now unless you think you'll need him in the next few hours."

"I'll do as you suggest and then take my bag up to my room, which is…"

"Top of the stairs, second door to the left."

"The room the Larimers had," I said, nodding to myself.

Rosalie shepherded us out to the main hall as if we were wandering sheep and then I hurried up to dress for dinner.

At the top of the stairs, I waited for Rosalie. When she arrived a half minute later, I asked, "Has Cummings returned? What did he learn about automobiles in the village?"

"The viscount was seen parking near the church and a few minutes later roaring away. A green saloon that matched the description of Perkins's automobile arrived sometime during the church service and parked near where the viscount had parked before."

"Does anyone know about what time, or how far into the service, the green car appeared?" I asked.

Rosalie shook her head. "Cummings couldn't find that

out. He did learn one other thing. Two people were seen by Walter Winthrop during service walking along the back lane near Mrs. Cole's cottage. He didn't recognize them, but Walter isn't known for being sober enough to recognize anybody or knowing what time it is."

"In other words, someone was there at some time, but we already knew that. Can we trust that it was two people?"

Rosalie spread her fingers out. "Not necessarily."

"Male or female?"

"He said one of each, and that made him quite certain there were two people."

"It could have been the Oswalds or Valerie Northcott and Daniel Perkins. But why would either of them search Mrs. Cole's cottage?" I shook my head.

"Oh, there was one other thing. Cummings learned a car was seen roaring toward the village very early this morning from the direction of Silverthorn Manor, running a young farm worker off the road on his bike. He said it could have been either the viscount's car or Perkins's car."

The inspector had mentioned that. "Or your car, I imagine," I told Rosalie.

She was about to disagree, but then she stopped and smiled. "Or ours. They all look the same in the dark, don't they?"

"How many automobiles are still on the road in this area with the petrol shortage?"

Rosalie thought for a minute. "Ours, as you know. Dr. Hamelstein, but he only uses his when he has a house call at an outlying farm. The same with the vet over in Wilsley Bridge. Neither man was called out last night. Then there's Mr. Perkins when he's in the village doing work for one or another of us. The viscount. The old earl's car has long been put up on blocks, so we can't count that. I don't think there's one at Marshburn Lodge. The funeral coach has been put away and they've brought out the funeral wagon and horses, black plumes and all. The vicar was thinking of buying a small second-hand car when war broke out, but now he's glad he didn't."

"So, there are very few choices for the vehicle who nearly ran down the young man on his bicycle," I said. "This was Freddy Croft? The inspector mentioned something about him."

"Yes. There would be more if you counted delivery trucks coming in from Lancaster, but Freddy said it was a saloon, not a truck. And we use wagons and horses on all the farms, and Freddy said it wasn't that, either. Livvy," she said, looking at me with widened eyes, "there are very few possibilities unless it was someone passing through."

"And that doesn't help us at all," I told her.

* * *

When I came back downstairs with Adam, I found both Sir Malcolm and Viscount Norrington in dinner jackets. Both men seemed constantly prepared to dine with the aristocracy. "Do you want me to send those detectives away?" the viscount was booming out.

"There's no need. They're not in the way," Thorpe said.

"And they have a duty to perform."

"Oh. You mean poor Northcott," the viscount said.

"And poor Larimer," I added.

"At least I think I've convinced them my uncle was not murdered."

"Despite what his caregivers said?" Rosalie asked in a mild tone. Something about her expression and lack of looking in the viscount's direction made me think she didn't believe him anymore than I did.

"It's obvious, isn't it? They mishandled him somehow and killed my uncle, and then made up that ridiculous story to cover their mistake. He was an old man, very frail, and it wouldn't have taken much to do him in. I don't want them to get into any trouble. They've always been devoted servants. No sense in them suffering for an accident."

I had trouble picturing an accident that put marks of suffocation on the old earl.

The Oswalds appeared and Rosalie said, "Shall we go in to dinner?"

I sat between Thorpe and George Oswald. It could have been much worse. Poor Rosalie sat between the viscount and Sir Malcolm.

After three murders in a few days, general conversation that didn't twist off into death and destruction was growing harder to start or to keep going.

"I heard you're going back to London tomorrow morning," I said to George Oswald.

"I'm expected back in the ministry Tuesday morning as

usual. No more shooting for me."

"I should stay here and wrap up my uncle's affairs, but I need to go into London and get proper approval for what I guess will be a lengthy absence," the viscount said. "Could you give all three of us a ride to the train station tomorrow, Thorpe?"

"What will you do with your car?"

"Leave it in a barn at Silverthorn until I return."

After that, the talk turned to shooting, or rather, the viscount talked about shooting in that loud, domineering voice of his. Thorpe and George Oswald made suitable responses at intervals, Downing made a comment once or twice. The rest of us enjoyed the otherwise delicious dinner in silence.

When we finally rose from the table, we moved to the main drawing room for coffee. Adam sat in the chair Rosalie had placed with the best location and height for him, and I chose one as close to him as I could.

"Will you be going back tomorrow?" Betsy Oswald asked me.

"No. We still have a few days' leave left."

"I wish I could stay with you. I don't look forward to going back to London with all the bombing."

Neither Rosalie nor I responded to her words. We had had enough of Betsy Oswald and her comments. And I suspected her of being in contact with Fleur every time she wandered off and of being a blackmailer.

If Perkins or Mrs. Northcott was the killer, trying to

blackmail them would be dangerous. Anyone who would murder someone with a battle axe had to be crazy.

"If you stay here, who's going to take care of me?" Betsy's husband asked.

"As if you couldn't stay at your club."

"No, I couldn't. I want to go home and I want you there with me." George sounded stubborn.

Betsy looked at Rosalie, who shrugged in return as if there was nothing she could do. Betsy then gave her husband a bright smile. "So, we're both going home tomorrow morning."

I breathed a sigh of relief. I hope I did so quietly.

After that, no one seemed to have much to say, except the viscount, and even Thorpe and George Oswald were having trouble listening to him enough to respond appropriately. Thorpe announced he needed to retire, and several of us said it sounded as if it was a good idea, the day having been so dismal with the death of the old earl.

We all wandered upstairs, first Thorpe and Adam in the lift and then the rest of us slowly climbing the stairs. The viscount brought up the rear, saying "No fancy dress party, no Sunday shooting, and now we're going to bed with the farmers. Makes you wonder what we're fighting for."

No one replied. We'd all had too much of the viscount.

Chapter Twenty

Adam was already in our room by the time I reached the top of the stairs, and Cummings was pushing Thorpe into his room, Rosalie following.

Cummings hadn't been in the elevator with Adam and Thorpe, I realized, and he hadn't been on the stairs with me. Of course, the manor house was old enough to have a warren of corridors and staircases unseen by the guests and useful to the servants.

Various guests called out "Good night" as they entered their rooms, myself included.

I shut the door and went over to Adam, who was dressing in his pajamas. "Sir Malcolm has me working tonight."

Adam growled.

"I'm to hide by the French doors and see who leaves to go over to Marshburn Lodge."

"And follow them." He looked at me angrily.

"No. I'm to wake up Sir Malcolm and he'll set everything

in motion. And then I can go to bed." I was looking forward to the end of my work that night.

"I think he has a bee in his bonnet about Marshburn and German spies. We've incarcerated or turned all of them. There's no one left to help Fleur." Adam looked at me as if he found me as mad as Sir Malcolm.

"He thinks there are some Englishmen—well, English people—that no one has caught yet. He thinks it's important that we do."

"I think he's wrong, but if you're going to hide out downstairs, you'd better take your turn in the washroom first."

I washed and dressed in a heavy dark tweed suit and thick stockings and shoes. "I'll be in the small drawing room."

"Get me before you go to wake up Sir Malcolm. I don't want anyone to get the wrong impression and think we'd reverted to the Edwardian era of house parties."

"I thought that was more Victorian."

"Livvy." Adam's tone was dry.

I walked over and we kissed. "I'll return as soon as I can."

"Get me before you go to Sir Malcolm."

"Are you jealous?" I'd never thought of Adam as the jealous type before. In a way, I was pleased.

He gave me a look that said not to tease him.

I nodded and went down the stairs on tiptoe. I heard a door shut along the grand hallway in the opposite direction from where I should be going. Of course, I headed that way, and I saw a gleam of light under the door to the study.

I opened the door but didn't see any light or movement. Not having a torch or lantern, I flipped on the overhead light switch.

Henry Downing was leaning against one side wall, a torch in his hand.

"May I help you?" I asked.

"No." He sounded cheerful. He'd undone his tie and looked relaxed, as if this were his home.

"I'll have to tell Rosalie I caught you in Thorpe's study after we'd all gone to bed."

"She'll ask what you're doing here."

"She knows what I'm doing, and she's asked me to do it. But not you, I don't think." I watched him closely.

He smiled, walked over, and sat down behind the desk. "You realize I can't tell you what I'm doing here. Official secrets."

"For which part of the government?"

"Now that would be telling."

"Is Henry Downing your real name?"

"Yes. It makes life easier."

"Good," I told him. "The man I work for is high enough up in the government that he'll be able to find out what you are doing sneaking around my friends' home, taking advantage of their hospitality."

"Then you'll have to do it. I can't divulge any secrets." He smiled at me. "Good night, Mrs. Redmond."

Furious, I turned out the light and shut the door none too quietly, leaving him in the dark.

When I reached the French doors, I found the best place to hide seemed to be behind the window curtains about ten feet from the exit. I sat in the window box and waited. After what felt as if it'd been a century but was less than an hour, a figure came into the room and went out the French doors, quietly closing them behind him. There was enough light from the moon to show me the wanderer was George Oswald.

George? Not Betsy? Was he going after Betsy? Were they working in tandem?

I climbed out of my hiding place and rushed upstairs to get Adam. "It was George Oswald," I hissed as he struggled to his feet to follow me down the hall.

I opened what I hoped was the correct door to find the light on and Sir Malcolm sitting in a chair waiting for me. "I saw George Oswald," I told him. He had already turned off the light before marching past me to move around Adam in the hall.

Sir Malcolm paused at the top of the stairs. "Hurry up."

I should have known Sir Malcolm wouldn't let me go peacefully off to bed. I looked at Adam who shrugged and turned his sticks around to hobble back to bed. I wanted to follow him, but I knew at that moment that Sir Malcolm might need me more.

Sir Malcolm went out the front door, pounded on the side window of the automobile to wake his driver, told him something I was too late to overhear, and ran past me to go back inside. I followed Sir Malcolm through the house and out the French doors.

Fortunately, I knew the path from using it several times, because Sir Malcolm would have blundered off once we reached the woods even with his torch turned on. I tried to walk along quietly, not disturbing the fallen leaves so I could tell if someone was ahead of us. Sir Malcolm, not used to forests, marched along as if he were on pavement and made enough noise to cover the sound of a tank.

Once we reached the fence dividing the two estates, I grabbed Sir Malcolm by the arm to slow him down. "Turn off your torch and walk quietly. We're almost to the lodge," I whispered in his ear.

Surprisingly, he didn't argue over my instructions.

We skirted around a tenant's cottage and the stables before we came to the back of the lodge. In what moonlight there was, I saw a figure backing along the side of the building toward us.

Backing toward us? What was going on in front of the lodge?

At that instant, bright lights shone on the front of the lodge and men's voices and heavy running footsteps could be heard. A woman screamed. The figure made a headlong dash at us and I caught her, pinning her between the stone foundation of the lodge and my body.

Sir Malcolm shone his torch on my captive. Betsy Oswald.

"What are you doing here?" I demanded.

"What are you doing here?" Betsy snapped at me.

"Apparently catching you."

"I wanted to see who George was sleeping with this time." She sounded furious.

"Who he was...?"

"I heard him call her Fleur. He went inside, and then I realized there were all sorts of men around the outside of the house, so I decided to leave. And here you are."

"Where is your husband?"

"How would I know? Inside, probably. Why don't you let me go?"

"Not until we find your husband and Fleur," Sir Malcolm said and walked away toward the back of the lodge, shining his torch all around at chest height.

In the darkness, I seemed to hear Sir Malcolm's voice from all directions at once. I held on to Betsy Oswald, who had stopped struggling and protesting as she watched the action around us.

"How many people are you blackmailing?" I hissed into her ear.

"Just Valerie Northcott. Did you guess or did she tell you?"

"I saw you."

"Well, you can't have me arrested for it. That solicitor of hers will make sure she doesn't admit she's done anything to be blackmailed for." Betsy gave me a nasty grin.

"Got 'em," a man shouted, and figures were seen being hustled toward the front of the lodge.

When I hesitated, Betsy said, "Oh, come on," and we

moved to the front while I kept a firm grip on her arm and shoulder.

In the lights—automobile headlights, mostly—I saw Fleur Bettenard and George Oswald. I tried to take in as much of the scene as I could before the lights had to be doused for the blackout.

Sir Malcolm shouted out my name and told me to bring my friend with me. We went in the front door of the lodge to find Sir Malcolm and a few of his staff with George Oswald and Fleur Bettenard in a well-lit drawing room where the blackout shades had been pulled shut.

Fleur sat with her wrists cuffed and her back straight on a tartan-patterned chair. When she saw me, she said, "You couldn't resist telling, could you, Livvy?"

"The first time I came up here, I saw the antenna wire in a tree that had lost most of its leaves. It made me wonder if you were Burke's prisoner or his supervisor. I'm still not sure."

"And where does my husband fit into this? Have you been sleeping with her, George?" Betsy demanded, moving forward. I kept a tight grip on her arm, not certain what she would do.

Fleur and Oswald looked at each other, looked at her, and shrugged. I saw he was also wearing metal wrist restraints.

"You should have put a bed in the attic with the radio. Would have made that story more convincing," one of Sir Malcolm's men said.

"You were caught actually in the attic with the radio?" Sir Malcolm said, his smile as frightening as if he'd waved a saber around. "That was sloppy, Fleur."

"You've caught me now. The question is, what are you going to do with me?" Her smile was as broad and as insincere as Sir Malcolm's.

"What would you want me to do with you? With any of you?"

"I want to know if you're having an affair." Betsy Oswald, not understanding the situation at all, was sniffling now as she reached for her handkerchief in a jacket pocket.

"Madam, your husband is being detained for espionage. Your petty domestic problems are not the concern of the government," Sir Malcolm told her.

Betsy burst into tears. Not tragic sniffles but big, loud sobs. She buried her face in her hanky, making it impossible to tell if her eyes were wet.

I pushed her into a chair and kept a hand on one shoulder to keep her there. Everyone else ignored her.

"You want to turn me the same as you have so many of my colleagues." Fleur made it a statement of fact.

"You're much more dangerous than your fellow spies. I think we'll have to lock you up. Someplace more secure than here," Sir Malcolm told her before turning to George Oswald. "Would you care for an adjacent cell?"

"No," Betsy wailed. "Don't lock him up." Her face was still covered by the handkerchief.

I pulled it away and looked. No tears. "You may want to

lock up Mrs. Oswald, too."

"I had nothing to do with this." She snatched back her hanky but stopped the pretense of crying. Her eyes weren't red.

"I think you were aiding Fleur and your husband by passing messages." I glanced at Sir Malcolm.

"Certainly worth investigating. Cuff her too."

"No." Betsy was screaming now. "It was all their idea. I didn't know what they were doing."

"Quiet," her husband shouted.

"I'll tell Rosalie you won't need that ride to the train station in the morning, shall I?" I couldn't resist saying.

"I'm glad I destroyed that amateurish sketch of yours. You think you're an artist. Hah!"

"At least I'll be free to keep improving my sketches." It was childish, but I couldn't resist arguing with a traitor.

Betsy gave me a dark look but kept quiet as her husband had demanded.

Sir Malcolm's men carried armloads of radio equipment and papers out of the lodge. When they finished, the three prisoners were taken to three different cars for transport to whatever prison they would be held at for a while.

Sir Malcolm and I were the last two to leave, turning off lights and shutting the door. "I'll give you a lift back to Briarcliffe Hall," he said.

"Thank you." I didn't look forward to wandering through the woods on my own in the dark. "What about Burke?"

"He swears he knows her as Marshburn's bit on the side

and as such he organized her meals and the house cleaning. He said he'd never been in the attics, nor had any of Marshburn's tenants who'd been cooking and cleaning for Fleur."

"Do you believe him?"

"There is no evidence he'd helped her with the shortwave transmissions. We'll keep an eye on Burke, but I don't see him as a danger."

"I wonder who put the antenna up in the trees." It was dark in the car and I couldn't see Sir Malcolm's expression as I spoke.

"We'll check to make certain no more transmissions go out from the area of the lodge, but I don't think Burke will give us any trouble. Especially since there's no one to pay him for any 'extra services.'" I could hear the emphasis on the last two words in his tone. "And we have the radio."

Chapter Twenty-One

"Who was paying Burke?" I asked. "Fleur or Marshburn?"

"We don't think it was Marshburn. We have his money tied up, since he's having to pay the government for his incarceration on his main estate."

"With his wife?"

"Oh, no." Sir Malcolm chuckled. "She's in the London townhouse living on an allowance set aside by the government from Marshburn's income."

"That's good. I wouldn't want to be the jailer keeping Marshburn and his wife from strangling each other." Sir Malcolm might give me terrible assignments, but being Marshburn's keeper would be much worse than anything I'd had to do.

"I'm going to pack my things and leave when we drop you at Briarcliffe Hall. Please give the earl and countess my thanks for their hospitality. I would myself, but I'll be needed elsewhere before the night is out."

"Of course, Sir Malcolm. By the way, do you know a government person named Henry Downing?"

"Government person?" I could hear the laughter in his voice.

"Henry Downing?" I repeated.

"No."

"He's been searching through Briarcliffe Hall at night and no one seems to know who invited him to the shooting party. He claimed official secrets when I asked him what he was doing."

"And you want me to check him out?"

"Yes. He may find himself locked up before the day is out."

"Might do some of these government johnnies good to be locked up for sloppy work." He sighed. "I'll check him out."

When we arrived, I said good night and went straight up to bed, not checking to see what else Sir Malcolm did. I peeled off my clothes in the dark and climbed under the covers.

Only then did my movement wake Adam. "Everything all right?" he murmured, turning over.

"Yes. I'll tell you about it in the morning." Well, as much as I could.

I went to sleep, snuggled into the blankets with Adam's arm protectively over me.

* * *

Morning came too soon, and I wandered down to the breakfast room in the heavy tweed suit I'd worn the previous night. My first thought was for coffee. It was hot, freshly made, and I sank into a chair at the table with a cup clenched in my fist.

"Good morning," Rosalie said. "Cummings gave me a message for you."

I looked up and noticed her for the first time. "Good morning. It was a late night last night."

"So I gathered."

"What was the message?" I'd forgotten asking Cummings anything.

"He said the letter inviting the viscount here was dated three days after Mr. Northcott's last visit."

The news woke me up. I sat straight up and took a large gulp of steaming coffee. There had been time for the old earl to have talked to the viscount after Northcott's visit.

"Have you seen anything of Sir Malcolm this morning?" Rosalie's expression was wide-eyed innocence. I didn't believe it for an instant.

Adam sat down beside me with a full plate. I resisted the urge to applaud his increasing dexterity. "When Thorpe gets here, I'll tell all three of you at once."

It was as if I'd conjured him up when a moment later Cummings wheeled Thorpe into the breakfast room, made him a plate, and shut the door as he left.

"Sir Malcolm, having made his arrests, packed up his things when he dropped me off and left to take care of business. He said to thank you for your hospitality and he was sorry he couldn't thank you in person."

"Be thankful he didn't wake you in the middle of the night to tell you himself," Adam said, not hiding the grumble he always used when talking about Sir Malcolm.

"Where are the Oswalds?" Thorpe asked.

"They went wherever with Sir Malcolm, but they weren't free to pack up their things or thank you in person for your hospitality."

"Both of them?" Rosalie asked, her eyes widening.

I nodded.

"What was going on over at Marshburn Lodge?" Thorpe asked, and there was no mistaking the air of command in his voice. He was born to be an earl.

"A woman was staying there that I'd met before the war. Fleur Bettenard. She is a Nazi spy and assassin. She had set up a means to transfer British secrets to Germany, secrets she was getting from people such as the Oswalds."

"No wonder the Oswalds were so keen to come out here and shoot. It was all just a cover," Thorpe said. "Rotten traitors."

"All three have been arrested by Sir Malcolm," I added.

"What?" Rosalie sounded shocked. "And I never guessed."

"I'm sorry. I've probably already said too much."

"An assassin? Do you mean she killed Northcott and—?" Thorpe asked.

"No. I don't think she ever met any of them or even knew they were here. She had no interest in them or Briarcliffe Hall. And the Oswalds were too busy passing secrets to worry about killing anyone who didn't know their secret. We have to look elsewhere for the killer," I told him.

"So, Sir Malcolm didn't solve our mystery," Rosalie said. "I hoped he would. I was counting on it."

"Fleur and the Oswalds have no ties to the village or the estates here, not yours or Silverthorn's. Maybe we should talk to someone who knows the history of the area. All the old feuds, especially as Northcott and the old earl were related and have ties to the Silverthorn estate."

"The only old feud I can think of is the younger son taking over and pushing aside the older son's illegitimate son. But that was one hundred and fifty years ago," Thorpe said.

"We should talk to Mrs. Cole," Rosalie said.

"I was told to talk to old Mrs. Petrie," I replied.

"I'd forgotten about her. And I owe her a visit." With a smile, Rosalie added, "I think my plans for this morning have changed."

"May I come along?" I asked.

"I wouldn't have it any other way."

"Well," Thorpe said, "shall we again plan to play chess in the garden?"

Before Adam could reply, I said, "Has Cummings learned any more about cars or people wandering around the village during the church service?"

"Yes," Rosalie said. "The viscount's car left almost immediately after the service started. He couldn't have searched Mrs. Cole's cottage. Mr. Perkins's car was seen arriving during the service, but the old man who gave

Cummings the information doesn't own a clock. And he didn't watch to see where they went."

"So, either Valerie and Perkins or the Oswalds could have searched Mrs. Cole's cottage, which we knew before," I said. "I take it no one was seen actually entering or leaving her cottage?"

Rosalie shook her head. "It gets us no further forward."

"Meanwhile, your study was searched last night."

"What?" Thorpe demanded.

"I saw Henry Downing sneak into your study last night when I came down to watch out for who left here for Marshburn Lodge. I followed him in and turned on the light. He was just planning to use a torch."

"Did he say why?" Rosalie asked.

"He claimed official secrets."

Adam, Rosalie, and Thorpe all groaned.

"Ring for Cummings, please," Thorpe said. When Cummings appeared in the blink of an eye, the earl said, "Would you please ask Mr. Downing to meet me in my study at his earliest convenience?"

His tone told me Cummings would see that Downing's earliest convenience would be very fast.

"Your lordship, Mr. Downing was seen coming out of the estate agent's office when Cook returned from church on Sunday."

"Was he? Thank you." Thorpe's tone said Downing would have a great deal to answer for very soon.

It was nearly eleven before Rosalie and I were ready to

go. She came from the direction of the kitchen carrying a small pot of something. When she saw me looking at it, she said, "A lotion Mrs. Petrie is fond of for taking the stiffness out of her joints. My cook makes it up for her. We'll take this with us to smooth our way."

It was a sunny, warm morning and Adam and Thorpe were already into a chess game. I didn't ask what had happened with Downing. We said goodbye and walked down the hill to the village. The Ivys' cottage was near the edge of the village in one of the newer homes, not picturesque but undoubtedly warmer and easier to clean.

Mrs. Ivy opened the door to us while carrying a baby. Nevertheless, I detected a tiny curtsey before she stepped back so we could enter.

"I've brought your grandmother a pot of that salve she likes."

"She'll be glad of it. She's almost out. If the weather had been colder this autumn, she would be out. She's in the kitchen, but if you wait a moment—"

"I don't want to disturb her. Would it be all right if we talked to her in the kitchen?" Rosalie asked.

"It's a mess." Mrs. Ivy looked at the countess with wide eyes.

"We promise not to look," I said and grinned.

We followed her to the back of the house where an ancient woman in a heavy sweater sat in a well-stuffed chair next to the radiator. The kitchen was well scrubbed with everything put away. At our flat, my rarely used kitchen never looked so clean.

After the social pleasantries and introductions were completed, Rosalie and I pulled up wooden kitchen chairs to face the old lady while Mrs. Ivy took the baby into another room.

"Milady, you have too much going on at the Hall to be visiting me unless you wanted to know something." The old lady's eyes were faded, but I saw a twinkle in them.

Rosalie smiled. "You know me too well, Mrs. Petrie."

"It's nice to see you whatever the reason. What do you want to know?"

"A reason why Mr. Northcott, a cousin of the old earl, and the old earl should both be murdered within days of each other."

"Why are you asking me? I hardly set foot outside the door anymore." Her innocent expression clashed with her gleaming eyes.

"If anyone knows the reason for these terrible crimes, you would." Rosalie tilted her head and studied the old woman.

"I don't know if it's the reason, but Mr. Northcott came to see me a month or so ago."

Rosalie and I both sat up a little straighter.

"I thought that would get your attention." The old woman's laugh was a cackle.

"Why did he—?" I asked and then looked at Rosalie. "Sorry."

"Don't be sorry. You won't learn if you don't ask." The

old woman was enjoying her time as the center of attention.

"Did he stay with you, Rosalie?" I asked.

"No. I only know he'd visited in the village and stayed with us two weeks ago, and I heard that from Thorpe."

"You were off at your government place," the old woman said. "We had a good natter in the front room, out of hearing range of my granddaughter. He wanted what we discussed kept secret."

Chapter Twenty-Two

"Why did Mr. Northcott come to visit you a month or so ago?" Rosalie asked. I willed the old lady to answer quickly and with information that would quickly solve the murders.

"He wanted to know about his great-grandfather."

"The bastard? From the reign of George III?" Rosalie said.

"So he's always been known. The younger brother, even before he inherited the title, took the little fellow in and saw to his care and education."

"What happened to the older brother?"

"He and the baby's mother, having been hounded out of England, were crossing the Channel to go to France when the ship they were on sank. They'd left the little boy with the mother's parents, so he survived."

"Why didn't they just get married as soon as they knew the baby was on the way?" I asked.

"She wasn't aristocratic enough," Mrs. Petrie told me. "His parents would have disowned him and neither wanted to be penniless."

"They couldn't disown him from his title and the estates that came with it," Rosalie said.

"The story is his father was a mean old tyrant. He might not have been able to keep the son from inheriting, but he could make his life a misery until then. And the tale was the old man had made a pact with the devil and would live forever."

"Surely people didn't believe that," Rosalie said.

"It was believed in the village and beyond," Mrs. Petrie assured her.

"Why is Mr. Northcott a Northcott and not a Norrington?" I asked.

"Northcott was the baby's mother's name. Mr. Northcott was very interested in that. No one had ever told him before how that came to be his family name." She pulled her shawl tighter around her shoulders as if she were cold.

I was sweating.

"What did you tell Mr. Northcott about his family? I'd like to hear all of it," Rosalie said.

"About his great-great-grandparents drowning when their son was a baby, but after the baby was christened in the local church. Here. In the village."

"The grandfather didn't stop that?"

"He insisted on the baptism being held here, insisted on naming the godparents. The younger brother was one."

"What else did you tell him?" I asked.

"The baby grew up to be a solicitor in Lancaster and took care of the affairs of the estates in the shire, as did his son.

Mr. Northcott's father went into banking rather than the law, but no one knows why. They all led unremarkable lives."

"Unremarkable?" Rosalie asked.

"No scandals. No pacts with the devil. Nothing to be gossiped about in church." Once again, the old woman cackled.

"Anything remarkable about the women marrying into the Northcott line?" I asked.

"Women weren't allowed to be remarkable in Victorian times." There was that twinkle again in the faded old eyes.

"Did any of them inherit large sums of money, for instance."

"No. Everyone was properly upper middle class, with the sons inheriting the money."

I leaned forward. "Mrs. Petrie, the day Mr. Northcott visited you, where was he staying in the village?"

"With the old earl. Mrs. Smith will tell you."

So far, Mrs. Smith hadn't felt it necessary to tell us much of anything. "Why do you think Mr. Northcott was murdered?"

"It's not for me to say."

"You must have some thoughts on it."

"Oh, I have thoughts on it, but I don't care to share them."

"Afraid the house will be torn apart the same as your niece, Mrs. Cole's?"

"My grandchildren don't have the freehold on this cottage. I don't want to say anything to hurt their tenancy."

I glanced at Rosalie, who said, "I imagine you rent from Silverthorn. Most of the houses around here belong to their estate."

"While Mrs. Cole owns her cottage?" I asked.

"Yes," the old lady told me.

"Someone is certainly getting their message across. Murder, intimidation. We need to find out who's behind this, Livvy," Rosalie told me.

Murder trials made good copy for the *Daily Premier*. I was sure I could convince Sir Henry Benton, the publisher and my employer, that this was a story worth following. Especially since, for once, Sir Malcolm wouldn't interfere.

"Do you know where the record is of the baby's christening?" I asked.

"Those records are stored in the rectory. My niece and the vicar can find them for you. Look under June 1795."

* * *

When we left the house, Rosalie turned in the direction of the path to Briarcliffe Hall. "I think we should go to the rectory first," I told her. "The way things are going, we need to see this baptismal record before it disappears or is torn up." I didn't want anything potentially important to vanish.

"But it's nearly time for lunch and Thorpe will expect me back." Rosalie sounded conflicted between Thorpe's immediate needs and the long-term need to find a murderer.

"Adam will tell him to blame your tardiness on me. I'm completely unreliable where time is concerned."

Rosalie shrugged, appearing a little relieved that she

wouldn't be the one upsetting Thorpe. "We do need to get to the bottom of this."

We walked in the direction of the rectory. When the Reverend Shaw opened the door, noise in the form of children's voices flowed out from behind him.

"I need the parish records for 1795," Rosalie told him after they went through the usual greetings in loud voices to be heard.

"Come in. They're in the office." He led the way, shutting a door, which seemed to cut down on the shrieks and screams. "I wish Mrs. Cole was here today, but she had to go into Lancaster."

After a search, we found the earliest records stopped at 1850.

"They must be in the boxes in the attic. I'm sorry."

"Don't be sorry, vicar. Just lead the way," Rosalie said.

We climbed up stairs to the top of the house. Fortunately, the attic had been wired for lights hung from the joists so we could see the many boxes stored there. The vicar wrung his hands at the sight, so Rosalie and I began to check boxes.

"1642 to 1644," I called out in amazement.

"Interesting, but not relevant. Remember, I need to get home for Thorpe's luncheon," Rosalie called back.

We dug in, the vicar standing by the door, saying, "I'm sorry everything is in such a mess," as we ignored him.

Rosalie was the one to find the records for 1795. I closed up a box from the sixteenth century and maneuvered around boxes and old furniture to join her.

The paper was dirty, the ink faded, and neither of us could make much sense of the spidery handwriting. The Reverend Shaw peered at the page and finally said, "June 14, a boy, Edwards Nathaniel Christopher, to Maria Northcott and Viscount Nathaniel Norrington of this parish."

"What is that?" I pointed to a spot above the mother's name on the page.

"An ink blot?" Rosalie suggested.

The vicar carried the book over to directly below a bare bulb. "No. It looks as if it's an addition to the record. A 'nee' above the mother's name."

"Indicating she was married." I looked at Rosalie, my eyes widening with surprise. "Whoever put the 'nee' there was telling us the parents were married. And that means the baby was legitimate and should have been the next earl."

Rosalie looked at the book again under the light. "I still think it's an ink blot. It's not even on the same line as the other information."

"It's just above the line. I think it's a hint of what Mr. Northcott was thinking. What he was trying to find out when he was killed."

"If they really were married, why did no one know it?" Rosalie asked me.

"If they were keeping it a secret until after his father died, they might have planned to bring out the evidence of their marriage then, but they died first in that accident in the Channel."

"Where would that evidence be? Vicar, do you have any idea?"

"Somerset House?" he asked.

"No," I said. "Somerset House wasn't used for keeping records of births, marriages, and deaths until 1837. I learned that while researching an article for the *Daily Premier.*"

"What about a special license?" Rosalie asked.

"You'd have to be upper nobility to do that," Shaw replied.

"He was a viscount, heir to an earl." Rosalie looked at me and said, "Can you check that out?"

"I'm sure I could. We're going to have to pool all our knowledge of these people if I'm to find the record that would prove this marriage happened."

"They believed in infant baptism back then, didn't they, vicar? Early infant baptism?"

"Oh, within a few days. A week at the most," he told Rosalie.

"So the wedding would have been late 1794 or early 1795. Before she was showing too much," I said.

"Surely, you don't think..." the Reverend Shaw said.

"Oh, yes," Rosalie and I said in unison.

"Where would you get a special license that would allow you to marry anywhere, not just in your home parish?" I asked.

"Why not in their home parishes?" Rosalie asked.

"Because we know they didn't marry here, the earl wouldn't have allowed it, and I'm sure he'd have made it impossible to marry in her parish either. They'd have to publish the banns, and the earl would have had someone listening for that."

"The only way to avoid reading the banns would be to get a special license from the Archbishop of Canterbury," the vicar said.

"How do you know that?" I asked. The Reverend Shaw seemed the same as just an ordinary vicar, unfamiliar with the workings of the church hierarchy.

"My dear child, I have one of those brains that can't seem to shed facts once they've been seen. And I had a course, a most interesting course, in Canterbury many years ago that covered the history of the church and its inner workings from the dissolution of the monasteries until the present time."

"Looks as if you'll need to start your search in Canterbury," Rosalie told me.

"Oh, no, those were handed out in Doctors' Commons in London in the Faculty office," the Reverend Shaw told us.

"That's where I'll start then."

"There's a problem," the vicar said.

I moaned as Rosalie shook her head.

"Doctors' Commons was demolished in 1867. After the ecclesiastical courts were abolished. Now let me remember…"

Shaw stood there thinking while I was conscious of wanting to hold my breath. Rosalie started to get nervous or impatient, taking a step or two in one direction after another between the boxes.

I knew she wanted to get home to Thorpe, who'd be wondering what was taking us so long, but she also wanted to learn the identity of the murderer. Two of the murders had occurred in her own home and the third was a defenseless old man, a friend of hers. There would be no peace in her village if the killer wasn't caught.

There didn't seem to be any peace downstairs either. The noise from the kitchen or wherever the children congregated was growing louder.

Rosalie took a deep breath and stood leaning against a support, apparently relaxed, while I was growing restless. Instead of moving around, I wanted to scream.

Suddenly, a thudding of little feet raced up the stairs and burst into the attic complete with high-pitched, excited voices.

Shaw turned to the children, which turned out to only be five for all the noise they made, and asked, "What seems to be the trouble?"

Their kickball was missing. "It's been stolen," one of the boys kept saying over and over.

"Are you sure you haven't misplaced it?"

"It's been stoled," a younger boy cried out.

"Where do you usually keep it?"

"In the cupboard."

"Did you put it there last time?"

"Yes."

"It's been stoled," the little boy shouted as he jumped up

and down.

"None of you looked out on the green," Rosalie said, looking out a dirty, cobweb-covered window.

Two of the boys ran over to her, pulling themselves up on the windowsill to see outside. "The big kids have it," they shouted and all five careened down the stairs.

All three of us adults took deep breaths after the invasion. I found my voice first. "Where were the records sent after the Doctors' Commons was demolished?"

"Oh, yes. Now, where were they sent? They'd still belong to the Archbishop of Canterbury. They must be in the archives of Lambeth Palace."

"Are you sure?" I asked.

"It's just a guess, I'm afraid. But I think it's a good guess."

Chapter Twenty-Three

We managed to go downstairs and out the front door without being run over by a clutter of children. Once outside, Rosalie said, "You now know everything to check in London."

"Adam and I will head back tomorrow morning." A day early, but as a reporter, I knew I was the one best placed to hunt out the records.

"Nonsense. Adam can stay here and continue his recovery and you can come back as soon as you find the information in the archives of Lambeth Palace." Rosalie started up the hill at a good pace.

"What if I can't get more time off from the newspaper? What if the records aren't there? What if that wasn't how or where they were married?" Adam and I had been separated for far too much of our married life, and the only good thing I could see about his injuries in France was that we were able to spend more time together now.

While Rosalie proposed to separate us again.

"Don't be so negative. Just check with Lambeth Palace

and tell your editor you're working on a triple murder with implications in the inheritance of an earldom."

I could picture Sir Henry salivating over such a juicy story.

We walked back talking about the possibilities of what I might find in the church archives, but I still was unhappy at the thought of leaving Adam behind.

But was I being selfish, since this was helping Adam?

Fortunately, Adam didn't want to be left behind. When we returned and Rosalie made her "suggestion" about our separation, Adam put his foot down. "For all the time we've had together since we married, we're still newlyweds, and while I appreciate everything the two of you have done for my recovery, I'd prefer to go back with Livvy. Besides, I have a couple of doctor appointments I really shouldn't miss."

"Are you certain? We'd love to have you," Rosalie said.

"That's very kind, but I'm sure Thorpe wants a better chess partner than me," Adam said and smiled. "And I do have to see those doctors. I'm still in the army and they don't like soldiers not showing up. Tends to make them line up a firing squad."

"We want the two of you out here again as soon as you've seen your doctors and Livvy has undertaken some research for us," Rosalie said.

"What are you two up to?" Thorpe said, suspicion in every word. "We never make Cook hold lunch, and I can't imagine why Livvy has to search Lambeth Palace."

Rosalie and I took turns telling him our findings and suspicions. When we finished, the color had drained from

Thorpe's face.

"You realize the ramifications of this, if you find a record of a marriage back in the eighteenth century? The College of Arms will have to rule on who is the rightful earl. You would be asking them to overturn a century and a half of tradition and decisions."

"Worse than that, darling," Rosalie said.

"Oh, you can't think so." Thorpe made a face. "He's an ass, but a killer? Never."

"That's for the police to figure out," I said, "but tell me more about this College of Arms. If we find proof of this marriage, will we need to take it to them?"

"Teds Northcott, the late Robert's older son, is the one who will have to apply to the College of Arms since he would be the alternative earl. He's the one to officially supply the evidence. Since he's a minor, he'd need to bring along his mother and I hope Daniel Perkins, who is a good solicitor and can deal with the formalities. Valerie couldn't deal with all the details. It would be too much for her. The three of them will need to request a hearing as soon as possible to present the information to the College of Arms so the viscount can't be named to the title of earl as a formality, not knowing of a rival claimant."

Thorpe paused. "The College is in the City. I seem to remember it being on Queen Victoria Street, if they haven't been bombed out. The first thing they'll need is the proof of the marriage and the baptism proving the first Northcott was a legitimate Norrington. The College will have everything before that time—they're great genealogists—but they'll need the birth, marriage, and death records for the generations afterward." He gave me a smile that said nothing could be easier.

I hoped he was right. "Somerset House should be useful for most of the later records."

"Then all we need is the marriage license of this long-ago Norrington to get thing moving," Rosalie said with satisfaction.

"Meanwhile, is Downing still here? Was there some reasonable reason why he was in your study after everyone had gone to bed?" I asked.

"He was telling the truth when he told you it was covered by official secrets," Thorpe said. "Finally, he came clean when I threatened to ring up Scotland Yard.

"The Munitions Board found evidence of theft at our factory. Since we're the owners, they suspected us. Downing went through our records in the study and in the estate office—during church services, if you can believe that."

"And no one noticed he was missing," Rosalie said in wonder.

"He's very good at fading into the background," I told her. "He must be a very good investigator."

"Not to mention a terrible thief, enjoying our hospitality," Thorpe said. "I pointed out some things he hadn't noticed, and that led him to who had been stealing from the factory. Our last estate agent."

"Is Downing still here?" I asked.

"No, he's gone to turn in his report and start the hunt for our former estate agent, who, instead of working for the government, has apparently disappeared."

"Well, I'm glad he's gone," Rosalie said. I wasn't certain which man she meant.

"But how did he get invited to begin with?" His presence didn't make sense to me from the start.

"Downing said his ministry 'convinced' one of the viscount's party to drop out and suggest him in his place. Apparently, he's a fair shot and can fit in. Then it was just a matter of finding opportunities to search the place for incriminating documents," Thorpe told me as he smiled bitterly. "He was rather frustrated when he couldn't find anything pointing to us as the thieves."

I shook my head in amazement as I looked at Adam.

"We'll leave in the morning and get started on what needs to be done in town," Adam said.

"Are you sure you won't stay here while Livvy carries out the research?" Thorpe asked.

"No, I want to go back with her."

Thorpe gave Adam a nod. "Then we'd better ring for lunch if it hasn't burned to a crisp, and we'll expect to see you at the weekend."

I walked over and gave Adam's hand a squeeze before we all headed into the dining room.

* * *

The next morning, armed with every detail Rosalie and Thorpe could think of, Adam and I had a hearty breakfast and then rode to the station to catch an overfilled train to London.

It seemed to take forever to reach London, which was mercifully still standing in the area of our block of flats. Any efforts by the Luftwaffe to take out the railway lines and stations seemed to be failing, but we could see pockets of destruction in the streets surrounding them.

Once in our flat, Adam immediately stretched out on the bed to rest his legs while I called the *Daily Premier*. After being transferred a few times, I reached Mr. Colinswood.

"Livvy," he said when I identified myself, "I thought you were on vacation for another day or two."

"I am, but I've run across a story that you will love. Three modern-day murders in an attempt to hide the theft of an earldom one hundred and fifty years ago."

"Have you got this on exclusive?" was, unsurprisingly, his first question.

"Yes, but first we have to find the missing evidence. What do you know about special licenses for aristocrats in the time of George III?"

"Nothing. Let me think who..." There was silence on the telephone line for so long I thought we'd been cut off. Then at a distance I heard Colinswood say, "Get me Cutheridge."

"I think this would be ecclesiastical," the editor said when he came back on the line. "I've called for our C of E reporter to come in here to talk to you."

"Good, because I've heard what I need is in Lambeth Palace," I told him.

"You might have told me that... Oh, here he is now."

Another man's voice, both deeper and weaker, came over the line. "Cutheridge here."

"Livvy Redmond. I'm on a story involving a possible special license and marriage one hundred and fifty years ago. The man was the heir to an earl, so he could have paid well for the license, but he needed to keep the wedding secret from his family, at least until his father died and he inherited."

"Why didn't he tell everyone then?"

"A few months after a baby boy was born to the couple, they, the parents, drowned in the Channel. The baby was treated as illegitimate, but if there was a secret wedding, he would have been the next earl."

"And you want to know where the records of such a license and such a wedding would be kept?"

"Yes."

"Why?"

"There have recently been three murders and it's possible they were designed to hide the truth about that baby boy's legitimacy."

"Good grief." As a reporter, Cutheridge could see the possibilities. "What is the year we're looking for?"

"Late 1794 or early 1795."

"The Lambeth Palace archives. I'll meet you there at nine tomorrow morning."

"Meet me there?" I wasn't expecting that.

"You're a woman, and a civilian. You're going to need me

to help you get through the front door, much less the labyrinth. It's the palace of the Archbishop of Canterbury. They are very traditional in their outlook."

We made our arrangements to meet and then he put Mr. Colinswood back on.

"When can I get the story?" was his first question.

"Once we have the proof, it's delivered to the College of Arms, and the police make an arrest. Then you may have your story."

"By then everyone will have it. We'll go with it once the claim is formally made for the title. That's quite a story all on its own."

"It will take a few days to gather all the paperwork. Once I have all the information I need here, I'll head back to Lancaster and get the people involved to file their claim. Once they do, I can write up the story for you."

"I'll tell Sir Henry you're on assignment for me. I can't wait to watch his reaction when he sees this written up." Mr. Colinswood chuckled over the telephone line.

"How much time may I have with Mr. Cutheridge?" I had a feeling he'd be very useful on the church side of this story.

"A day or two. If you need more, let me know. It's bad enough I have one of you running all over England on a story I haven't heard the details of yet. Two of you is a bit much. Reporters are hard to come by in wartime. It's as if employees are rationed, too."

"Don't worry. You've got the best of those available," I assured him as I rang off.

Adam awoke and dressed in his uniform in time to go out to dinner. He knew better than to ask if I had anything on hand to fix us to eat. I wore an old evening dress. We planned to go to one of the hotel dining rooms since they still had decent food.

We walked, the closest nice hotels not being a great distance. The blackout was rigorously enforced and we had to be careful crossing streets. I wore my coat with the reflective tape sewn on; I had tied bands of the same tape on Adam's canes.

There was hardly a man out who wasn't in military uniform, though so far few of them were on crutches or canes. I noticed more women in uniform than before, but still not too many. With the blackout and the general drabness, there was no doubt we were at war.

When we reached one crossroads, I looked over my shoulder and saw a beefy, middle-aged man in a raincoat and fedora turn away and look into a shop window. Strange, since with the blackout, no one could make out what was displayed in the shop windows at night.

I hurried Adam across the street.

Inside, the hotel dining rooms were keeping the specter of rationing and dreariness away. Outside, all the windows were taped and dark. I wondered how much longer hotel restaurants could keep up with pre-war standards and pre-war food.

Adam and I enjoyed ourselves, feeling alone as we hadn't on the train or at Briarcliffe Hall. Or would later when we had to go down to the air-raid shelter. Unfortunately, we timed our dinner too late and had to use the hotel shelter when the sirens started.

At least we had our meal, but I had been looking forward to finding out if their coffee was better than the usual served in London lately.

We found seats in the shelter, but there was no place for Adam to stretch out his long legs. I knew he'd be in agony before long. A man in naval uniform asked Adam with a gesture toward his canes if he'd been in France. I felt Adam stiffen on the bench next to me, but the man's empathetic expression melted Adam's hostility.

By the time the all-clear sounded, it was well into the early morning and we were exhausted. Adam had stiffened up and was in pain until he had walked a few streets toward home. We walked slowly back in the dark to find our block of flats was still standing. Adam may have been even more relieved than I was, and I know I was thrilled.

We caught a few hours of sleep, remembering how nice a full night's sleep had been at Briarcliffe Hall. Then we washed, dressed, had weak tea, and while Adam went off to see one of his doctors, I headed south of the river to meet Mr. Cutheridge by the entrance to Lambeth Palace.

Two Underground stations south, I looked over to find the beefy man from last night standing behind some people in the aisle of our carriage. I jumped off at the next stop and raced to the lift, jumping in just before the doors closed.

The beefy man was left on the platform.

Once on the street, I walked over to the next stop on another line and headed in the general direction of south. Once across the river, I had a long walk through heavily bombed areas to reach Lambeth Palace. I didn't see the beefy man again.

I almost missed Mr. Cutheridge. I wasn't expecting a tall, thin youngish man, and he wasn't expecting a fashionable ginger-haired beauty.

We both stood there for a moment before I said, "Mr. Cutheridge?"

"Mrs. Redmond?"

That sorted, we went up to the front entrance and rang the bell. Mr. Cutheridge knew the man who answered the door and was let in, but then the ascetic-looking man in black with a clerical collar and a large silver cross on a chain around his neck blocked my way.

"I'm afraid we can't allow women inside."

Chapter Twenty-Four

"I need to research some old records that are kept here," I told the churchman.

"You'll need to find a man to go through our records for you." He remained in my way even though he looked as if a stiff breeze would blow him aside. I considered running into him for a moment, but I didn't think it would help me find the particular record I needed.

"I'm here to assist her," Mr. Cutheridge said, standing behind the thin churchman. "We work together. She's the only one who will recognize the correct record."

"Nonsense. What was the year of this record?"

"1794 or 1795, but it's important today to prevent a miscarriage of justice," I told him, righteousness ringing in my voice.

"Nonsense."

"Then you approve of murder."

"No. I—"

"Good," I said, sliding past the frail-looking man.

"Because if you don't help me, a man will get away with three murders in the present day. Now, which way is the archives?"

"Madam—"

"It's this way." Cutheridge led the way with me on his heels and the man who answered the door following. We were in a medieval-era building with long corridors and many steps. The steps we took led down into a crypt-type area where musty volumes sat on shelves and two more black-suited men with clerical collars and large shiny metal crosses were studying a faded ledger.

"Excuse me. I'm Thomas Cutheridge and I'd like to see the special license register for 1794 and 1795."

One of the two men walked away without challenging us. When I looked behind me, I found the doorkeeper hadn't followed us into this cave-like cellar. I stood next to Cutheridge, who didn't seem surprised at the silence from either man, and tried to copy his air of respectful patience. It was driving me mad.

The man brought over a thick volume covered with the dust of ages. He blew across the cover and then handed it to Cutheridge. "Those bombs seem to send dust everywhere. Even down here."

Cutheridge carried it over to a tall table and laid the huge ledger down. He brushed at the dust smeared on his jacket while I edged around the table to peer over his shoulder.

He found 1794 easily and I had him begin in June, one year before the christening of the Norrington-Northcott baby. He carefully turned over page after page, not finding the license we hoped to find. When we came to the end of 1794, I took a deep breath and nodded to Cutheridge to search through 1795.

We didn't have to look long. The license was taken out by Edwards Nathaniel Norrington on January 25, 1795, and was marked with the stamp for a twenty-one guinea fee and the four-pound stamp tax. "He could use this to marry anyone at any time at any church without publishing the banns," Cutheridge told me in hushed tones.

"Any idea where?" I asked.

"I don't know. I'm not familiar with these records," he told me and looked around for the man who had brought him the volume.

When the black-shirted and suited churchman reappeared, Cutheridge signaled him with a small gesture of one hand, and the man came over silently.

"Was this particular license used? Is there any way to tell?"

The man leaned over the book and peered at the page. "Yes, it was used. See this mark here?"

"Are you able to tell where?" I asked.

The man ignored me.

Cutheridge said, "Any idea which church this was used in?"

"From this book, no. But many of the licenses from this time were used at one of the nearby churches. St. Mary-at-Lambeth, just next door, or perhaps the Church of St. Saviour and St. Mary Overie. You know it as Southwark Cathedral."

He glanced at me and then back to Cutheridge. "After going to all the trouble of getting, and paying for, a special license, I can't imagine they went far."

"May we get a copy of this?" I asked.

The cleric looked at Cutheridge, who nodded. He took the book away, returning in a few minutes with a copy certified at Lambeth Palace. I paid the fee, but the copy was handed to Cutheridge.

Then we found our way out of the palace, with the door opened by the same man who hadn't wanted to let me in. This time, the door was firmly shut on my heels.

"Shall we try next door first?" I asked.

"Makes sense." Cutheridge led the way, but I followed closely. I wasn't going to chance having another door shut in my face. Not when we were so close.

Here, an older woman heard what we wanted and led us to a musty back room in a sort of half-basement. She found the volume, as dusty as the one in the Lambeth Palace archives, and opened up to the date we gave her. "Nothing on that date."

"Could we check the next week or two?" I asked.

"Of course." The woman peered nearsightedly into the book, slowly running her finger down one page after another. "Norrington-Northcott, you say?"

"Yes."

"Here it is. January 30."

"Wonderful. May we have a certified copy, please?"

"Oh, no. We can't do that. Rector isn't here."

Before I had completely swallowed my gasp, Cutheridge said, "When will he return?"

"We expect him back tomorrow. He's gone to visit his brother in Oxford."

"And do you think he'd make a copy for us tomorrow?" I asked, sweetness dripping from my words.

"Oh, yes, I'm sure he would. For the usual fee."

We fixed a time for the next morning and Cutheridge and I left by the main doors.

"You've found what you wanted," he said in a tone of amazement.

"If the Germans level this place tonight, you will have to witness what we've seen and heard at the College of Arms," I told him. I would not rest easily until these records were handed in to the proper authorities.

We went back to the *Daily Premier* building, where I found the beefy man loitering on the pavement near the front door. I studied his face as I dashed into the building. It was square with a smushed-in nose, deep-set eyes, and thin lips. A scary, brutish face.

I was certain he was the same man I'd seen the night before and earlier that morning. Perhaps it was coincidence, but I couldn't convince myself of that.

I went up to Mr. Colinswood's office. There weren't as many cigarette stubs in his ashtray for this time in the late morning, and the air was not so thick with smoke. He looked up when I knocked and walked in. "Livvy. How's the story going?"

I told him about the murders and how the death of the old earl meant rumors of two claimants and how I'd found records disputing the official version. "But you must remain silent until the evidence of the rival claim is presented to the College of Arms," I finished.

Mr. Colinswood lit a cigarette and said, "Tobacco is so hard to get—I have to ration myself. Now, what about these murders? Any arrests? And what about the College of Arms?"

"You're going to have to wait until the police make an arrest, and so far, they don't have enough evidence. What I'll have for you first is the background to tie the murders into this rival claim to an earldom. Of course, that's only if the killer is who I think it is."

He raised his eyebrows.

"Let's not get ahead of ourselves," I told him.

He grinned at me, knowing I was already ahead of what I could prove.

I gave him a reproving look. "Right now, I'm working on a story of deceit a century and a half old, with a young lad of today whose father was brutally murdered trying to get the inheritance that should have been the father's, and now his."

"We can definitely play up the human-interest angle. How long do you think it will take?"

"A few days. Maybe a week. I'll have my hands on the last piece of missing evidence tomorrow morning. Then I'll have to go back to Lancaster and get the rival claimants to undertake a journey to London to present one hundred and fifty years' worth of records to the very formal College of

Arms. They haven't been bombed out, have they?" That was a frightening thought.

"No, they're all right. When do you think we can publish?" Colinswood said directly, smoke rising above his head.

"Once everything has been presented, it should be safe then. But not before."

Mr. Colinswood leaned back in his chair, thinking for a moment, and then nodded. "Keep in touch with me about this. I'll want to know how this is progressing."

"I will. And now I better tell Sir Henry what's going on." I went up to the top floor and faced his secretary across her heavily laden desk. "Is he available?"

"He's leaving for lunch with the Ministry of Information heads in about five minutes."

"That's all I need."

She waved me in, and I knocked and entered the large, impressive office of our publisher. "Livvy," he said from his raised chair behind his massive desk. "How are things going in Lancaster? Has Sir Malcolm found any more spies?"

"Yes, but I don't think you can print any of that."

"Pity." Sir Henry had been at this for so long he didn't get upset by an inability to report on everything newsworthy due to the censors.

"I just talked to Mr. Colinswood about a story that will have two surprises."

"I have to leave in a few minutes. The Ministry of Information does most of their pontificating at lunch meetings, but at least the food is good." He smiled at me. "So, give me a quick synopsis."

The Ministry of Information was where the viscount worked. It would be a place that spent a lot of time on lunch meetings. I filled him in on what had happened in 1795 and how I thought it led to three current-day murders.

He looked at his watch as I finished. "That's a good story and I don't think the censors will cut it. And now I have to hurry."

"Don't breathe a word of this to anyone. Except Colinswood. I'm reporting this to him. If word gets back to the wrong people, the story is dead. And maybe a few more people," I added.

He smiled. "I haven't heard a thing."

I knew I could trust his discretion.

We rode down in the elevator together while he asked if Adam had regained his strength yet. I assured him my husband was making progress, pride evident in my voice.

"I'll tell Esther the next time I talk to her. She and the children are staying at the house I bought in Oxfordshire, and James is going down there whenever he can." Then he laughed. "She took the cook and the servants with her, and they've managed a decent garden. If he wants a decent meal, he has to visit them."

"I suspect you visit your grandchildren frequently and get country-cooked meals as a bonus."

"You won't believe how they've grown." We reached the lobby and Sir Henry was about to head outdoors. "Tell Adam

I'm thinking of him."

"Tell Esther I'll write to her." I waved and walked toward the stairs and the photography section where my old colleague Jane Seville worked.

Thank goodness she was in.

After we greeted each other and caught up on what had occurred in our lives since the fall of France and the Blitz began, I told her, "I have a favor to ask. I'm being followed by a large man and I want you to get a photo of his face."

"I have an hour or so free. Where is he now?"

"He was loitering outside the front door when I came in."

"You go out the front and I'll follow with my camera. He's not dangerous, do you think?" Jane held her camera protectively.

"Not so far. I'll come by tomorrow morning for a print."

Jane shook her head as I smiled and said, "Thank you."

She readied her camera and held it by her side, the strap around her neck as we went to the lobby. Then I walked out, followed by Jane, as if we'd reached the doors at the same time.

Jane hurried past us as I started up the pavement and the stocky man followed. Then she swung around, raised the camera and snapped.

I hesitated a moment because of the flash in my eyes. Behind me, I heard the heavy steps stop also. Jane rushed to the side against the building's wall.

When I glanced back, he had taken a step or two toward her, but there were people on the pavement between the two of them. I made a small squeaking noise in my throat and moved on. After a moment, he ignored her and I was aware of again being followed by the heavy-set man and his heavy footsteps.

I hurried into the Underground and jumped into a lift at the last moment. However, when I reached the platform, there were no trains to board. By the time one appeared, my shadow was standing practically next to me.

Hanging on to my bag where I'd put the copy of the license, I stayed away from the edge in case he wanted to shove me in front of a train. Every time he moved toward me, I scooted around another person, trying to keep my distance. Then my train came in and I jumped on, grabbing a seat between an old lady and a woman with a baby.

He stayed at the other end of the carriage the entire ride and I could have relaxed, except every time I glanced in his direction, he was staring at me. And it wasn't a friendly stare.

Once we reached my stop, I hopped out and hurried upstairs on the escalator, knowing the beefy man was following me. I worried about him learning where I lived until I realized he'd followed me from our block of flats. He knew where I lived, so why was he following me? Was he going to try to get in past Sutton? I thought our doorman could stop him.

At the last cross street but one, I was waiting for a bus to pass when I felt a shove on my shoulder and a pull on my bag. I shrieked. The twin movements of the shove and the pull naturally swung my body around to the side, twisting away from my attacker and into a couple. They began to protest.

I continued to turn and found the heavy-set man had a grip on my bag and we were nearly nose to nose. Opening up my mouth, I screamed as loudly as I could, startling him. I kept up the scream until I had no breath left.

He loosened his hold as he stepped back and I jerked my bag out of his hands. People moved toward and away from us, a crowd began to form, the couple complained loudly, and he stepped back, disappearing into the crowd.

* * *

I was jumpy the rest of the day and dithered over what to fix for dinner until Adam took pity on me and offered to take me out. "What's wrong?" he asked as he made certain his uniform tie was straight.

"You haven't told me what the doctor said yet." That wasn't the only thing bothering me, but it was the most important. Adam had worried about what the doctor would say the whole time he was walking around the garden at Rosalie's.

"He liked the improvements I've made while staying at Briarcliffe Hall, but I'm still not where he'd like me to be. The left leg especially. I have to return tomorrow to be seen by another doctor. This one is talking about a permanent desk job." He looked at me with his lips pressed together.

I could see the doctor's words hurt him. "I thought the idea was to get you declared fit enough for the training brigade. That at least isn't all from behind a desk, is it?"

"No. This doctor's saying he doesn't think I'll ever be fit

enough for a training position, even one with a great deal of desk duty."

"He's wrong. I'm sure of it." I gave him my determined look. "You just need a little more time. More time at Briarcliffe Hall, out of all this bombing, with good food and rest and more walking."

He squeezed my hand. "Thanks for having faith in me."

"Of course. I know you can handle this."

"So, what is it that's really bothering you?"

After all he had on his mind, I hated to admit what I was thinking. "I found an important piece of information about the inheritance of the Silverthorn title. But I couldn't get a copy signed by the rector until tomorrow when he returns. I'm afraid the records will all be burned up by a German bomb tonight, and that horrible viscount will get the title. And there goes my scoop for the *Daily Premier,* and Sir Henry and Mr. Colinswood will be disappointed in me."

I wouldn't tell him about being followed or the attempt to steal my bag.

"Come on, get dressed, and we'll have a nice dinner. Forget all about the war and our disappointments," Adam said.

It sounded exactly what we needed.

Chapter Twenty-Five

The next morning, our moods not improved by hours spent in the damp, cold, hard-benched shelter in the basement of our building, we dressed and as Adam went to another doctor's appointment, I went to St. Mary-at-Lambeth.

It was my lucky day. The church was still standing, the rector had returned, and I didn't see the stocky man following me. I paid for and received what they called an official copy and headed to the *Daily Premier* building.

Fortunately, Jane was in and had made a copy of her photograph of the stocky man. I thanked her and slipped the photo into my bag along with the official copy of the wedding record.

Then I headed back to the flat to wait for Adam. As soon as he returned, we could head out to Lancaster and get a decent dinner and a good night's sleep that night.

About two streets away from our flat, in the middle of the pavement, I suddenly felt my bag being ripped from my arm. Since I had been holding it close to my body, I was able to swing around and throw my body between my bag and my attacker. I found myself facing not a heavy-set man but a thin young man. We tussled for a moment before a bobby came between us, grabbing the young man and allowing me to gain control of my bag.

"What's going on here?" the bobby demanded.

"He tried to steal my bag," I said, holding my bag against my stomach.

The young man broke free, and the bobby chased after him, blowing his whistle. I hesitated a moment but then I saw the stocky man across the busy street coming toward me. I ran as fast as I could in three-inch heels the rest of the way to my building, darting inside just before the beefy man reached me.

He continued down the pavement at a fast pace.

I made a trunk call to Rosalie and let her know I'd been successful. "Great. I'll call Valerie and let her know to get the rest of the papers together to present to the College of Arms. When are you coming out?"

"As soon as Adam finishes with this doctor. We're already sick of the shelters. I can't wait to spend an entire night in bed again. You've spoiled us, Rosalie." And I wanted to get out of London, where someone wanted to get the papers I'd had copied for Valerie Northcott and her son, Teds.

"Adam has spoiled Thorpe with his presence."

"About that. The doctor is saying Adam isn't progressing enough and should be permanently assigned to a desk job, which he doesn't want. Adam's trying for—something else, which would mean only part of the time behind a desk. I don't know if he'll be pushing himself harder or moping around, but you might warn Thorpe he won't be the best company."

"I'll warn him. Which train do you think you'll be on so I can send Miles to meet you?"

We made our plans and hung up, trunk calls being horribly expensive.

When Adam returned, I had packed my own things and started getting his things ready. He dropped down to sit on the side of the bed, his canes at angles.

"What's wrong?"

"I'm having a final assessment next Thursday. If I don't pass, I will be sent to a desk job. Immediately."

"But you have so much to offer in the training brigade," I assured him.

He gave me a weak smile. "We know that, but the doctors don't see it."

"Well, let's go out to Briarcliffe Hall and see if we can't get you a little stronger."

"There's something else."

He sounded so hesitant I began to worry. "What's wrong?"

"I ran into Viscount Norrington near the building here. He asked me what you and Rosalie were up to. When I told him I didn't know that you were up to anything, you were covering some story for the newspaper, he kept pressing. He obviously didn't believe me."

"Did he tell you if he was going to stay in London or go back to Silverthorn Manor?" I decided he must be behind the attacks on me and had hired the beefy man and the thin youngster. I didn't like or trust the viscount.

"When I asked him if I'd see him this coming weekend at Briarcliffe Hall, he said he'd show up when I least expected to see him."

"Wonderful." I understood why Adam sounded hesitant. If Norrington knew what Northcott had been hunting down, he must suspect that Rosalie and I were searching for the same information.

That would explain why there had been two attempts to grab my bag.

After taking a detour around an unexploded ordnance and a massive hole in another street, we made the train with little time to spare. At least my shadow didn't reappear. Our first-class tickets got us seats, so the trip was not unbearable. It had been dark outside for hours, riding with the blackout curtains down, when we finally reached Lancaster.

I think Adam was exceedingly glad to see Miles waiting for us outside the station. He took our cases from me and we climbed into the back seat, Adam's canes whacking my legs as I sat down next to him.

"I'm sorry," he said, readjusting his sticks as I yelped in pain.

"It's all right. It's good to see you again, Miles," I added to the chauffeur as he entered the car.

"London still getting pounded?"

"I'm afraid so."

Miles and I continued our conversation as he drove off toward Thorpe and Rosalie's. Adam remained silent. In a few minutes, he was asleep, and the chauffeur and I stopped our discussion.

I woke Adam as we pulled up in front of Briarcliffe Hall. I climbed out and let Adam struggle to his feet as Miles carried our cases in. Rosalie and Thorpe met us in the great hall with hugs and handshakes.

"You have the paperwork with you?" Rosalie asked.

"In my bag." I patted it, having kept the fashionable leather handbag clutched to my side the entire trip. Even though I hadn't seen the stocky man or the thin young man on the train, I hadn't felt safe.

"Good. Valerie, Teds, and Mr. Perkins are all here with their paperwork. We'll go over it tonight, and hopefully find they have everything they need. Then in the morning, they'll drive to the station and take the train to London," Thorpe told us as Rosalie wheeled him toward the large drawing room.

"How long will it take them to get an appointment with the College of Arms?" I asked from behind them.

"Mr. Perkins has already set that up for tomorrow afternoon."

"Is that quick?" Adam asked.

"Yes. He mentioned this was in light of a counterclaim for the earldom of Silverthorn. It grabbed their immediate attention."

"Has the viscount already sent in his claim?" I asked.

"Yes. That's why they want to hear the other claim so quickly."

"Does Norrington know there's another claim?"

"I suspect so," Thorpe said. "He must, now that the College of Arms knows."

Adam and I exchanged a glance.

We walked into the large drawing room to find Valerie Northcott, Daniel Perkins, and a lanky young teenaged boy waiting for us.

"This is Edwards Northcott, the next earl of Silverthorn," Valerie said. "We call him Teds."

The boy blushed a deep rose.

"I'm pleased to meet you, your lordship," I said.

The boy turned a brighter red shade as I called him by his new address.

We all sat, the men with brandy, the women with wine, Teds with tea, and pulled out the various pieces of paper involved in the claim.

"Here is the baby's christening record from here at the local church. Here is the wedding certificate from St. Mary-at-Lambeth for his parents. I don't have anything for the parents' death. I didn't think about that," I said, showing them the special license and the church records.

"The College of Arms has that, as it was part of the younger brother's claim in 1797," Mr. Perkins said.

"You've been thorough."

"Any solicitor would be in the same position," he told me

gravely.

We were almost finished going through the rest of the paperwork for the generations in between when a maid came in to tell Rosalie there were sandwiches and cakes in the dining room in case the visitors were hungry.

For the first time, I saw Teds brighten.

"You've had dinner already," his mother said, seeing his face.

"We can share," I told him. "You're a growing boy. Adam needs his because he's had to survive on my cooking far too often."

We moved into the dining room, where the abundance of sandwiches and tea cakes tempted all of us. Teds ate three finger sandwiches and a tea cake before he took breath to say "Thank you."

"They don't feed you well at school." I made it a statement of fact, since I still remembered the food at St. Agnes.

"It's horrid. The school's all right, except for that," he quickly added.

"Where do you go to school?" Adam asked, having already eaten more than Teds since the boy had been interrupted and had to answer.

"Meadowbrook. It's near York."

"How do you feel about becoming an earl?" I wondered if I had done damage to his life by finding the evidence, at least in the short term.

"Golly. I don't know. I don't have anything to say about

it, do I?"

"I'm afraid not," Thorpe said. "Of course, I didn't have it sprung on me. I'd known about it from the cradle. You'll find people will treat you differently. Perhaps not so much at school," he hastily added.

"I'm not going to tell my friends if I can help it," Teds said and dug into another sandwich. Nothing could spoil the appetite of a growing boy, I decided.

"And nothing may come of it," Mr. Perkins said.

"Now, Daniel," Mrs. Northcott said, setting a hand on his wrist.

"You must be practical, Valerie. The College of Arms is a very traditional group, leaning toward following past decisions. Until they make their determination, no one knows what they'll decide, but tradition favors the viscount."

Daniel? Valerie? Rosalie and I exchanged glances. Mrs. Northcott seemed to have recovered from her husband's murder quickly, to now be openly displaying a close personal friendship to her solicitor.

"This is what my husband discovered, isn't it?" Mrs. Northcott asked.

"I believe so."

"And then he was murdered. Is Teds in any danger?"

"Keep a good eye on him, but I don't think so. I've had two people try to snatch my bag since I found this information, but they seemed to be more interested in retrieving the paperwork than attacking me. Make certain no one knows where the evidence is hidden, or how you're proceeding," I assured her.

"You think this is why my father was killed?" Teds asked me.

Oh, dear. "I think so."

"Then I have to go through with this. It's what my father would have wanted." The boy sounded resolute. His mother looked frightened.

Adam said, "You have to understand I saw Viscount Norrington in London this morning. He was very interested in what Livvy and Rosalie were investigating. I would assume he knows what kind of records you may have in your possession and may try to steal them. Take precautions accordingly."

Perkins thanked him.

"I have a photograph of one of the two men who tried to grab my bag." I passed it around, but no one recognized the stocky man. I then told them what had transpired.

"How did you get that?" Thorpe asked.

"I work for a newspaper, and I've made friends with one of the staff photographers. I had her take it in front of the *Daily Premier* building when he was following me."

Perkins took the photo. "Thank you for this. We're forewarned now."

As we headed upstairs to bed, I heard Thorpe instruct Cummings to make sure every outside door and window was locked and bolted. Adam was already yawning. By the time I climbed under the covers, he was already snoring.

In the morning, we went down to breakfast to find everyone intact. Perkins told us he was driving the Northcotts to York to the train station and then the three of them would travel to London on an express for their appointment that afternoon. He even mentioned the hotel where he had reservations for them in London. He might have been telling us out of caution so that others would know of their plans in case they didn't arrive, but after three murders, I thought his fear was only prudent.

They quickly finished their breakfasts and loaded up the car to be on their way. While Teds helped Perkins load the luggage into the green saloon, and Thorpe said goodbye and was helped back inside by Adam and Rosalie, I pulled Valerie aside. "I think you should apologize to Mrs. Cole for searching her house."

"What? But...? How?"

"You and Mr. Perkins have been following your husband's footsteps, trying to find where he hid the proof of his right to the title. You came to the village during the church service, knowing the Cole cottage would be empty. And you made a mess of her house."

"I'm sorry about that. Truly. Daniel wasn't as neat as he should have been."

"Did you find his proof?" I asked.

"No. Do you know where Robert hid the papers?" Valerie clutched at my arm.

"Valerie, come on. We need to catch the train," Daniel Perkins called to us.

I stepped back and Valerie Northcott hurried over to climb into the automobile. After I waved them off, I went back for more tea to find Adam telling them about his final evaluation in less than a week that would determine his next position in the army.

"Anything we can do," Thorpe told him. "The house and grounds are at your disposal. Cummings is available for massages. I'll even work the stop watch."

"I appreciate it. If I can get down to one cane, do some stairs, that will help me get the assignment I want."

"Did the doctors give you any exercises to make the improvements?" Thorpe asked.

"No. They're overworked with soldiers worse off than I am. They're more interested in whether I'm shirking and getting me back to work, even if it's shuffling papers all day," Adam said with a resigned tone.

"Surely they're not trying to get you back on the battlefield," Rosalie said.

"With these legs? They're not that foolish," Adam replied. "I suspect my time on the battlefield is over, but I've had a lot of training and I'd like to pass it on. Can't do that from a desk all the time."

"If you like, I could call in Doctor Hamelstein. He's been treating me for paralysis, but he knows a great deal about muscles and nerves and he might be able to come up with good exercises," Thorpe suggested.

"If you could, that would be very helpful." Adam and Thorpe reached across the table and shook hands.

"And I'll be here full time. The letter came yesterday officially releasing me for mill and factory management,"

Rosalie told us with a big smile.

I gave her my heartfelt congratulations.

"Downing has made his report on our former agent who stole from the government, which helped to get me released quickly," Rosalie said.

"And we received the apology I demanded for Downing's bad manners in staying here with a shooting party while he searched through our papers," Thorpe added.

When we rose from the table, Rosalie excused herself to tend to the running of Briarcliffe Hall and a nearby factory. Thorpe and Adam went into the study to call the doctor about a visit to see Adam.

I went upstairs to get my sketch book and pencils. I had promised to do a drawing of the house from the clearing up the hill, and my first attempt had been destroyed by the unknown attacker in the woods who turned out to be Betsy Oswald. I wanted to try again to complete the drawing as a gift to Rosalie and Thorpe, since they had been so kind to Adam and me.

I dressed in my tweed suit and put on a brown cloche to match over my reddish curls. With thick stockings and flat-heeled shoes, I was ready to brave the chill in the morning air. At the last moment, I pulled on soft leather gloves so my hands wouldn't get cold while I held a pencil.

I was about to go down the stairs when I found Adam trying to climb up them. He put his right foot up on the next step, gripped the railing harder, and dragged his left foot up to rest next to the right. He'd left his canes behind.

"Oh, well done, darling," I called down. I started down the stairs as he tried one more step. Then he turned awkwardly and started down, still gripping the railing.

I didn't try to reach the ground floor until Adam had both feet set on it and reached his canes again. "You've done well for a start."

"I need more than a start."

"You'll do it." I kissed his cheek. "I'm going up the hill behind the garden to attempt a sketch of the hall again."

"We'll be in the garden in a little while. Adam is going to try to speed up his walk," Thorpe told me.

I went out the French doors and across the garden to climb the path toward the Duke of Marshburn's land. When I found the spot I had worked from before, I spread out a blanket and sat with my sketch book, ready to begin.

The roof was beginning to take shape as the sunlight made the air a little warmer. I pulled off my gloves and continued sketching. I looked up, leaning to the left around a tree trunk to get a slightly different view of the corner of the building.

Boom!

Chapter Twenty-Six

Something whistled over my shoulder as a blast of sound echoed through the woods. Was someone hunting near where I was sketching on Thorpe's property?

Rolling over on the blanket, I called out, "Hey! I'm here. Don't shoot." And found myself looking up into the barrel of Viscount Norrington's rifle.

"Don't worry. It will just be put down to a hunting accident. I didn't know you had returned from London." He smiled. He was planning to kill me, and he smiled.

I was angry, and I made certain to shout. "Thorpe never gave you permission to hunt in his woods."

"I was following an animal I wounded that crossed over to his lands. And it won't do you any good to shout. No one will hear you."

"I'll shout if I want," I bellowed. I'd seen how successful I could be against my London attacker with a scream. "No one will believe you. Especially when they learn this is all about the title."

"How could it be about the title? There is no evidence of any other claim."

"There is, and it's been found. That's what your hireling should have told you. Or was I too good at giving him the slip?"

"No, he knew where you were. You just weren't in the right places. I found the records Northcott obtained and destroyed them." The smile slid from his face as he turned red and raised his rifle to aim directly at my head.

"Where were they hidden?" I was determined to keep him talking, particularly since I wanted to know the answers to the questions I asked.

"In the old wing. In the helmet of a suit of armor." Norrington smiled. "I was determined to find out where they were hidden and so I stayed up all night. Robert came in sometime after two in the morning. He led me right to them. I took them after I killed Robert."

"Unfortunately, you stayed there too long and were seen by Mr. Larimer."

"Why had he followed Northcott?" The viscount sounded as mystified as I was.

"Perhaps Larimer wanted to know why Robert Northcott had crept into the old wing?"

"Possibly. I was as surprised as anyone when Larimer showed up."

We'd never know the answer to that question, but there were details the viscount and I needed to straighten out between us. "You grabbed Northcott's copies, yes, but not the original records. They're still there and another copy can be, and has been, made and attested to." I rose slowly to my hands and knees along the edge of the blanket. My hand closed on a rock. "And now there are all sorts of people who know the truth of what happened one hundred and fifty years ago."

"But not the College of Arms. They're the only people who matter."

"Don't be too sure those records your hireling didn't get away from me aren't at the College of Arms now." I wanted to smile, but he was holding the rifle, and somehow, I didn't want to antagonize him further. I just wanted him to keep talking.

"It's not fair. That title should be mine. It is mine." The rifle wavered slightly as the viscount fumed.

I rose to my feet. If I could distract him, I could make a break for running down the hillside. There were enough trees to hopefully stop any bullets. But there were few enough leaves on the trees and bushes that they wouldn't serve as any sort of camouflage.

"This must be frustrating. You've been counting on the title all your life. When did you learn Robert Northcott had proof he was the rightful heir?"

"The old earl told me after Robert had been to see him. Only two weeks ago or so. He positively gloated when he told me, 'You won't get it, my boy. You're not half the man Robert is.'"

"That had to hurt." The sympathy in my tone wasn't

completely faked.

The rifle was leveled at my face again. "Don't think you can distract me."

"Was that when you wrote to Briarcliffe inviting your shooting party to the hall?"

"Yes, and stop trying to distract me," he shouted, his face red again.

"How did Downing join your shooting party?"

"A friend of mine had to drop out, but he suggested Downing. A friend of his, he said, and a good shot. Now, stop trying to distract me."

"There are too many people who know where the evidence resides. Shooting me will accomplish nothing." I raised my voice again. Someone or something was out there. If it was human, I hoped it would rescue me. Distract him. Anything.

"I don't believe you."

"Believe me. I've told people. Left notes. Remember, I am a newspaper reporter. This makes a good story. I have editors. Friends." I kept my voice raised. Yelling. Angry. Out of the corner of my eye, I'd seen movement.

"You didn't." His tone held scorn.

"I did. I'd have to be a fool not to after three murders. Give this up and go home."

The rifle lowered slightly. "I don't have a home to go back to. I'll be a laughingstock."

"You've been disappointed by something you had nothing to do with. No one will laugh. It's just chance. Bad luck." I didn't mention the three dead bodies he'd left in his trail. No sense in upsetting him more, not when he still held the rifle.

There was something else I wanted to know. "Did you hire Daniel Perkins to defend Dermot Young against the charge of murdering Robert Northcott?"

"Why would I do that?" Norrington scowled at me, scorn dripping from every word. "He took the fall for the thefts from Silverthorn Manor. Why not for the murders, too? Big lump of a chump."

Then behind me, down the hill in the garden, I heard Adam call out, "Hello. Livvy. How's the sketching coming?"

He was a perfect target out in the open in the garden, and with glee, the viscount raised his rifle with his finger on the trigger.

He was not going to shoot Adam. He'd been through enough already. I threw the rock at the viscount's head, making him jerk the rifle upward as the shot rang out, and in an instant, I jumped on top of him.

He had strength and weight on his side, I had fury and fingernails on mine. It nearly balanced out our struggles.

He hit me with the butt of the rifle. The pain seared my shoulder, but I hung on, my fingernails clawing his face. I aimed a knee at his groin and only slightly missed, delivering a sharp blow to his hip.

The viscount flipped me over, pinning one of my hands under his shoulder, but I still had one hand free to mangle his face. He forced the gun barrel across my neck, cutting off my air. I pushed on it with my free hand, giving him two hands to push the rifle down on my airway.

As the world went black, I felt a great weight lifted from me and heard men shouting. Then a weight fell across my legs as I gulped in cold fresh air.

"Are you all right, Mrs. Redmond?"

I opened my eyes to find Cummings looking down at me.

"I think so," came out as a hoarse whisper. My throat was on fire.

"The police should reach us any moment. When his lordship and your husband heard the shot up here where they knew you were sketching, they sent me up from around the side. They gave me a few minutes while his lordship called the police and then your husband came out as a distraction."

I looked down at my legs and found the viscount sprawled out, unconscious across my knees. "Thank you," I whispered.

"You're welcome," Cummings replied without a hint of irony. He helped me rise by rolling the viscount off me.

I brushed off my skirt and stockings. "What are we going to do with him?" came out through an ache in my throat.

"The police are here. They'll take care of him. Let me help you to the house," Cummings said as he handed the rifle to a uniformed bobby.

"I'll need a statement from you," Inspector Andrews said. "From both of you."

I nodded and helped Cummings gather my things before

we made a slow progress to the hall. Adam dropped one of his canes in his rush to hug me and didn't seem to notice as we made our way indoors hanging on to each other.

"My big, brave hero," I whispered in his ear.

We both collapsed into the first sofa we came to and Rosalie rang for tea. It seemed to arrive instantly, although I still wasn't completely aware of everything around me. The tea was hot, heavily sugared, and welcome as it slid down my bruised throat.

Inspector Andrews came in and sat across from me as a teacup was pushed into his hands. "I need to know what happened out there."

I told him in little more than a whisper what the viscount had told me about his dashed hopes and how he'd taken and destroyed Robert Northcott's proof that he was the rightful heir. How the old earl had told him, gleefully, that Robert Northcott would succeed him to the title.

Andrews made notes, and when I finished, asked, "Did he mention the three murders?"

"Not really, only Northcott's, and he tried to kill me and Adam to keep his secret. He shot at both of us."

"That's enough to hold him for now," Andrews said as he snapped shut his notebook.

"And you should lie down. You look as if you're going to drop at any second," Rosalie told me. Adam led me over to the lift. I did notice someone had brought him his second cane.

"Won't Thorpe...?"

"He's busy in his study with Inspector Andrews, explaining what Robert Northcott found and where his widow and son are headed now. You ride upstairs," Rosalie said and hustled Adam and me into the lift.

I barely remember reaching the first floor or climbing into bed.

When I woke up, Adam was still sitting in our room watching me. "How long have I been asleep?" My throat was still a little scratchy but felt much better.

"It's nearly time for lunch."

"Good. I'm hungry."

"Your powers of recuperation never fail to amaze me." He smiled when he said it, so I was sure Adam wasn't frustrated with me.

I looked around the room. "How did my sketching supplies get up here?"

"The maid brought them up a while ago. Rosalie was in a short time ago to see if I wanted her to call the doctor and to say Inspector Andrews left to question Norrington about the murders, shooting at us, everything."

"I hope you told her not to call the doctor. I'm much better now."

Adam nodded. "For you, yes. He's coming out this afternoon to see me. To see if he has any suggestions to strengthen my legs."

"I hope he does. He has more time than the army doctors. Maybe that will allow him to find something else that can be done." I slid off the bed and walked over to grip

Adam's hand. "Good luck."

* * *

The next several days slid by in an unprecedented number of trunk calls and telegrams between London, Lancaster, and Briarcliffe Hall. Thorpe kept in touch with Daniel Perkins about the questions and decisions of the College of Arms concerning Teds Northcott. Whatever they wrote to each other, Thorpe kept to himself.

Questions concerning the trial of a possible earl for murder were now involving Whitehall and Downing Street, Scotland Yard and the chief constable for Lancashire. I got a hint of this when Inspector Andrews came out to Briarcliffe Hall with the chief constable to go over my statement again with the rigor of adversaries.

After an hour of having every word I said questioned, the chief constable proclaimed himself satisfied that I would make a reliable witness. When he left the room to speak to Thorpe, Andrews said, "I apologize. This case has us all tangled up in knots."

"It's a murder case. I would expect the chief constable to make certain all the details were scrutinized."

"It's not just him. He has to answer to Scotland Yard and the government. It's the title that has everyone upset. The government wouldn't be involved if Norrington were a shopkeeper."

"And wasn't a high-ranking member of the Ministry of Information."

I was keeping Mr. Colinswood aware of where

everything stood as far as my story was concerned. So far, the inspector had kept the arrest of the viscount out of the papers, but it wouldn't be for much longer. I had to keep telling the *Daily Premier* to wait until the College of Arms ruled. The story wasn't complete without the connections between the murders and the title, because the motive was where the best part of the story lay.

And we were the only newspaper to have that.

Doctor Hamelstein was in contact with Adam's army doctors in London, discussing various treatments and getting details on the final assessment Adam would undergo. Then they would close themselves off in one room or another to practice various exercises. Thorpe came along for moral support. Rosalie and I were banned from watching.

On Tuesday, two days before Adam's assessment, the phone rang in Thorpe's study. I was passing by, so I answered.

"Countess?" a man's voice said.

"No, this is Mrs. Redmond. I'll get the countess for you."

"No, wait. This is Daniel Perkins. I have a message for the earl. The College of Arms has ruled in Teds's favor. He'll be named earl in their written decision."

"Oh, that is wonderful." It balanced out a wrong from a century and a half ago, but it made the murders of three men pointless.

"We'll be heading back to Lancaster tomorrow with the official documents. You will tell the earl and countess?"

"Of course. You haven't had any trouble with the stocky man who tried to get the copies of the records away from me?"

"We were followed from the train station to the hotel, but nothing after that."

"Probably because after that, he heard Norrington was arrested for murder and attempted murder," I told him.

"So the Earl of Briarcliffe told us. We're grateful to you, Mrs. Redmond."

"Glad to help. But I would like to know…"

"I imagine I can guess. Yes, I volunteered to provide Dermot Young's defense."

"Why?"

"Isn't it obvious? Young was innocent. Without having him to blame, the police might find out who really killed Northcott."

"And this is important to you?"

"Of course, just as it is to you, Mrs. Redmond."

I had no more than hung up the telephone when Rosalie came in. "Was that the telephone I heard?"

"Yes. It was Daniel Perkins. They've named the Northcott boy the new earl. They'll be returning with the proclamation tomorrow."

Rosalie hurried to me and gave me a hug. "Thank you. You found the link we were missing. Now, let's tell Thorpe the good news."

I followed her to the large drawing room. When we opened the door, we found that the furniture had been rearranged and three grown men wore the expressions of guilty little boys. Books, delicate china, and priceless silver candlesticks were scattered about. "We needed to set up an obstacle course. I hope you don't mind," Doctor Hamelstein said.

Adam stood looking at me using one cane. Since I knew that was part of the final assessment, I could have cheered.

Rosalie gulped before she said, "Not at all. May we see what you have accomplished so far?"

"Of course," Thorpe said. "Adam?"

"I feel as if I'm a trained dog," Adam muttered, but he gamely did a circuit of obstacles. I could see how much it was costing him in pain and effort. One leg was carrying his weight and doing much better. The other tended to drag and it was opposite the one that Adam kept his cane.

When he finished, I was grateful he avoided all the expensive obstacles. Rosalie's sigh of relief was audible.

"Well done, Adam. Sit down," the doctor said.

Adam dropped into the closest chair.

"Will he pass the test, do you think?" Thorpe asked.

Chapter Twenty-Seven

Adam watched the doctor, wanting to know his assessment.

"They have some latitude in conducting these tests, because they are, after all, subjective. I think you have a good chance of passing to get into the brigade you want, but it's not a certainty. Remember, final isn't final. We can do more work later and get you retested."

"They don't like anyone to request retesting. They consider it a waste of time," Adam told him.

"Then you'll just have to pass this time. I'm sure you will. You've made great strides," Thorpe said. "No pun intended there."

"I thought you did wonderfully," I said with enthusiasm.

"Just take your time. Think about what you're doing, and you'll do well," Doctor Hamelstein said.

"These are timed tests," Adam said.

"Designed to make you worry about the time and not pay attention to where your feet are going," the doctor replied. "Don't fall for their tricks."

"In other words, you can do it. Just don't let them distract you. We've seen you do it. Believe in yourself," Thorpe said.

"If I pass the test, it will be due to you, Cummings, and the doctor," Adam told him with a hint of a smile.

"There's no if. You'll do it," I told him. And then "Thank you," to the other men.

"This is a good day," Rosalie said. "You're doing brilliantly, and the College of Arms have decided in Teds's favor for the title." She went on to repeat what I'd told her to general cheers.

"We'll have good neighbors," Thorpe said. "I hope luncheon is worthy of a double celebration."

"It always is," Adam said with feeling. I suspected he was thinking of the food he'd be eating at his new duty station if he passed the physical for the training brigade. Or perhaps he was thinking of my cooking if he ended up in a desk job in London.

"I think we need to tell Inspector Andrews about the decision to grant Northcott's son the title. He needs to tell Norrington. That might make the former viscount an easier prisoner to get a confession out of," I said, looking at Thorpe.

"It might break him completely," Thorpe said in funereal tones before he nodded and Cummings wheeled him out of the room.

That night, Inspector Andrews called back, to tell Thorpe that Viscount Norrington had indeed confessed to all three murders after hearing the decision of the College of Arms. "Without the title, I have nothing to live for," the viscount supposedly said.

Inspector Andrews added, "He regrets killing the old earl. I think he'll almost welcome the scaffold."

"You mean, life isn't worth living if you're not an aristocrat?" Adam asked, looking perplexed.

"You remember what he was like. Ordering everyone around," Thorpe replied. "As if he was always in charge."

"And Larimer was just in the wrong place at the wrong time?" I asked.

"Yes. Norrington said Larimer shone his torch on Northcott's bloody corpse and turned around and ran. He never saw the viscount, but the viscount couldn't have him sounding the alarm." Thorpe shook his head.

"How awful," Rosalie said.

* * *

Thursday was the day everything came together. The *Daily Premier* reported the confession of Norrington to the murders of Northcott, Larimer, and the old earl along with the decision of the College of Arms to give the title to the rightful heir, Teds, the son of Robert Northcott. While I'd given them all the details to the story, someone else wrote what appeared in the newspaper.

I was used to that. It didn't make me less hurt and annoyed that someone else saw their words in the *Daily Premier*, but it no longer came as a surprise.

What I wasn't used to was Sir Henry phoning the news

desk I worked out of and telling my editor to send me up to his office. I went upstairs, hoping nothing had occurred to render the story I'd given them false. At a nod from his secretary, I knocked on Sir Henry's office door and walked in.

"There she is," he boomed. "Livvy, you have a talent for sniffing out stories. I don't know where we'd be on these murder cases without you."

"I wish people would stop dropping dead around me."

"But it's convenient for our purposes. You've given us some great stories."

Sir Henry had always paid me far better than I could get with my lack of talent or experience. I knew this wasn't preliminary to giving me a raise. "I'm glad you're pleased."

I managed to say the words without letting my sarcasm show.

"Now," he said, getting to what I suspected was the real reason I was called to his office, "are you going to stay in London for a time?"

"I suppose so. If Adam passes his assessment for duty today, he'll be sent who knows where, but I doubt it will be London. And I'll be here." I let my feeling of being left behind seep into my voice.

"I've been left on my own, too, with this war. Esther has taken her children to the house I bought in the countryside. By the time this war is over, my grandchildren will have forgotten me."

"Oxfordshire's not that far," I assured him. "I'm sure you visit every time you get a chance. Besides, Esther isn't going to let her children forget their grandfather. Any more than Adam's going to forget me."

He shrugged and scrunched up his face. "Then I suppose we'll both be here in London for the duration."

"Oh, I hope this is a short war," I said with all the fear and anger everything about this war had stored up inside me.

I finished up the day at my desk without hearing from Adam. I didn't know if that was good or bad news about his testing. I hurried home to find he wasn't there.

There was nothing to do but wait. Wait until I'd worn a path in the drawing room carpet. After an hour, I checked to make certain he hadn't already packed and left for a new duty station. He hadn't.

I knew something had to be wrong. I hoped if he failed the assessment, he hadn't jumped off a bridge into the Thames. I hoped he hadn't been run over in the blackout. I hoped he'd come home or call this instant.

Finally, I heard a key in the lock of the front door of our flat. I ran to the hallway to see his face so I would know immediately how he'd done. And whether he was all right and hadn't been attacked or injured in the blackout.

Adam, when he came in, relying on both canes as his shoulders slumped from exhaustion, had the most amazing poker face.

"Well?"

He walked over to me and then smiled. "The good news is I passed. The bad news is I have to report Sunday to a place in the middle of nowhere where there's no place for you to stay."

I wrapped my arms around him. "Congratulations. I know how much passing the test means to you. How much being of use to the army means to you."

He nudged me toward the drawing room where he dropped onto the sofa. "I'm happy about it, but I don't like leaving you behind with this nightly pounding by the Luftwaffe."

I sat next to him and snuggled close. "I'll be fine. I'll be working at the newspaper, and if the bombing comes too close, I'll stay with my father. His house is far enough out that no self-respecting German is going to pay any attention to his area."

"I'd rather you stay with Esther or your cousin Abby. They're both out in the countryside with no targets around for miles. Your father isn't far from the Underground."

"It's been quiet out there," I insisted. The real question was what would my father say if I tried to move in with him. The only way he'd agree to it was if I told him it was Adam's idea.

Adam studied my face for a minute. "You're determined to stay in London and keep working for Sir Henry?"

"Yes. They say we should keep calm and carry on. Well," I said, straightening, "that's exactly what I'm going to do. I won't let Hitler win."

"You make me feel as if I'm abandoning you while I sneak off to a castle in the north and pull up my drawbridge."

I had to laugh at that image. "If we're going to turn this

war around, or at least defend our country, we need well-trained soldiers. That's your job. My job is to report the news."

"Your job is to find scoops for Sir Henry for others to write. I heard you complaining when you didn't get to write the article about the Northcott boy getting the title." He chided me, but I could hear his teasing tone.

"Reporting the news sounds better than sticking my nose in to uncover misdeeds for Sir Henry to put in his paper." There was some truth in my joking words.

"You know your work is more important than that. I don't think that's what's bothering you. You're sure you're all right about me leaving for a distant military base for my new assignment?"

He seemed genuinely worried about my feelings, although he couldn't do anything to change where the army was sending him, the German bombing—anything. "You've worked hard to get this position. You deserve it. I'm proud of you. And I hope you're proud of me working for Sir Henry and the paper."

"I'm prouder of you getting justice for people such as Robert Northcott and his son and the old earl. If you hadn't, I don't think anyone could have."

"The police would have eventually," I told him.

"The inspector said the only thing that got them the confession they needed was the loss of the earldom. You did that. You got them justice."

We were wrapped in each other's arms and I didn't want

to ever move. But Sunday would come too soon, and Adam would be gone for who knew how long. I'd grown accustomed to him being home since he returned from France and then the hospital.

I had been so frightened since the shooting war started and Adam was gone. I had nearly lost him when he was shot in France. He was safer now, training recruits, but I couldn't help worrying.

I wished the war was over. I wanted the bombing to stop and I wanted Adam home every night. However long it took, I'd worry about Adam and my friends and our country.

I knew someday all this worry and killing would stop, and I hoped Adam and I could have a normal married life. Until then, we'd just have to make the best of whatever time we had together.

"Promise me you'll be careful," Adam said.

"I will. And I'm not letting go of you until Sunday." I snuggled closer.

"I love you, Livvy. I always will."

Whatever happened, I'd feel safe in his arms.

I hope you've enjoyed Deadly Manor.

If you have, please be sure to read the rest of Olivia's adventures in The Deadly Series. And go to my website www.KateParkerbooks.com to sign up for my newsletter. When you do, you'll receive links to my free Deadly Series short stories you can download from BookFunnel onto the ereader of choice.

If you want to let others know if you found Deadly Manor to be a good read, leave a review at your favorite online retailer or tell your librarian. Reviews and recommendations are necessary for books to be discovered and to get good ratings. Thanks for your help on behalf of all good books.

Notes and Acknowledgments

The inspiration for Deadly Manor came from the many country house mysteries set in the inter-war years in England, both those written at that time and those that are being written today. After all, who doesn't love the stealthy servants, the lavish dinners, the secrets, the surprises, the murders.

I had known that Adam would go on a secret mission to France as the German army was overrunning the country in June, 1940. I couldn't leave him in a POW camp for the duration of the war because I have plans for him in future stories. However, what if he was wounded? And what if those wounds will haunt him through succeeding books?

It was a short hop from there to an invitation to a country house for rest and recovery, and what better country house than that belonging to Rosalie Billingsthorpe who had been so useful to Livvy during Deadly Cypher? I've given Rosalie and her husband Thorpe some new challenges to go along with a shooting war and Britain's isolation.

The return of Fleur Bettenard from Deadly Fashion illustrated the work Britain did early in the war to imprison or turn all the German spies and German sympathizers. In fact, the British government turned enough of the captured spies that they were able to send all sorts of misinformation to Berlin and had it believed.

I'd like to thank Ken Gates for the name of the older son

of the Northcotts, based on a friend of his. Teds is a great nickname.

I'd like to thank my first reader, my daughter Jennifer, my editors, Eilis Flynn and Les Floyd, my proofreader, Jennifer Brown, my formatter, Jennifer Johnson, and my cover artist, Lyndsey Lewellen. Their help has been invaluable in making this book as good as it can be. All mistakes, as always, are my own.

I thank you, my readers, for coming along with Olivia on this journey. I hope you've enjoyed it.

About the Author

Kate Parker grew up reading her mother's collection of mystery books by Christie, Sayers, and others. Now she can't write a story without someone being murdered, and everyday items are studied for their lethal potential. It had taken her years to convince her husband she hadn't poisoned dinner; that funny taste was because she couldn't cook. Her children have grown up to be surprisingly normal, but two of them are developing their own love of literary mayhem, so the term "normal" may have to be revised.

For the time being, Kat has brought her imagination to the perilous times before and during World War II in the Deadly Series. London society resembled today's lifestyle, but Victorian influences still abounded. Kate's sleuth is a young woman earning her living as a society reporter for a large daily newspaper while secretly working as a counterespionage agent for Britain's spymaster and finding danger as she tries to unmask Nazi spies while helping refugees escape oppression.

As much as she loves stately architecture and vintage clothing, Kate has also developed an appreciation of central heating and air conditioning. She's discovered life in Carolina requires her to wear shorts and T-shirts while drinking hot tea and it takes a great deal of imagination to picture cool, misty weather when it's 90 degrees out and sunny.

Follow Kate and her deadly examination of history at

www.kateparkerbooks.com
        And www.facebook.com/Author.Kate.Parker/
        And www.bookbub.com/authors/kate-parker

Made in the USA
Thornton, CO
08/30/23 12:17:06

0f15f02b-1a2f-4b15-8ec0-ba3bd0ae4766R01